"A love story that will have your heart racing and maybe tears too...Nelle has a way of conveying a tasteful, believable, endearing story. If there was one word to describe Undying Love, it would simply be beautiful."

—*Mary Tatar, Mary Elizabeth's Crazy Book Obsession Blog*

"I really loved the author's writing...The story was beautiful...I could feel the emotions in her writing, and the love the characters had for each other was simply amazing."

—*Loverlys Book Blog*

"I sobbed and then smiled through my tears. The devotion, the pure love, and the unbelievably strong characters of Ryan and Allee took my breath away."

—*The Book Hookers*

"I haven't been this emotionally invested in a book in a very long time...This story was just plain amazing...It was so well written...I felt their pain like it was my own and couldn't put it down. I can't praise this book enough."

—*Maria's Book Blog*

"I will tell you that this is a beautiful story. One that I loved HARD, swooned for HARD, and cried for HARD."

—*Book Boyfriend Reviews*

"This isn't a superficial feel good book...This is a book about love, pain, heartbreak, lust, and strength. If you want a book that makes you FEEL something, then you need to read this book."

—*The Book Reader Chronicles*

"So beautiful and heartbreaking."

—*Adriane Leigh, author of* **Steel and Lace**

"I cried and I'm still teary-eyed. What a beautiful and sad story...This story will stay in my heart forever."

—*The Bookaholix Club Review*

# UNDYING LOVE

An Erotic
Love Story

Undying
L♡VE

NELLE L'AMOUR

This is a work of fiction. Names, characters, places, and
incidents are products of the author's imagination or
are used fictitiously and are not to be construed as real.
Any resemblance to actual events, locales, organizations,
or persons, living or dead, is entirely coincidental.

Copyright © 2013 by Nelle L'Amour. All rights reserved.

NICHOLS CANYON PRESS
Los Angeles, CA USA

Undying Love
By Nelle L'Amour

ISBN-13: 978-1484941416
ISBN-10: 1484941411

Cover and Interior: Streetlight Graphics

All rights reserved. No part of this book may be used
or reproduced in any manner whatsoever without
written permission, except in the case of brief
quotations embodied in critical articles and reviews.

*Dedicated to my dear readers who make
the long, hard journey so worth it*

# UNDYING LOVE

"True love doesn't have a happy ending
because true love never ends."

—Barbara Johnson

# ONE

I could have asked the tall, willowy blonde with the mile-high legs and the Kate Moss face to show me a painting, but instead I chose the bookwormy, bespectacled brunette. She looked like the type who knew where a secret treasure would be and would just get down to business. The blonde, who was already eying me flirtatiously, reminded me of all the girls I grew up with and dated—including Charlotte, my soon-to-be ex-girlfriend. Both were wearing the basic tour guide uniform—a gray pleated skirt and navy blazer with their Metropolitan Museum of Art employee badge clipped to the lapel. Except, while the blonde's skirt fell to the middle of her toned thighs, the brunette's fell below her knees, leaving a lot to the imagination.

"Excuse me, can you possibly show me something that is, in your opinion, one of the museum's hidden treasures?" I asked her.

"What for?" she asked suspiciously.

Her raspy voice was heavy-duty New York. Not the cultured kind associated with the tony Fifth

Avenue neighborhood I grew up in, but rather BBQ. Someone who lived in Brooklyn, Bronx, or Queens and called the Big Apple "New Yawk."

"I'm doing an article on the city's secret art treasures," I said.

"Oh, so you're a reporter." The tone of her voice was snide, in fact, borderline belittling.

"I like to think of myself as a writer. One day, I'm going to write a novel."

"Really? And what do you write now?"

"Articles for *Arts & Smarts.*"

She rolled her eyes at me. "That's such a piece of crap magazine. Intended for tourists and wannabes in the art world."

Her cutting words stung me, but I hid my hurt feelings. "Hey, it's a living."

"You don't look like you need to make a living."

I was taken aback. "What do you mean?"

"You're rich."

"How can you tell?"

"You're wearing pressed, premium denim jeans, a three-thousand-dollar designer motorcycle jacket, and expensive, black leather loafers with no socks." She paused. "And because I'm not."

I had to give it to her that she was observant. Mental note to self: I need to tone it down.

"So, Allee, what can you show me?"

"How do you know my name?"

"It's on your employee badge."

"Right," she said, with a flash of a smirk.

*Score one for me.* I followed her as she led me

to the elevator. She moved quickly, with a blend of authority and grace. I couldn't help wondering what she looked like underneath that oppressive uniform. There was something about her.

Thick silence accompanied the elevator ride to the museum's third floor. Alone, we stood side by side, facing front. Twice, I stole a glance at her. Despite the oversized, tortoise-shell spectacles, she was actually rather pretty. Maybe even beautiful, in an unconventional way. She had a strong, dimpled chin, upturned nose, and cheekbones the size of Golden Delicious apples. And there was that slender, long neck that gave her height and elegance. Her skin was milky white and made a stunning contrast to her lustrous, ebony hair that was gathered in a messy bun. I had the crazy urge to pull down her hair to see how long it was.

Having gone to cotillion (Man, did I hate it!) and way too many debutante balls, I was accustomed to holding doors open for women and letting them exit first. When the elevator hit the third floor and the doors slid open, my formal etiquette education went up in smoke. She shot out like a bullet, leaving me helplessly behind. I had to sprint to keep up with her.

"Follow me," she said. She walked briskly, with long strides, and while I was used to speed—being a runner—it was challenging to keep up with her. Maybe because I was distracted by her toned calves and thin, elegant ankles that peeked out from below her longish skirt. I also kept thinking about what her ass looked like every time it shot out between the vent of her blazer.

She led me to a painting. I studied it. At first, I couldn't make it out. And then I gaped. It was an abstract of a man and woman fucking face to face!

"What do you think makes this painting so great?" she challenged me.

I studied it further. "It's in fifty shades of gray."

She scowled. "What else?"

My eyes stayed fixed on the painting. "Their bodies are one."

She nodded. "Okay... and what's the artist communicating about sex?"

*Hold on.* Wasn't I was supposed to be the one asking the questions? Instead, I was pondering them.

She tapped her foot and folded her arms across her chest. "I'm waiting for an answer."

My eyes focused on her contoured chest. There was definitely a nice set of tits under her blazer.

She harrumphed. "You know, Golden Boy, I don't have all day."

I studied the painting again. "That sex is the union of two souls," I stammered.

She smiled for the first time. I was taken in by her upturned, ruby lips, which wore no lipstick, and the little dimples that bracketed them. Even without makeup, there was something about her.

"Excellent. Tell your readers that if they want to get laid they should visit this painting. It's a little known Picasso."

I pulled out a notebook and pen from my satchel. There was definitely a story here.

As I started to scribble down my thoughts, she yanked my pen away. "You don't need notes. When you write your article, write it from your heart."

She glanced down at her watch, an inexpensive cloth band one. "Sorry, time's up. It's my break."

"Let me take you for coffee," I insisted. "To thank you."

"Let me take you. I get a ten percent employee discount."

The museum café was busy, but we managed to find a table for two.

We had something in common. We both liked our coffee with a lot of cream, no sugar. Despite my protest, she still insisted on paying for the coffees, but I bought a dessert. One to share. A crème brûlé. My favorite. I was ravenous as I hadn't eaten lunch.

"So, Golden Boy, what's your name?" she asked after sipping her coffee.

"Ryan."

"Nice. Now we're both on a first name basis." Though she was still wearing her glasses, her eyes, the color of espresso beans, burnt right through me.

"Why did you agree to have coffee with me?"

"I felt sorry for you."

"So if you think I'm such a loser, why don't you just leave?" I made an "L" with my thumb and index finger on the word "loser."

She flashed that dimpled smile. "Because I like the way you hold your coffee cup."

Pinky out. Fifth Grade. Miss Primrose's Etiquette Class.

I took it as a compliment, especially coming from her, and thanked her.

We dug into the dessert. "So, how long have you worked here?" I asked, fumbling for small talk to make a conversation. She wasn't exactly what I'd call easy to talk to. Or maybe it was just the unnerving effect she was having on me.

"Almost a year. I was an intern first."

Her tongue languidly rolled around her upper lip, savoring every last bit of the creamy custard. Beneath the table, my cock tensed.

She glanced at her watch. "I need to go because I wanna keep my job."

She pushed back her chair and stood up. "Here's your pen."

I took it from her and twirled it between my fingers. "Are you going to watch the marathon tomorrow?"

"I haven't given it much thought. Are you?"

"I'm running in it. My first time."

"Good luck, Ryan." She reached into her purse. "And here's a couple of bucks for my share of the dessert. No backsies."

I was stunned when she slapped the money on

the table. What was with this girl?

Before I could say a word, she tore off. Maybe, next week, I'd visit the museum again. There were lots of beautiful and interesting works of art to look at, and she was one of them.

# TWO

Though it was November, the weather was unusually warm. This was definitely not going to help me through my first New York City Marathon. Stretching my calves, I stood gathered with thousands of runners of all ages who had come from all over the world to run this famed race. I was number 1212. Along with the identification bib, I was wearing an official marathon t-shirt and blue runner shorts that complemented my worn-in Nike athletic shoes. I was ready. I had trained all year. And had loaded up on carbs both at dinner last night and breakfast this morning.

The minute the race started, adrenaline shot through my veins. A team of co-workers, led by my best bud and colleague, Duffy McDermitt, cheered me on. Crossing the Verrazano-Narrows Bridge, which was closed for the event, I took in the magnificent view of the city and felt exhilarated. Though I wanted to run as fast as I could, I knew I had to pace myself. Covering all five boroughs of the city, the distance spanned a little over twenty-six miles. I had to be careful not to burn myself out early on.

I was doing well, running at a solid, even pace. My goal was to complete the race in less than five hours. While the various ethnically diverse neighborhoods I ran through were a blur, the sound of so many spectators cheering me and all the other runners on was motivating. As the temperature rose, I was grateful to all those who handed me a cup of water or Gatorade along the way. New Yorkers could really be there for you when they wanted to be.

About halfway through the race, I slowed down. My legs were lead; I was sweating like a pig, and my breathing was labored. I was questioning if I'd be able to finish, but I knew, by the worn-out looks of other runners, I wasn't alone. My father had drilled into me the value of not quitting. Once an all-star quarterback at Harvard (MVP '72), he never quit. I wasn't allowed to either.

But, man, let me tell you, as I crossed the Queensboro Bridge heading back into Manhattan, I wanted to throw in the towel. The climb up the bridge was agonizing, so far the most difficult challenge in the race. My thighs were burning, and so were my lungs. Sweat was pouring from every crevice of my being. I didn't think I could go on. While there were only ten or so miles left, these miles were going to be far more challenging than the sixteen I'd already run. No matter how much I had trained for this race, it was not enough. "Hang in there, Madewell," I said to myself, my breathing now short, constant pants.

"How ya' doin', 1212?" came a voice from behind me a little after I exited the bridge.

There was no mistaking that sexy, raspy voice. I stole a glance over my shoulder. Sure enough, it was Allee, her dark hair gathered into a long ponytail and a wicked grin spread across her face. She was running right behind me, holding a bottle of water. She was so close I could feel her warm breath on my neck.

"Have some water." Instead of handing me the bottle, she poured the icy cold contents over my head. Aah! It felt so good! Rubbing the water out of my eyes, I found her right beside me. I couldn't get my eyes off her body. She was wearing a tight Metropolitan Museum of Art graphic T-shirt that exposed her pert breasts and nipples, even under her sports bra, and black running shorts that revealed her toned mile-high legs. I'd imagined she'd had great legs but nothing like these gams. They were smooth and taut, flaunting a rippled muscle that ran down the side of her thighs. What turned me on most was the substantial space between her inner thighs. Man, she was hot.

"I thought I'd go for a little jog," she said. "Hope you don't mind if I join you."

Mind? Are you kidding? She was just what I needed to get through the last leg of the race. For the next ten miles, she kept pace with me. I shot her little looks that didn't go unnoticed. She wasn't wearing her glasses. I was awed by her profile and bouncing ponytail that made it even more electrifying.

As we passed through Harlem onto Fifth Avenue, she sprinted ahead of me. "Betchya you can't keep up with me, Golden Boy," she shouted with a turn of her head and a smug smile.

"Betchya I can," I yelled back at her. What a tease! Calling upon every muscle in my body, I charged ahead. I don't know if it was the competitive value that my father had instilled in me ("Son, Madewells are born to be winners.") or that I wanted to catch up to her and wrap my arms around her, but nothing could stop me.

Damn, she was fast. Then again, she hadn't run twenty-four grueling miles across the city. On the other hand, I enjoyed watching her run. She ran with the grace of a gazelle, her long, muscular legs kicking up their heels to propel her forward. From time to time, she glanced back at me, firing me a mischievous smile. A smile I wanted to wipe off her face with my lips.

Just as we edged into Central Park at Columbus Circle, I caught up to her. I clasped her hand tightly so that she couldn't get away. And so that she would pull me over the finish line with her. As thousands of spectators cheered us on, we crossed the famed finish line together, a bundle of hot, sweaty human flesh. I clocked in at 4:40:30. Just a little under five hours. I did it! Wasted, I sunk to my knees, wrapping my arms around Allee's long legs. She sunk down with me, wrapping her arms around me. Her hard nipples brushed against my soaking wet T-shirt. Beads of sweat clung to her like fairy dust, making her ethereal. Otherworldly. I couldn't stop panting. She met my gaze with her espresso bean eyes, and I broke down in heaves from the pain and the emotion of it all. In the background, Lady Gaga's "Edge of Glory" blasted. Here I was hanging onto this gorgeous, sexy girl I hardly knew—wanting her like a child wants a forbidden candy. She gently brushed sweat off my forehead with her long fingers and looked straight into my eyes, burning a hole in them. With a broad smile and her husky voice, she said, "Congratulations, 1212!" I could hear well-wishers in the crowd shouting out my name, but I saw only one beautiful person—a girl named Allee.

A marathon volunteer passed by us, carrying a box full of bottled water. I grabbed two bottles, one for her and one for me. We gulped down the contents down greedily. As parched as I was, what I most thirsted for was her. Her hot sweaty body, her long legs, her lush lips. I drank it all in and could practically taste her.

Slowly, I rose to my feet, lifting her with me. "I need to go to my health club and take a cold shower and get a massage," I said.

"Save your money," she said. "I give an excellent massage."

My skin prickled.

"And besides, I owe you for winning the bet."

"So, you have a driver," she said with that maddening roll of her eyes.

"Yeah," I said, on the verge of embarrassment, as my black, tinted-window Escalade pulled up to us as we stood on Fifth Avenue. "You were right. I'm rich."

"I underestimated you," she smirked. "You must be a very prolific writer."

"I'm just lucky." Indeed, I was.

My uniformed driver, Marcus, opened the passenger door. An ex-marine, he had a brick shithouse build, ruddy complexion, and buzzed bone white hair that contrasted sharply with his perpetual black shades and belied his fifty-something years.

"After you," I said to Allee. A little hesitant, she slid into the leather backseat with me following behind her. She deliberately stayed her distance, though I longed to cradle her in my arms.

I admired her long muscular legs and inhaled her delicious scent, a blend of sweetness and sweat, as the SUV headed downtown to my loft. The place I called home was located on the Lower East Side. A far cry from my parents' stuffy Fifth Avenue apartment and lifestyle, it suited my downtown sensibility and was close to my office.

We cruised down Broadway, steeped in silence until we reached my residence. Marcus jumped out of the car and let us out.

"So, you live in a warehouse," she said, eying the three-story depression-era brick building. Her wide eyes communicated a tinge of surprise.

"Actually, it's an old millinery factory that manufactured nurses caps during World War II," I said, leading her inside.

"I hope those caps saved a lot of lives," she said, taking in her surroundings.

The ground floor served as a storage area for things like my skis, bike, college papers, and textbooks. And a whole lot more, including a bunch of ancestral typewriters. I had to admit, I was somewhat of a hoarder. I was always afraid of tossing a possession—be it an old photograph or a treasured childhood toy—thinking it might be an inspiration for the prize-worthy novel I aspired to write.

"You've got a lot of stuff," Allee commented as she followed me to the former freight elevator to our right. "You know, there are lots of needy kids out there."

Oh, so now she was doing a guilt trip number on me. The number of ways this girl could get under my skin irked me. Though, I suppose she was right—I could give some things away.

After swiping a security card over the elevator call button, I pushed it and the wide, original metal door creaked open. We stepped into the massive elevator carriage together. Her intoxicating scent filled the air. I pushed the button for the second floor, and the car rose slowly. Again, more silence.

The elevator door jerked open and let us out in my loft. True to fashion, Allee bolted out. She surveyed my living quarters, taking in everything with an analytical eye. If she was awed, she didn't show it.

"This place is like a museum," she finally said.

Well, it wasn't exactly a museum, but the space was vast, filled with interesting artifacts, photographs, and art, each a souvenir from my travels around the world. The exposed high ceilings, gleaming hardwood floors, industrial lighting, and floor-to-ceiling windows made the perfect backdrop for my collection. Charlotte, an interior designer, had done the decorating—sleek, high-end Italian furniture that included oversized black leather couches, a burled wood dining table and chairs, built-in shelves for all my books, plus an antique Persian rug—her gift to me. At the far end, there was a state-of-the-art kitchen and, in a corner, a winding polished-metal staircase that led to the third level where I slept and showered.

Leaving me behind, my companion freely explored the space. I trailed behind her, observing her gorgeous ass. It was firm, rounded, and shaped like a heart. The kind you want to squeeze in your hands. Or take a bite out of.

Her raspy voice diverted my attention. Focusing on a photograph of me posing with a giraffe from my trip to Kenya, she asked, "Did you use to write for a travel magazine?"

"Yeah. Before I wrote for *Arts & Smarts*, I

worked for *Travel & Fun*." Another one of those magazines she'd probably pooh-pooh. Travel aimed at the Silicon Valley nouveau riche.

Sure enough, she rolled her eyes. "Did you ever write an article on Paris?"

I shook my head. "I've been there several times, but I've never found the words to describe the City of Light."

"Probably because you've never fully experienced it."

"And you have?"

"Not yet," she said wistfully.

Paris apparently meant something to her. I changed the subject. "What about that massage?"

"Yeah, Golden boy, what about it?" Her eyes roamed around the loft. "Where's your bed?"

"Upstairs." My cock twitched. The thought of having her in bed any way I could was turning me on.

"Well, what are you waiting for? Move it. There's an expiration date on this free massage... today." She shot me a wry smile.

With Allee right behind me, I strode to the spiral stairs and mounted the winding metal steps. My bedroom, along with the adjacent state-of-the-art bathroom, occupied the entire second floor. It was my kingdom where I wrote and dreamed.

Allee's eyes took in the expansive, minimally furnished room and landed on the king-size mattress lying in the middle of the floor. It was covered with a plush white duvet and a mountain of fluffy pillows. "That's your bed?"

"Yeah."

She gave me a scornful look. "C'mon, don't tell me you can't afford a real one."

I simply shrugged, feeling a little embarrassed that I had never gotten around to buying one. Truthfully, I liked sleeping so close to floor. It kept me grounded and expanded my mind when I gazed up at the skylight above.

"Take off your t-shirt," she commanded. "I'll deal with the rest."

I lifted the damp cotton tee, my marathon souvenir, over my head and tossed it onto the floor.

She surveyed my torso, her eyes passing over my broad shoulders, toned pecs, and washboard abs. All 6'2" of me. A regular at my health club, I had to admit I was in great shape. Her impassive expression did not confirm that. All that came out from her mouth was a throw away "hmm."

"Lie down, facedown," she ordered.

I got down on the bed, following her instructions. The cool, soft cotton duvet was soothing under my aching, heated body.

"Where's your bathroom?" she asked.

"Behind you." With my face pressed into a pillow, my voice was muffled.

"Don't move. I'll be right back."

I heard her step away, and then the sound of running water filtered into my ears.

"That's quite a bathroom, for one person," she said with sarcasm, the sound of her footsteps getting closer. She was right—with its steam room, it was almost like a spa. It was Charlotte's idea, but I didn't owe her an explanation.

She dropped to her knees beside the mattress. With swiftness, she tugged off my running shoes and damp, clingy socks. My sore feet were at last freed prisoners. Around each one, she wrapped a hot, moist towel, gently squeezing them as she did. The sensation was exquisitely soothing. A loud sigh escaped my throat. She removed the towels and began to work my right foot with her soft, warm hands. I let out a moan as she dug her thumbs into the sole. She circled them around, pressing deep, releasing all the pain and tension that had gathered there from the long race. She worked every part of my foot, from my heel to my toes. Oh, God, it felt good! My whole body was letting go. Except one part. The mound of flesh between my legs. The hard circular motions were arousing my erogenous zone, sending little electrical pulses there. Balls! I was getting hard.

I jolted a little as she pulled each toe, one at a time, and then splayed her fingers between them. My other foot was screaming for equal treatment, and she did not disappoint. I was moaning and getting harder.

From my toes, she moved on to my tight calves, squeezing and kneading each one. The delicious pain was almost unbearable. I let out a deep groan.

"No pain, no gain," she said in that deep, raspy voice.

I was craving more and got it when she moved up my thighs to my hips, pressing deeply into the sore sockets. Man, she was good. My back couldn't wait for her skilled hands.

However, it wasn't her hands that made contact with my back. A warm, wet sliver of velvet slithered up my spine. Her tongue! The movement was slow, fluid, and focused. Tingles spread through my body, pooling in the engorged area between my inner thighs. She was driving me crazy. My balls were filling up. She was giving me a boner! I wanted that aerobic tongue in my mouth. And then I wanted it all over my cock.

When she reached the nape of my neck, her hands took over. With her magic fingers, she kneaded my neck, upper back, and tight shoulders. Oh, yeah! I was in heaven. Except for my pulsing dick.

"You carry a lot of tension in your neck and shoulders," she said, squeezing the flesh along my shoulder blades.

"I sit in front of a computer too much," I mumbled, wanting to tell her that I was carrying a lot of tension between my legs.

"You need to stop doing that, Golden Boy." It was another command.

"Turn over," she ordered before I could respond.

I rolled over onto my back. There was now a serious bulge between my legs. It was hard to miss. I was blessedly well-endowed. She shot a glance down at me and muttered another one of those hard-to-read "hmms." She smirked at me.

Gripping my shoulder blades, she leaned into me. Her warm breath heated my cheeks. "How do you like your massage so far?"

"I'll show you how much I like it." I couldn't help myself. Grabbing her ponytail, I yanked her down toward me and covered her lips with mine. Not resisting, she moaned into my mouth. I moaned back before parting her lush lips with my tongue. It immediately found hers, and I massaged her mouth all over. She tasted delicious.

A roguish blend of guilt and desire surged through me. Here I was kissing this girl I'd just met, who was making me as hard as rock. And damn it, I wanted to ravage her every which way I could. *Stop it, Madewell!*

Lucky for me, unable to refrain, she abruptly pulled away first.

"This is not part of the deal." Her voice was gruff.

She was right. And I was wrong. What right did I have engaging in this lewd behavior? "I'm sorry," I apologized.

"I've gotta go and you've got an article to write," she said, climbing off the mattress. With her long legs, she jogged down the spiral stairs. Still bare-chested, I trailed behind her, unable to keep my eyes off her backside. *Holy shit! That ass!*

"I recommend taking a hot bath," she said, seductively leaning against the elevator. Her eyes roamed down my body and stayed locked on my crotch. "It'll make you feel better."

My cock was throbbing. She had successfully

managed to blue ball me.

I pushed the elevator button, resisting the urge to thrust my body against hers. The door jerked open. As she gracefully stepped backward into the car, she said, "Good luck, Golden Boy, with that article. I might even buy a copy of that schlock magazine and read it."

The door slammed shut before I could say a word.

Following her advice, I trudged back upstairs and drew myself a hot bath in my antique copper tub, one of the few things I installed without my soon-to-be ex's approval. Charlotte had insisted on a built-in Jacuzzi tub, but I had always wanted one like this. Deep and soulful. No girl had ever shared it with me, including Charlotte.

Leaning my head against the back of the tub, I stared at my swollen dick, which was shooting out of the water. I couldn't get Allee out of my head, and the more I thought about her, the harder and larger my dick got. It was crying out for relief. Holding my heavy, aching balls in one hand, I circled my fingers around my girth and moved them up and down the shaft. Harder and harder. Faster and faster, jerking myself off. Closing my eyes, I arched my back and fantasized Allee in the tub with me, her long, deft fingers taking over. My breathing grew ragged as I raced with brutal speed and force to a climax. As my cock exploded, I growled her name. She was right. The bath made me feel better. Damn that girl!

# THREE

I was not looking forward to the rest of the day. It was my mother's birthday, and she was giving a small formal dinner party at my parents' Fifth Avenue apartment to celebrate. I was expected to dress up, bring her an expensive gift, and indulge her as she talked about her society friends and accomplishments in between glasses of Dom Perignon. I could be sure that neither she, nor my father, would have any interest in hearing about my marathon achievement. Hell no! They didn't even bother to come watch me run the race. I hadn't expected them to.

Reluctantly, I donned my requisite preppy finest—chinos, a crisp blue and white Turnbull shirt, and a navy gabardine blazer. Attending my mother's birthday party was the last thing I wanted to do after the grueling marathon. It meant having to spend time with my father.

My parents' twenty-room Fifth Avenue apartment

enjoyed one of the most coveted and prestigious addresses in the city. Famous people lived in the elegant pre-war building, including several award-winning movie stars, one former U.S. president, and numerous Forbes-List billionaires like my father. With only one apartment per floor, the gilded elevator brought me directly to an elegantly appointed corridor, facing the rich mahogany door to their apartment. After a ring of the doorbell, I was greeted by my parents' longtime housekeeper, Maria. Having practically raised me as a child while my mother fluttered between beauty treatments and social events, she was always delighted to see me. The handsome Honduran woman, her hair now graying, wrapped an ample arm around me and warmly ushered me into the spectacular duplex.

"Darling, how good of you to come," came a voice from the sweeping staircase. My mother, Eleanor Madewell. Needle thin, Botox-beautiful, and always on the best-dressed list, she made the perfect trophy wife for my father, Ryan Madewell III. What made her even more perfect was the fact that she could look the other way despite his many rumored indiscretions.

Wearing a long, silk sheath that exposed her jutting hipbones and a long strand of sparkling diamonds with matching teardrop earrings (last year's look-the-other-way birthday present from my father), she draped a bony arm around my neck and pecked each cheek. Her other hand was wrapped around a half-drunk glass of champagne.

I'm sure not her first.

"Help yourself to a drink," she said as I followed her into the spacious, elegantly furnished living room that housed a well-stocked art-deco bar. "Charlotte will be here shortly."

Charlotte was coming? A shudder ran through me. I thought she was still away on a trip with her parents and not due to come home until next week. After I'd told her a few weeks ago that I thought we should cool our relationship and see other people, she blew up and seized the opportunity to travel with her parents to their chateau in the South of France. She was convinced I would come to my senses upon her return. Except while she was abroad, I had decided I wanted out and planned to break up with her permanently as soon as she came back. The five-carat Tiffany's engagement ring that she coveted wasn't going to make it to my credit card. Or her finger.

I was not looking forward to seeing her. Dread seeped through my veins. My mother had no clue that I wanted to break up with Charlotte; I hadn't yet told her. Or my father.

As I made myself a martini, contemplating how I was going to handle seeing Charlotte, my mother continued in her clipped voice, typical of old-money Manhattan wealth. "Since she's practically family, I thought it fitting to invite her to our little soirée after I ran into her this afternoon at Bergdorf's. I would have, of course, invited her parents had they not still been on holiday abroad."

My parents and Charlotte's parents, the Vanowens of steel industry fame and fortune, had known each other forever. Their ancestors even came over together on the Mayflower, and Charlotte's mother Sylvia, like my mother, served on the board of Daughters of the American Revolution as well as other prominent cultural institutions and philanthropic organizations across the city. Her father, like my father, went to Harvard and Harvard Business School. They played golf together whenever they retreated to their upstate New York country manor homes.

Both sets of parents believed that our union was destiny and had pushed us together. On paper, Charlotte and I were the perfect couple. Gorgeous debutante daughter and New York's most eligible Ivy League bachelor. We were the kind of couple that was feature-worthy in the wedding section of the *Sunday New York Times.* Beautiful and aspirational. In truth, beautiful and dysfunctional.

Over the past few months, Charlotte had been getting on my nerves, pressuring me to get engaged when I wasn't sure if I was really in love with her—or ever had been. A rising interior designer, whose clients included New York's elite, she was becoming more and more like my mother every day. Bouncing from one social event to another and seeking media exposure. It was all about her. She was a *Page Six* regular as well as a fixture in *Women's Wear Daily* and the *New York Social Register*. It didn't hurt that she was Uma Thurman beautiful and dressed to the nines. More often than not, I was featured in the photos, labeled as Charlotte's "handsome billionaire boyfriend." I could care less. All I wanted to do was stay home and write. We'd grown incompatible. I finally told this to Charlotte. Bickering replaced her one-way conversations. When she demanded an official engagement date, I'd had enough.

As I finished my martini, Charlotte came sweeping into the room. Her long, wavy platinum hair curled around the exposed shoulder, her one-shoulder sequined gown left bare. Its thigh-high slit gently revealed her long, toned legs.

"How good to see you, darling!" she said with one of her perfunctory high society embraces. "Did you miss me?"

I quirked a nervous half smile. Words were trapped in my throat. She was acting like nothing had gone down between us before she'd left, and this was making it harder.

"Mummy and Daddy send you their love." She casually helped herself to some champagne.

"Why are you back so soon?" She was only gone for ten days.

She sipped the champagne and, with her free, perfectly manicured hand, flung back her shiny mane of hair. "Muffy Malone's baby shower. It was this morning at The Carlyle. I just couldn't miss it."

Sheesh! She knew damn well I was running the marathon. That I'd trained a year for it. That it was important to me. But some classmate from Spencer, whom she openly despised, was more important to her. She didn't give a shit...Just like my mother, who couldn't miss her waxing appointment, and my father, who couldn't miss his weekly Class of '74 Harvard Club brunch (and who, quite frankly, didn't consider running a marathon a sport). I shrugged my shoulders. It didn't matter to me. I had someone there for me. And I still couldn't get her face out of my head. Maybe later tonight I would call it quits with Charlotte.

"Where's Father?" I asked my mother.

On cue, he strode into the room. As dapper as ever, he was clad in tan twill slacks and a black cashmere blazer that buttoned over a crisp white dress with monogrammed gold cufflinks and a silver silk tie.

His steely gray eyes met my blue ones. "Son, you could have at least put on a tie for your mother's birthday."

He was always critical of me. From the day I was born, he'd never had a nice word to say. I dared not to challenge or defy him. Or could I ever rub in his face the shit I knew he was capable of doing. It was not what Madewells did. Reluctantly, I mumbled two words. "Sorry, sir."

The five-course dinner was served by Maria and her staff in the grand dining room that overlooked the sparkling city. The table, which could seat twenty, was scaled down to make the evening more intimate. My parents sat on opposite ends, Charlotte and I in the middle, facing each other. Most of the conversation zigzagged back and forth between my mother and Charlotte as they exchanged small talk and gossip. Charlotte, who barely touched anything on her plate, was only one glass of champagne behind my mother, who had consumed four. I swear when I looked at the two of them, Charlotte could easily be mistaken for my mother's daughter. They say that boys are often attracted to women who remind them of their mothers. I suppose that's what attracted me to her in the first place. A big mistake. In retrospect, I should have known how things would turn out.

My father said few words and consumed his elaborate rack of lamb meal with a blend of grace and gusto. "Did you see what Madewell Media closed at on Friday?" he asked me.

Madewell Media was a Fortune 500 company that owned newspapers and broadcast outlets around the world, as well as a sizeable chunk of the Internet. My father was the revered and feared Chief Executive Officer. Worth over three billion dollars, he was number ten on the Forbes 400 List of Billionaires. He wouldn't be happy until he was number one.

"Well, son?" His tone was irritated.

My mind was elsewhere. I was thinking about Allee. Reliving my run with her. Her massage. And that kiss. *Holy fuck! That kiss.* I was getting an erection under the table! Finally, I brought myself back into the moment and replied, "Sorry, Father, I wasn't paying attention."

My father's lined, but still handsome, face hardened. "For your information, the stock closed at an all-time high."

So, he was richer. How much richer could he get?

My father's voice grew harsh. "Ryan, if you're going to take over Madewell Media one day, you had better start paying more attention to these kinds of things."

That's what my father was grooming me for. To follow in his footsteps and take over the business. But that's not what I wanted. I just hadn't worked up the courage to tell him.

Sensing the rising friction between my father and me, Maria suggested opening my mother's birthday presents while she cleared the table. Charlotte presented hers first—a lovely Hermès scarf, something my mother could never have enough of despite already owning dozens. I gave her a rare Baccarat unicorn that I'd found on eBay to add to her menagerie, and finally, my father presented her with a twenty-carat Burmese ruby ring. She gasped and instantly put it on her middle finger.

"It's absolutely beautiful, darling," she drooled.

"You deserve it, dear," my father replied in a cold, monotone voice.

Yes, she did deserve it for all the nights he never came home. Given what this ring must have cost, there must have been many of those this year. Inside, I was seething. My mother deserved better.

Following more champagne and birthday cake, my father called it a night. My mother was slurring her words, and her eyes were glazed. Another typical birthday. I kissed her good night. "Ryan, darling, don't forget about the Met gala tomorrow night."

Charlotte's face lit up. "How exciting that the Madewell Gallery of Old Masters is finally opening." She shot me a sharp look. "Of course, we'll be there. Right, Ryan?"

To be honest, I'd almost forgotten about the event, having been focused for the past month only on work and the marathon. "Yes," I stammered, frustrated that I would have to put off our breakup. It was a big night for my mother, and I didn't want to ruin it in any way. Then I brightened. Perhaps, Allee would be there too. The thought of seeing her again made my skin prickle and put a smile on my face.

My driver, Marcus, was waiting for me outside the building. Charlotte, in one of her moods, asked me to take her home. Not wanting to be an asshole, I reluctantly agreed. Sitting side by side in the back seat, there was a thick layer of ice between us.

"You didn't exactly pay a lot of attention to me tonight," she said, finally breaking the ice.

"What do you mean?"

"You could have told me how much you liked my new dress. Or asked me about my trip or Muffy's baby shower, which, by the way, was divine though she's as fat as a cow."

I wanted to say, "And you could have asked me how it felt to run my first marathon." But instead, I said, "I'm sorry. I've had a lot on my mind." Right now, there was only one thing on my mind. Allee. Why the hell couldn't I get her out of my head?

"Don't we all," Charlotte scoffed, folding her arms tightly across her chest. She went back to giving me the silent treatment, which was fine by me. Tomorrow night after the gala, I was going to tell her that is was over between us. Over for good.

Marcus arrived at Charlotte's Sutton Place apartment in no time. She invited me up for a nightcap. I politely declined, telling her that I was too beat from the marathon. I didn't want to spend any more time with her than needed.

"Fine." She stabbed the word at me. "I'll meet you at the museum tomorrow night."

Not waiting for Marcus to help her out of the car, she yanked the passenger door open and slammed it behind her.

I leaned my head back against the leather seat and closed my weary eyes. The image of a girl with a messy bun and big tortoise-shell glasses filled my head. Beneath my slacks, I felt my dick harden.

# FOUR

W hen I got to my office in the morning, I was in for a big surprise. Everyone was gathered in the kitchen area cheering me on for completing the marathon. My Copy and Layout Editor and best friend, Duffy McDermitt, popped a bottle of champagne. "Way to go, Madewell!" he toasted. I felt myself blushing and humbly took a bow. Several employees helped Duffy pop additional bottles and pass glasses of the bubbly around to the magazine's staff of thirty. I counted myself lucky to have such a great team of young writers, editors, and graphic designers working under me. Each of them had a bright future ahead of them.

Unlike my father's other companies, *Arts & Smarts* was more of a start-up, and the environment was relaxed rather than corporate. The headquarters, a gutted Tribeca townhouse not far from my loft, lent itself to creativity, self-expression, and a high level of energy. Much to my father's chagrin, employees dressed casually and worked in an open space rather than in cubicles or boxed-in offices. Even I, Editor in Chief, wore jeans and didn't sit in an office. My style of management was very different from my father's. It disturbed him.

Grabbing a cup of coffee, which I planned to drink instead of the champagne, I headed to my desk. My legs were still sore from the marathon, but not as bad as I had expected. Allee's deep-tissue massage had worked wonders. But between my legs, I was throbbing. I had woken up with a boner having dreamt about fucking her brains out. In my dream, we were on a deserted island, our side by side naked bodies one—just like that Picasso painting at the Met. As I thrust my cock inside her, she moved her hips toward me, making the penetration deeper. I could feel her squeezing her muscles around my thick, heated erection, adding to the outrageous pleasure she was giving me. As I slid in and out of her faster and harder, she met my every thrust. Her throaty moans harmonized with my deep groans. Our arms were wrapped around each other, and our eyes were half-open. I enjoyed watching the expression on her face, one of pure ecstasy, as she built toward climax. "Come for me, Madewell," she shrieked. I shouted out her name as I convulsed inside her, her own waves of ecstasy and screams of pleasure mingling with mine.

In the shower, I jerked myself off as the steely water fell onto my face and body. Charlotte had never had this effect on me, I thought, as I toweled myself dry. And in reality, I'd never had such a mind-blowing fuck with her.

"Dude, you seem distracted," said Duffy, who

was walking beside me. His laid-back voice, typical of a California surfer, brought me back into the moment.

"Sorry, paly. Charlotte's back." Duffy was one of the few people I confided in about my personal life; he knew about our trial separation. The other was my older sister Meredith—Mimi, for short—who lived in Boston and was married to a dynamic woman she had met while attending my mother's alma mater, Wellesley. My parents had sent her there so that she would be ripe material for marrying a Harvard man or Yalie. Well, that didn't happen. When she told my father that she was gay and engaged to a fellow Wellesley girl, he disowned her. That didn't put an end to our close relationship, and fortunately, she told me Mother still secretly talked to her and sent her money.

Duffy dug into me. "This has been going on too long. When are you going to end it with her for good?"

"Soon."

"Yeah, right." A dubious smirk played across my best friend's face. He was eager for me to say goodbye to Charlotte. And I understood why. He didn't care for her one bit. Why should he? Anytime she met him, she was rude, cold, and condescending. The former USC surfer dude, who could be Owen Wilson's ginger-haired twin, was way beneath her league.

At my desk, Duffy and I reviewed a proof of the upcoming issue of *Arts & Smarts*. Everything seemed on target. Things were also coming together for the popular online edition, which I proudly took credit for launching, although my father would never acknowledge me. Since I had taken charge of the start-up magazine, our advertising revenue had grown, and we were now almost at a breakeven point. My father, however, would never be proud of me until the magazine was showing a strong profit. Something he could boast of in his annual stockholder meeting.

I reviewed a couple of articles and caught Duffy up on what needed to get done this week.

"What's your schedule like, dude?" he asked, brushing a strand of his unruly ginger hair off his forehead.

I told him that I was going to edit a couple of recently submitted articles on the New York art gallery scene, and start writing my own contribution to this month's edition about hidden art treasures in the city. *Allee.* I also let him know that I would be leaving early to attend the opening of the Madewell Gallery of Old Masters. *Allee.*

"You going solo?" he asked.

"No, Charlotte's coming along. I don't have much choice."

He arched a shaggy eyebrow. "I don't get it. So, you're back together?"

"Not after tonight."

Duffy quirked a lopsided smile. "Good luck, dude." He gave me an affectionate slap on my back and loped back to his workstation in his laid-back way.

Finishing my coffee, I opened my laptop and started to type. *"Beauty can be hidden behind a pair of tortoise-shell glasses, or it can be hidden in the corner of a museum. Picasso's little-known masterpiece is just that. Tucked away on the third floor of the Metropolitan Museum of Art, it is a lyrical expression of sensual lines and flowing curves—a work of art that can make your heart stop and bring you to a mind-blowing climactic experience..."* Within one hour, I had completed the article. I reread it and felt my cock strain against my jeans. It was an accurate description of how I felt about Allee.

Limos were lined up on Fifth Avenue in front of the Met, dropping off anyone who was anyone among New York's social elite. Paparazzi were clambering on the street, eager to take a shot of the uber-glamorous crowd. Dressed in my tux, I scurried out of the Escalade and up the red-carpeted steps that led to the Met's majestic entrance. I heard several photographers shout out my name, but ignored them. Shielding my face with my hand, I ran up the stairs as fast as I could with my still sore legs.

The gala was a glittering spectacle of art and wealth. Moneyed men were in black tie, and elegant women were dressed to the nines in dazzling jewel-tone gowns and dripping with diamonds and gems. My mother, stunning in a ruby red ball gown that matched her new ring, was hobnobbing amongst the guests with her ubiquitous glass of champagne in hand, clearly proud of her cultural achievement. The Gallery, all her idea, had been in the making for two years and cost thirty million dollars to build. That was nothing compared to the hundred million dollar painting collection my parents had donated to the museum.

I made my way through the crowd to tell her how beautiful she looked and to congratulate her.

"Where's Father?" I asked, after kissing her on the cheek.

She fiddled with the ring and stiffened. "At the last minute, he couldn't make it. Some kind of crisis with shareholders." She forced a smile and then mingled again with her guests.

Damn him. This was one of the most significant accomplishments of her life. She had been dreaming about this day for years, and he couldn't be there for her. My blood was boiling. There was no shareholders' crisis. Just a crisis between his legs. He was out somewhere getting his balls sucked. Fuck him!

A familiar, deep, breathy voice in my ear catapulted me out of my thoughts. "Darling, you must come with me to get our photo taken."

I spun around. It was Charlotte. Dressed in a sleek, chartreuse silk sheath with matching emerald and diamond earrings and her platinum blond hair upswept, she looked like a goddess. She wrapped her long, toned bare arms around me and nuzzled my neck. All eyes were on her. And me. I hated her public displays of affection and just wanted to get away. Tonight, after the gala, I was going to break up with her for good. I just wasn't sure how.

"I'll get us some drinks. I'll be right back," I muttered, breaking away from her.

"Make it fast," she snapped.

Weaving in and out of the crowd, I took in snippets of conversation around me. Most of it was about who was wearing whom—be it Dior, Valentino, or another top designer. Then one conversation between two whippet-thin women made me stop in my tracks.

"I feel so sorry for Eleanor. Everyone knows what Ryan does behind her back."

My stomach churned. She wasn't referring to me.

The other woman nodded. "It's horrible. I think she knows but just closes her eyes."

I'd heard enough. My father was a scumbag. I'd always suspected that and now it was confirmed. I made a beeline to a white-gloved server and downed a glass of champagne in one gulp. The bubbly didn't numb the pain. Putting the empty glass back on the tray, I snagged two more, another for me, and one for Charlotte. When I got back to the spot where I'd left her, she was no longer there. Perhaps, she'd gone to the ladies' room to freshen up. Rather than stay put and wait for her, I decided to check out the new Madewell wing.

The wing was indeed breathtaking. Designed by one of the foremost architects in the world, it was a blend of old-world motifs and contemporary lighting that made my parents' extraordinary collection of Old Masters come to life. Each painting, be it an epic Rubens canvas or small Rembrandt portrait, was a masterpiece.

"The beauty of this Caravaggio is the milkiness of the subject's skin. When you look at it, you can practically feel her flesh beneath your fingertips…"

That raspy, know-it-all voice, with its distinct "New Yawk" accent. I'd recognize it anywhere. I wheeled around and there she was. Allee, in her museum uniform, her back toward me, giving a mini-lecture to a chicly dressed couple that I recognized from my parents' circle of friends. Still holding the flutes of champagne, I strode up to the entourage.

"So, what does the subject's skin feel like?" I asked matter-of-factly.

Allee whirled around, obviously recognizing my voice. Her bespectacled eyes met mine. If she was shocked to see me, she didn't show it.

"Sir, that's a very good question." Her voice sounded scholarly. "My sense is that the subject's skin is velvety, warm, and throbbing."

She was describing my cock at the moment to a tee. I felt heated. Man, she knew how to get to me!

The couple, having had enough of an encounter

with the painting, ambled off after briefly saying hello to me and commenting what a "fabulous" night this was.

I was alone with Allee. I offered her one of the champagne flutes.

"Are you freakin' nuts? You wanna get me fired? I can't drink on the job." She fired me a sexy smirk. "So are you like covering the event for that pseudo-intellectual, piece of crap magazine you write for?"

Man, she sure didn't mince her words. Her put down irked me, but I knew where she was coming from. *Arts &Smarts* was what it was, and didn't pretend to be some scholarly art journal. Before I could say a word in my defense, an old, matronly friend of my mother's wrapped her arms around me and kissed both cheeks.

"Why, Ryan Madewell, I haven't seen you since your graduation from Andover! You're as dashing as ever, looking more and more like your father every day!"

Inwardly, I cringed. Allee's eyes grew as round as saucers.

"Your last name is Madewell?" she asked after the matron had sashayed off. "Like in the Madewell Gallery of Old Masters?"

Embarrassed, I nodded. "Yeah, that's me. Ryan Madewell IV."

"See, I knew you were rich," she said smugly, quickly recovering from her shock.

"It's my parents who are rich," I said

defensively. "I have to work for a living."

She furrowed her thick, dark brows. "Come on. You really want me to believe that, Golden Boy?"

Jeez! You just couldn't bullshit this girl. Truthfully, I needed to work only for my sanity as I had a hefty trust fund. But I wasn't going to share that with Miss Put-Me-Down.

Lifting her glasses onto her ponytailed head, she eyed me from head to foot. She cocked a saucy smile. "You look good in a tux though I much prefer you in a pair of shorts."

My body temperature went up several notches. Holy shit! She was doing it to me again—making me hot and horny. I desperately wanted to pin her against the marble wall and shove my tongue inside her mouth. To my surprise, as if she had read my mind, she leaned seductively against the wall next to the Caravaggio. She thrust her pelvis forward and pursed her luscious lips in a sexy pout. "So, Madewell, what does this painting do for you?"

I glanced at the full, creamy-white breasts of the draped nude and then back at Allee. "It turns me on," I said breathily. *And makes me want to tear off your clothes.*

"That's a very profound effect." Her mouth curled into that wickedly seductive smile.

I wanted her. Badly. Nervously checking for onlookers—there were none as everyone had gathered at the other end of the gallery to hear my mother's speech—I moved in close, so close that our hipbones touched. Allee didn't flinch. I raised my arms above her and pressed my hands, still holding those two damn glasses of champagne, against the cold marble. Closing my eyelids halfway, I leaned into her and felt her warm, sweet breath heat my cheeks. My lips latched onto hers—oh, how delicious they were! —and as my kiss deepened with her moan, I felt my collar-length, sandy hair yanked from behind.

"What the fuck?"

Startled, I pulled away and spun around, sending one of the glasses of champagne crashing to the floor.

It was Charlotte. Her face was red with rage, her eyes narrowed into angry slivers. She grabbed the other champagne flute out of my hand and tossed the chilled bubbly contents into my face. Her eyes clashed with Allee's. "You low-life whore," she screamed. Hurt washed over Allee, but she remained silent and still.

Charlotte grabbed me by the lapel of my jacket. "We're leaving."

As she jerked me away, I turned my head. Allee still hadn't moved. Her gaze locked on mine as if we'd never see each other again. I felt sickened.

Charlotte made me take her to her Sutton Place co-op; the air between us during the ride was frigid. She stormed into her luxurious apartment and stomped straight to the bedroom. When she returned, she was holding a pile of my clothes that I had left there. She dumped them onto the floor. She disappeared again, returning with a large pair of scissors. Still in her slinky gown, she plunked down on the floor and immediately started shredding each and every piece. Every shirt. Every pair of jeans. Every pair of boxers. Every tie and tee. There wasn't a single tear shed. Or even misty eyes. Just pure, manic madness. She'd had her moments, especially when we bickered about getting engaged—she was ready, I was not—but I'd never seen her like this before. I watched with my eyes frozen wide.

"You fucking asshole," she shrieked. "Get the fuck out of my life."

I'd never heard her curse before tonight. Never. I didn't move.

"What the fuck are you waiting for?" she screamed, her voice shrill.

Suddenly, it hit me. *She* was breaking up with me. And not the other way around.

"GO!" Leaping to her feet, she grabbed one of her many Lalique figurines and hurled it at me. It hit me hard in the head, narrowly missing my eye, before it smashed to smithereens on the polished hardwood floor. I rubbed my throbbing forehead and felt warm blood trickle beneath my fingers.

The vicious assault left me dazed. But one thing was clear. That was it. I was out of there, and she was out of my life.

The breakup. That's how it happened. As simple and as fast as that.

# FIVE

The next day I was again the center of attention at my office with the Band-Aid I was wearing above my right brow to cover my nasty gash, courtesy of Charlotte.

"What happened, dude?" asked Duffy, stifling a smart-ass smile. "You get into a fight?"

"I broke up with Charlotte."

His eyes popped. "She did that to you?"

"Yeah." I told him the details of her rampage.

"Man, she's one crazy bitch." He high fived me. "You should be happy it's over."

The truth is, I was. I was a free man. Free to see another. Over lunch at my desk, I called the Metropolitan Museum of Art and asked if they could get a message to a tour guide named Allee. "A-L-L-E-E," I spelled out.

"You mean Allee Adair?" asked the operator, clearly impressed by who I was.

So, she was probably Irish. I should have guessed that by her coloring. "Yes," I said, sure that there wasn't another tour guide with her unusually spelled first name.

"Please tell her that I'd like to meet her for dinner. Have her call me on my cell phone." I gave the operator my number and hung up.

All afternoon, it was difficult for me to focus. My head hurt from the cut, and I waited anxiously to hear back from Allee. Finally, at four p.m., my cell phone rang. I recognized the caller ID number. The Met's. It had to be her.

"Hi," I said awkwardly.

"Hi," she said back in that raspy voice that completely undid me.

"So, would you like to have dinner with me tonight?"

"Sure. As long as I pay for my share."

Man, she was a strange bird. "Fine. I'll pick you up. What time do you get out of work?"

"Six."

"Great. Meet me in front of the museum."

"Look for me." CLICK.

I hit "END" on my iPhone and sucked in a deep breath. It had been a long time since I'd asked a girl out on a first date. That tingly excitement I'd felt as a teenager surged inside me. I knew the perfect place to take her. And since she insisted on going Dutch, it wouldn't cost her an arm and a leg on her meager salary.

The restaurant I took Allee to was a small Greek diner on Madison Avenue, just a few blocks away from the Met. It had been there forever. My nanny Maria used to take me and my sister there when we were kids. I remembered it having the best hot fudge sundaes in the world.

We sat facing each other in a red leather booth. The restaurant, which was extremely popular at breakfast and lunch, was not too busy at this time of day. It was filled mostly with older, neighborhood residents, many of them dining alone with a newspaper or book. After perusing the menu, we both ordered the Tuesday special—chicken potpie. When I added a glass of the house white wine, Allee followed suit.

I immediately imbibed the wine after the waiter set the two glasses on the table. My stomach bunched with nerves. What do you say to a girl on your first date? It had been such a long time. The stuff I used to talk about in high school and college would probably come across as plain out stupid. Like what's your major? Or what are you going to do after you graduate?

Allee didn't touch her wine. Instead, she scrutinized my face, zeroing in on the Band-Aid on my forehead. "So, Golden Boy, what the hell happened to your face?"

Although I really was tired of talking about it, I was glad she had started some form of conversation.

"Shaving mishap." Embarrassment mixed with shakiness as I flashed back to my violent breakup with Charlotte.

"Bullshit. I don't know any guys who shave their forehead." She paused as she studied my face further. "It was her. That blond psycho-bitch."

I grimaced. "Yeah."

"Your girlfriend? She looks like your type."

"Ex-girlfriend." It actually felt good to say that. Liberating.

She nodded pensively and took a sip of her wine. It was hard to tell what she was thinking. Finally, she said, "I hope she looks worse."

I couldn't help smiling. Her wicked sense of humor made her even sexier.

"So, Madewell, tell me something I don't know about your life."

She hardly knew a thing about my life. I told her how I was born into privilege, or at least, that's how others perceived it. Actually, it was more a life of neglect. "My mother was never there for me, and I literally had to make appointments with my father to see him."

"That's whacked." She chuckled. Her laugh was deep and sexy, and it made me smile again. I continued.

"My sister and I were raised by our nanny, Maria. I think if she hadn't been there for us, we would have run away or turned to drugs. She was loving and kept us grounded. When I turned thirteen, my parents sent me off to boarding school—Andover."

She snorted. "Bet they couldn't wait to get rid of you."

"Yeah. Seriously, if there was a boarding school for preschoolers, I would have been there."

She laughed again. I liked the fact that she enjoyed my sense of humor. Charlotte never had, finding my off-color comments totally unnecessary.

"So then what, Golden Boy?"

"No choice. Off to my father's alma mater, Harvard. He wanted me to major in finance. I wanted to major in English. After a long battle, we finally compromised. He let me major in English as an undergraduate as long as I went to Harvard Business School for grad school. His goal has always been to groom me to take over Madewell Media when he retires."

"And is that what you want to do?" asked Allee, leaning in closer to me.

"No. I want to be a novelist. But that's never going to happen. Okay, your turn."

Allee's life story was so different from mine yet, in some ways, so similar. At the age of three, she lost her parents, both artists, in a tragic auto accident. From that point on, she went in and out of the foster care system, landing with one unloving family after another. We were both orphans of sorts. What kept her going was education and books. She dreamed and worked hard, earning the grades to get her a partial scholarship and student loan to Parsons, a college known for its fine arts program. On a field trip to the Met in high school, she had fallen in love with art and vowed one day that she would work in a museum.

"Who are your favorite painters?" I asked, intrigued by her passion.

"I know it's mundane, but I love the French Impressionists. The Madewell Gallery is awesome, but it can't compare to the Met's Impressionist collection. I could hang out with those paintings all day." Her face grew dreamy, and there was yet another level of beauty to her. I think she had no clue how beautiful she was, even in that drab Met uniform.

"Why haven't you been to Paris?"

Her face turned somber. "I was almost going to go there my junior year in college."

"Why didn't you?" I immediately regretted my question because it probably had something to do with not being able to afford it.

She hesitated, running her forefinger around the rim of the wine glass. "I had to deal with some personal shit."

My eyes widened. "Like what?"

She drained her wine. "Oh, just some crap I don't want to think about." Her eyes darted to the right. "Hey, look, here come the chicken potpies."

She was obviously glad to change the subject. And I wasn't about to pursue an obviously sensitive issue this early on in the game. We both dug into the steaming dishes. I admired the gusto with which she devoured her crusty pie. So unlike Charlotte, who picked at her food (usually meager salads) like a bird. She even wiped the bottom clean with a chunk of bread.

"Dessert?" I asked.

"Sure… if we split it."

I ordered one of those delicious hot fudge sundaes that I so fondly remembered from my childhood. When the waiter set it down on our table, my eyes widened. It looked to be everything I remembered it to be. A mouthwatering, overflowing glass of vanilla ice cream, gooey fudge, and whipped cream.

"Do you want the cherry?" I asked Allee, remembering how my sister and I used to fight over it.

"Nope." She lifted the bright red candied fruit off the heap of whipped cream by its stem and then twirled it around. "Open your mouth," she ordered.

Taken aback, I did as she asked. She sensuously brushed the cherry around my lips and then dropped it into my mouth. "Swallow."

Another command. I swallowed it whole. Jesus! The cherry thing was having a strange effect on me. I was getting a serious hard on! Plus, it gave me X-ray vision. I could see Allee's tits right through her blazer and blouse. They were full and firm, dotted with rosebuds the diameter of the cherry I'd just consumed. I had the insatiable urge to tear off her uniform, lather the whipped cream all over her breasts and then lick it off.

"What are you waiting for, Madewell?" she said. Holy fuck! Was she a mind reader?

Her lips curled up into a saucy, dimpled smile that made me want her more. "The ice cream's gonna melt."

I was what was melting. Distracted by my arousal, I dug one of the long sundae spoons deep into the mountain of whipped cream and scooped up a heaping of vanilla ice cream that was dripping with rich chocolate fudge.

"Taste," I said. My turn to be in charge.

She parted her lush lips, and I slipped the spoon into her mouth. She clamped her lips over the spoon and moaned. It was such a deep, sensual sound that I felt my erection press against my jeans.

After savoring the creamy ice cream a little longer, she spread her lips. I slowly glided out the spoon.

"Mmm. That was so good."

"Let me give you another taste." I was getting off on feeding her.

"No, Madewell. Let me feed you." She reached for the other spoon and filled my mouth with a heaping portion of the hot fudge sundae. It was every bit as good as I remembered it. My eyes met Allee's. There was only one thing my mouth watered for more —her velvety tongue.

We continued this sensuous back and forth feeding until we were scraping the bottom of the sundae glass. I don't think I had ever shared a dessert with Charlotte as long as I'd known her.

Before the check came, I asked Allee if she wanted anything else.

"Yes." She smiled wickedly.

*A coffee?*

"I want to suck you, Madewell."

The temperature in the restaurant suddenly rose ten degrees, and my already hard cock boinged under my jeans.

My eyes stayed wide as she gracefully slid under the table. I squirmed as she unzipped my fly. My dick shot out. She wrapped her moist, sweet lips around the crown and rolled her tongue, chilled from the ice cream, around it. Holy shit! She knew how to give good head! Slowly, her mouth descended on the thick hard shaft. I could feel my cock growing bigger, filling the hollows of her cheeks. I was shocked by how much of me she could take in. When she reached the base, she slid her mouth back up and then right back down, her velvety tongue trailing along the back of the shaft. I arched my back and dug my fingers into the leather banquet. The elderly woman in the booth next to ours looked away from her book and eyed me strangely. God knows what she was thinking. As Allee went down on me again, I chewed my lip to stifle a groan. She picked up her pace, exerting gentle pressure with her teeth. My cock was throbbing. A tingling feeling spread from my head to my toes, and my face felt flush. The pressure was quickly becoming unbearable. I was building to a climax. On her next visit to my crown, her tongue flicked the tip. I helplessly could not hold off. My cock spasmed, and I pumped into her mouth with a hiss of relief. She lapped up my release with her tongue as if were creamy, flavorful ice cream.

Jesus. I had just gone to heaven. Charlotte had never done this to me. Never. She actually found oral sex repulsive. With a final titillating lick of my dick, Allee zipped up my fly and magically reappeared, her glasses perched atop her head. The little old lady across the way gaped, like she was about to have a coronary. Allee licked her upper lip and shot her a wicked smile. I stifled my laughter.

Man, this girl was too much. The check came before I could say a word. "Let me take care of dinner." That was the least thing I could do for the mind-blowing blow job she'd given me. She reached for it before I could and, from her purse, pulled out two crisp twenty-dollar bills. "My treat," she said brightly.

I thought about asking her to spend the night but, in the end, decided against it. Despite the outrageous blow job and my thirst for more of her, it felt too premature. I needed to slow things down, get to know her better, and wrap my head around this new relationship that was taking me to places I'd never been.

"Where do you live?" I asked once we were back on the city streets.

"Queens." Just as I suspected.

"Can I take you home?"

"Nah. I'll just take the subway."

I didn't like the idea of her going home by

herself even though it wasn't that late. "Are you sure?"

"Yeah, I'm sure, Golden Boy."

I ended up walking her to the subway station. She walked briskly and deliberately stayed a distance away from me, making it difficult for me to hold her hand or wrap my arm around her. Man, she was a hard one to figure out. One minute she was down on me, the next almost a stranger.

At the entrance to the subway, I gripped her by the shoulders and flipped her around so that she was facing me. A saucy, dimpled smile played on her face. Balls! It turned me on.

"Can I see you tomorrow night?" I asked.

"Maybe. I work some nights to help pay off my college loan and some other bills. It's one of those jobs where I'm on call. Sometimes I know in advance, and sometimes it's last minute."

"What do you do?" I asked, intrigued and sorry that she had to work two jobs.

"I'm a masseuse."

"That figures." The memory of her delicious massage flashed into my head. I suddenly yearned to have her hands all over me. And her tongue.

"I'll call you in the morning. What's the best way to reach you?"

"Just call the museum. They'll get a message to me, and I'll call you back."

I leaned in to kiss her but before my lips could reach hers, she gave me a peck on my cheek. "Keep your pants on, Madewell." With that, she flew down the steps to the subway.

# SIX

I woke up in the morning with another boner. I'd dreamt once again about fucking Allee's brains out. This time she came around me with multiple orgasms. After kicking my covers off, I jerked off, peed, showered, shaved, and got dressed. In that order. Before I left for work, I peeled the Band-Aid off my wound. I glanced at myself in the bathroom mirror. The nasty gash was already healing. With luck, there wouldn't be a scar to leave me with the memory of Charlotte written on my face for the rest of my life.

What surprised me most, however, about my reflection, was that I looked refreshed and relaxed. My bickering with Charlotte and sleepless nights had taken their toll. But this morning, for the first time in a long while, my blue-green eyes twinkled, and the dark circles beneath them had faded. What an effect this strange girl was having on me. I couldn't wait to see her again. Hopefully, she would be free tonight.

"Where were you last night, dude?" asked Duffy when I got into the office. "We missed you."

For a minute, I was perplexed, but then I remembered I had missed my weekly poker game with Duffy and a bunch of guys I'd bonded with at my health club.

"Something came up," I mumbled.

"Hot date?"

A sly smile whipped across my face. He read my lips.

Duffy chortled and we both got down to work. I reviewed a couple of articles, and just before noon, I called the Met and left a message for Allee. Fifteen minutes later, she called me back.

"Well, are we on for tonight?"

"Not sure."

"What do you mean?"

"One of my regular clients may need to switch his standing appointment to this evening. I'll know by five."

Balls! I was going to have to wait the rest of the day to find out if I could see her. My dick could fall off in the meantime.

I impatiently tapped my pen on my desk. "Call me as soon as you know."

"I will." She hung up on me before I could say goodbye. She could be so irritating. And distracting. It was hard for me to focus on my work when she was all I could think about.

To make matters worse, Charlotte left me five messages on my cell phone in addition to several more via text. The last one was a shouty, all-caps, CALL ME NOW! After some deliberation, I chose not to call her.

At 5:15, my cell phone rang. Charlotte? I breathed a sigh of relief when I saw the Met's main number on my caller ID screen. For sure, it was Allee. I eagerly swept my index finger across "answer."

"I can see you," she rasped before I could say "hi."

"Great." I had done some research. The Walter Reade Theater at Lincoln Center was doing a retrospective of Paris-based films. I was positive that this would appeal to her, so I'd reserved two tickets online.

"I'll pay you back for my ticket," she said after I told her about the plan for tonight.

I rolled my eyes, but there was no point in arguing with her. She simply didn't like to take anything material from me. I'd just have to give into her quirkiness—probably some kind of power play—although during the day I had fantasized taking her shopping at Barneys and buying her a wardrobe of fabulous designer dresses that would show off her amazing body. Wishful thinking!

"I'll pick you up the same time, same place as yesterday."

"Don't bother. I'll meet you at the theater at 7:30." CLICK. She hung up on me.

Man, she was infuriating.

Infused with nervous energy, I left my office early and headed over to my health club. I did forty-five minutes on the treadmill and another thirty lifting weights. I worked myself hard. My body showed it; sweat glistened on my well-toned muscles. I felt pumped. After a hot shower, I had Marcus take me to Lincoln Center.

With the tickets in hand, I stood outside the bustling Walter Reade Theater, eagerly waiting for Allee. The temperature had dropped considerably, and I was glad that I had worn my overcoat. I put my hands in my pockets to stay warm.

At 7:45, they let in the long line of ticket holders. Where the hell was Allee? A few minutes later, I checked my iPhone to see if she had texted or emailed me. No message. Eight o'clock. The movie was starting. My eyes darted around Lincoln Center in search of her. Was she standing me up?

Fifteen minutes went by. For sure, she was standing me up. With a heavy heart, I called Marcus to take me home. My disappointment morphed into anger. Damn her!

"Madewell," I heard someone from behind me call out breathlessly.

I whirled around. It was Allee, racing toward me at breakneck speed. She was wearing just her museum uniform and was not dressed properly for the chilly weather. I didn't know whether to be mad at her or to sweep her into my arms. I chose to contain myself. What stunned me was the range of emotions she'd made me feel in such a short time.

"Why are you so late?" I tried hard not to sound angry.

"I had to deal with some last minute shit." She was shivering.

I took off my overcoat and wrapped it over shoulders. She said nothing. There was no time to ask for details. "Come on, we probably just missed the coming attractions."

As I gripped her ice-cold hand and led the way into the theater, she shot me a quick guilt-ridden smile. That was likely as much of an apology as I would get.

Tonight's feature was *Camille,* the 1936 Hollywood tearjerker starring Greta Garbo as a Parisian courtesan who had to choose between the wealthy man who kept her and the promising young suitor who loved her. It was a good thing I had reserved tickets because the theater was packed. Our seats were toward the back, mine being next to an aisle so that I could stretch out my long legs.

I was right. We had only missed the coming attractions, and during the opening credits, I offered to get us something from the concession stand since neither of us had eaten dinner. As expected, Allee whispered to me that she would pay me back later. I'm sure she couldn't see me rolling my eyes in the dark. Five minutes later, I came back with two hot dogs, a giant popcorn, and two Cokes. Allee was already engrossed in the movie and didn't even notice.

As the movie progressed, we ate the hot dogs, sipped our sodas, and nibbled the popcorn. While Allee was intensely focused on the movie, my mind was elsewhere. Questions whirled around in my head. Should I take her hand in mine? Put mine on her thigh? Wrap my arm around her? The same damn questions I'd faced as an adolescent with those haughty Spencer girls. Even with last night's blow job, I felt awkward and anxious. I wondered if Allee felt the same way and was thinking about me. It was hard to tell in the dark, and she was so focused on the movie. I finally let myself just enjoy the film. It was a great love story, and Garbo was at her finest and most beautiful.

As the movie was nearing the end, Allee unexpectedly clasped my hand and began to sniffle. The character Garbo was playing had just died of tuberculosis in the arms of her distraught lover. Her sniffles quickly morphed into whimpers and then sobs. I'm talking loud, heaving sobs. Movie-goers turned around to look at her.

She continued to cry unabashedly. Her sobs moved me in an unexpected way. They made me want to take care of her. It was another side of her that I hadn't seen. Or anticipated. She let me brush away her tears with my fingers, and when that didn't work, I offered her my hankie. She blew her nose hard into the cotton swag and softly mumbled "Thanks." It was the first time she had ever thanked me.

The movie ended and the lights came back on. While the teary-eyed crowd made their way to the exits, Allee was unable to move. She kept sobbing and sobbing. She lifted up her glasses, and turned to me. I met her gaze. Her tear-soaked eyes made her even more beautiful than she was. I again wiped away the endless rivulets of tears. Without any resistance from her, I held her in my arms.

"Allee, what can I do?" I asked helplessly.

"Fuck me, Golden Boy."

Thirty minutes later, we stood facing each other in my candlelit bedroom. I thought fucking her would be fast and snappy, just like our first verbal encounter. But it was just the opposite. Slow. Methodical. Sensual.

Allee gazed at me for a long while. I was about to make the first move when she softly said, "Madewell, I'm gonna undress you."

I didn't move a muscle as she expertly lifted my t-shirt over my head, unzipped my jeans, and pulled them down my long legs. She then slid down my boxers and let them fall to my feet. I stepped out of them, the jeans, and my sockless loafers. I was totally naked. Her eyes roved up and down my body, lingering on the hard pillar of flesh between my legs. Smiling, she ran her fingers down my muscular arms, slowing over my defined biceps. Seamlessly, she segued to my ass, outlining the curvature, and then down to my thighs until she could go no further without squatting. My skin tingled beneath the pads of her fingertips. Her touch was so soft, so sensual, so soothing. So the opposite of the caustic girl who had verbally challenged me the first time I'd met her at the Met. Perhaps this was the real Allee or, at least, a different side of her.

She looked straight into my eyes. "Madewell, you have a nice body. It's meant to be painted."

"Thanks," I mumbled, humbled by her unusual compliment. She was no bullshitter.

Eager to see her in the nude, I reached for her blazer. She forcefully lowered my hand.

"Let me," she insisted. I had no choice as she shrugged the jacket off and let it tumble to the floor. I had to remember that she was very independent and somewhat of a control freak. For some reason, it was difficult for her to take things from me, be it money or a favor.

"You can watch," she said as she slowly unbuttoned her white blouse. With each button she undid, I felt myself getting hotter and hotter. At the same time, my dick was growing longer and thicker. By the third button, I could see a hint of her bra, and when she was done unbuttoning, she pulled the edges of her blouse apart, exposing her breasts in full view. Jesus! They were even more beautiful than I'd imagined. Firm and full, plumped up by the sexiest, lacy black bra I'd ever seen—the kind of bra that I least expected her to be wearing. Falling into the thick fold of her breasts was the single piece of jewelry she wore other than her watch—a gold locket on a chain.

She proceeded to unfasten her pleated skirt and pull it down. My eyes grew wide. She was wearing a sexy red lace garter belt over skimpy, high-cut panties that matched her bra. Slowly, one by one, she unhooked each garter, letting her sheer stockings slither down her toned legs to her slender ankles. She gracefully stepped out of the skirt and then yanked off her sensible work shoes and the crumpled hose. She stood before me in the bra, garter, and panties that rose on the sides to make her already long, shapely legs look longer.

Holy shit! Her body was beyond beautiful. Her creamy, unblemished skin shimmered in the candlelight, and I admired the curves and contours that made her deliciously womanly. Charlotte, in contrast, who still lingered in my mind, was a small-breasted, straight-as-an-arrow, stretched rubber band. Charlotte's body always screamed, "Don't touch." Allee's was screaming, "Take me all." I wanted her. It took all my willpower to resist ravaging her when she loosened her ponytail, letting her dark, wavy mane cascade over her shoulders like a whimsical cape. She looked like she had escaped a Botticelli painting.

She met my gaze. "How would you describe

what you see in that crap magazine of yours?"

For a writer, I was wordless. I was too shell-shocked to move my lips. Finally, I managed one word: "Hot." *Fucking hot!*

The corners of her lips curved into a sexy smirk. "Madewell, for a man of words, you surprise me. You could do better than that."

Her put-down actually turned me on. My fully erect cock twitched. I felt like a high-speed elevator going up as she slipped off her scanty undergarments and tossed them like a stripteaser across the room. My eyes never strayed from her nor did they blink.

"Fuck me now, Madewell."

Her directness sent blood rushing to my shaft. It felt like a volcano ready to explode. I scooped her up into my arms and carried her to my bed. I laid her face up and then lowered myself to the mattress, straddling her between my knees. Her milky white breasts quivered, and her pussy called my name. As hungry as my throbbing cock was, I wasn't ready to fuck her. I wanted to get to know every part of her.

Planting my hands on either side of her for support, I slathered my tongue up her torso. First stop—her navel. I dipped the tip into the pit and then circled around it. Pure sweetness! My tongue's journey continued across her ribcage until it landed in the thick warm fold between her breasts. I swept the locket aside with my hand and laved her warm cleavage. I felt like an explorer staking out a new territory. Everything about Allee was a discovery. The taste of her. The feel of her. The smell of her. The way she moved. My imagination had not prepared me for the riches I had found—or for those I would soon discover.

Lifting my head, I studied her breasts. Unlike Charlotte's, they were so full and sensual, tipped with glorious rosebud nipples. They were just as I had pictured them. Pink, pert, and perfectly puckered. I moved my hands to the mounds, and groped them between my fingers. They were dense yet so velvety soft. I squeezed and massaged them, circling my thumbs around her tender buds. "Beautiful," I said breathily. A moan escaped her mouth.

I wanted those beautiful rosebuds in my mouth. I wanted to taste them, suck them, roll my tongue around them... even bite them. I sealed my greedy mouth over one and nibbled it. It was indeed a rare delicacy. She moaned again. I worked the other one before running my tongue in a straight line to her neck. She tasted so, so sweet, and the scent of her was delicious. As I rolled my tongue up and down her neck like a paintbrush, her back arched and she let out a rapturous "aah." It was obviously very sensitive and linked to her erogenous zone.

"What do you want, Madewell?" she managed between moans.

I only wanted one thing. "I want to be inside you."

"Come," she rasped.

"Are you on birth control?"

She smiled wistfully. "Don't worry. You can't get me pregnant."

I took that to mean she was, and though I knew better, I was glad not to have to resort to a condom. To be honest, I wasn't even sure if I had any handy since I'd stopped using them with Charlotte a long time ago.

With my powerful knees, I parted her legs, repositioning us for the inevitable. I wanted our first time together to be as good for her as it would be for me. I stroked her folds, astonished how warm and wet they already were. I found her clit and played with it, rubbing and squeezing it. It grew hard beneath my fingers.

She shrieked. "Oh, Madewell, you're driving me insane."

I was turning myself on as I turned her on. Her pussy was so exquisite! And my erection was at its peak.

"You're so beautiful," I breathed into her ear, my fingers never leaving her clit.

"Now! Fuck me now!" she cried out.

She groped my heavy arousal and inserted the crown into her core. Inch by thick inch, I poured my cock into her until I could go no further. She was so tight. So hot. So wet. I groaned while she let out a dreamy sigh.

Slowly, I withdrew my thick length, and just as slowly, I slid it back down her hot, moist passage. As hungry as my cock was, I wanted to savor the sensation of being inside her. *God, she felt good!* After a few more delicious, soft strokes, I picked up my pace, pummeling into her deep and rhythmically. Just like in my dream, she met my every thrust, intensifying the outrageous pleasure she was giving me. She groaned each time I hit her magic spot, the erotic sound of her voice only adding to my ecstasy.

Oh, man! I was losing myself in her. Endless tingles shot down my legs, from the inside of my thighs all the way to my toes. I was on fire. She was taking me to the edge. To the point of no return.

I knew she must be close too. She was panting, her soft skin beneath me slick with sweat like mine. She dug her nails into my back, the pain bringing me closer to the brink. I pounded harder and faster; she began to scream.

"Oh, baby!" I found myself saying. I couldn't get enough of her. With one last hard thrust, and a grunt from deep within me, my cock exploded inside her as her own waves of pleasure met mine.

"Oh, God!" she cried out.

Wasted, I collapsed on top of her and buried my head in the hollow of her neck, inhaling her intoxicating scent. Slowly, I pulled out of her. She wrapped her arms around my back and, for the second time tonight, she sobbed—this time softly.

"What's the matter, Allee?" I asked urgently, brushing her damp hair out of her face. Was it not good for her? Had I hurt her?

She clutched her locket and gazed at me with

her tear-filled eyes. "Madewell, you were supposed to fuck me. Not make love to me."

I crushed my lips against hers, silencing her sobs.

# SEVEN

S he slept naked, spooned in my arms, that night. My palm held her heartbeat as I inhaled the sweet smell of her. I couldn't fall asleep. All I could think about was the mind-blowing experience I'd had with this sassy Irish girl from Queens. I had never experienced anything like it with any other girl. Especially Charlotte, whose idea of making love was along the lines of let's get it over with. She fucked with the reserve that colored her whole life. Beige. Quietly and dispassionately. "Mind-blowing" was not part of her vocabulary. She had never cared for me grunting or groaning, so when I came, I had to stifle my sounds. She would always assure me that she had come, but the truth was, I could never tell if she really had.

Not Allee. Like everything she did, she came with gusto and brutal honesty. And she had made me come the same way. Where the hell had she learned to fuck like that? I had the burning urge to wake her and make love to her all night, but the peacefulness on her angelic face held me back. I finally drifted off, the memory of her pussy dancing in my head.

When I woke up in the morning, I was greeted by the unmistakable smell of bacon and eggs—and freshly brewed coffee. Allee wasn't in bed. She must be downstairs cooking.

She trotted upstairs, carrying a wicker tray with breakfast for two. She was wearing one of my expensive cotton dress shirts that stopped midway on her sculpted thighs. It turned me on that she was wearing my shirt—that, in some way, she was inside me. Knowing her bare pussy was likely beneath my shirt turned me on even more. I felt the beginnings of a hard-on.

She lowered the tray to the bed and then crawled into it, facing me. She wasn't wearing her glasses, and her ebony hair was gathered into a high ponytail. Her skin was dewy and her espresso bean eyes twinkled. Sheesh! She was beautiful in the morning!

"What time to you have to be at the Met?" I asked, helping myself to a mug of the steaming coffee.

"I don't," she grinned. "I have the day off." She lifted a forkful of the scrambled eggs to her mouth and savored it, smiling as she swallowed. I loved the way she loved food.

I immediately reached for my cell phone on the floor next to my bed and hit Duffy's number. I was hoping to reach his voice mail but instead he picked up.

"What's up, dude?"

"I need you to cover for me today. I'm sick. I'm not coming in."

Allee giggled.

"Bullshit. Are you getting laid?" asked Duffy.

Damn. It was hard to pull the wool over his eyes because Duffy thought with his dick.

"How many times have you done it?"

"None of your business. I owe you."

"Just get me some of what you've got."

I rolled my eyes. Poor Duffster. He really needed to get laid. Assured that he would take care of things, I ended the call.

"Where were we?" I asked Allee.

"We were here."

She placed the breakfast tray on the floor and smothered me with kisses. The kisses led to another delicious session of lovemaking. A tangle of legs and tongues. Moans and groans. Two heated bodies that couldn't stay away from each other. After we exploded together, we showered.

Facing me, she lathered my balls and then my rod, making it thick and hard yet again. "Oh, Allee," I cried out as she ran her hand up and down the slippery shaft. Waves of pleasure were coursing through my entire body. I, in turn, rubbed her clit, turning it into a marble. Our breathing grew haggard. I held her as she arched her back and sensuously caught droplets of water on her tongue. She was so sexy. And beautiful. And mine. I thought I might have been dreaming until she cried out my name. "Madewell." As she convulsed around me, my own climax met hers. Before stepping out of the stall, I lifted her into my arms and showered her with kisses.

We never left my loft. In fact, except for retrieving the Chinese food I ordered in, we never left my bedroom.

"I'll pay you back for lunch," Allee said, sitting cross-legged on my mattress as she fed me a heaping of Lo Mein.

"I'll put it on your tab." Before she could insert the chopsticks into my mouth, I smacked her lush lips with a playful kiss. I had no intention of ever having her pay me back.

While we continued to feed each other the tasty noodles, my landline rang. I let it go to my answering machine.

"Ryan, darling. I think we can make things right. It was just a little skittish skirmish. Mummy says we're just having pre-nuptial jitters. Let's have dinner tonight. I love you. Call me back."

It was Charlotte. I knew it and so did Allee. The chopsticks that were heading into my mouth froze in mid-air.

"She's still into you," she said, matter-of-factly. "You and she belong together. You come from the same tribe."

I cupped her head in my hands. We were still sitting cross-legged on my bed, facing each other.

"Look at me, Allee Adair."

She slowly tilted her chin up until her eyes met mine.

"It's over between Charlotte and me. You've got to believe me." I looked into her eyes so deep I could practically see inside her.

"You're full of shit."

"I'll show you what I'm full of."

In a heartbeat, I tore off the shirt of mine she'd put back on. I left no part of her body untouched. It was all mine to stroke, suck, lick, and gnaw. She squealed with delight as I fumbled with the drawstring of my sweats and pulled them off. Spreading her legs, I thrust my hard thickness into her center and finished her off with an orgasm that rocked her body and mine.

I lost count of how many times we made love. Of how many times she'd come. And I'd come. Each orgasm was as spectacular as the one before, leaving us only wanting more. Finally wasted, we spent the rest of the afternoon cuddled up in my bed listening to music—she loved Adele, Edith Piaf, and Debussy—and talking about our dreams. She dreamed one day of living in Paris, working as a curator at the Musée D'Orsay.

"Do you speak French?" I asked, toying with her gold locket.

"*Bien sur*," she replied, her French accent

charmingly laced with her heavy New York one.

I, in turn, shared my dream of becoming a great writer. Like Hemingway, Fitzgerald, and all the greats before and after them.

"So, what else have you written besides bullshit articles for that piece of crap magazine of yours?"

Man, she could be acerbic. I thought my articles were good, for what they were, but instead of defending myself, I said, "Lots of short stories."

"Let me read one"

I was taken aback. I had never shared any of my personal writings with anyone. Not my father. Not my mother. Not Charlotte. Not even my sister, or my best friend Duffy.

I got up from the bed and crossed the room to the desk where I kept a file of my stories. I randomly pulled one out. It was about an estranged father and son who finally bond when they're both old men.

I returned to the bed, and Allee snatched it out of my hand. She immediately began to read. My eyes stayed riveted on her, my heart thudding. I wasn't sure if my anxiousness was tied to my desire for her or my fear of what she would think of my writing.

"Why are you staring at me, Madewell?" she asked as she flipped to the second page. She hadn't looked up once, yet she knew my eyes were on her.

"I'm not," I said in defense.

"Bullshit. You're staring at my legs. If you want me to finish this story, you'd better stop it."

Man, she was irritating. And such a tease. The deliberately sexy way she was sitting with her knees bent and apart was making me horny as hell. I wanted her to read faster.

When she was done, she handed me back the story and looked straight at me. She fidgeted with her locket.

"You're good, Madewell," she said in a matter-of-fact voice, saving me from having to ask her what she thought.

"Not great?"

"Good is the enemy of better."

"What do you mean?" She was pissing me off.

"Next time, write with your heart and not the tip of your dick."

Before I could ask her what she meant by that, her cell phone rang. I didn't want her to answer it, but she insisted. Her thick brows furrowed when she gazed at the caller ID number. "Fuck. I've got to take this." Her voice wavered.

"Hi, Sid... shit... okay... where?... okay... I'm on my way." She ended the call and leaped out of the bed. She quickly donned her clothes.

*Sid?* Was she seeing someone else? A pang of jealousy slashed through me. "Who the hell is Sid?"

"My other boss. I've gotta split. I'm late for a massage client." She hurried the words.

"Male or female?" While I was relieved that Sid wasn't some other guy she was seeing, the thought of her touching another man made me cringe.

"A woman," she said hastily to my relief.

She bounded down the winding stairs, with me, naked, trailing behind her.

She grabbed her purse, which she'd left on a couch, and hurried to the elevator. I pressed her against the metal door and pinned her to it with my body. I leaned into her, my lips heading straight for hers. To my surprise, she jerked her head away.

"Madewell, I've gotta go. Please." Her pained eyes were begging me to release her. As much as I wanted to hold her in my arms forever, I let go of her. I pushed the call button, and the elevator door slid open. She scurried inside it.

"Can I see you later tonight?" I asked, holding the door open with my body.

She shook her head. "No, not tonight."

I let go of the door and she disappeared.

Balls. She was out of my life again. Her sudden departure left me bereft. I was frustrated and restless. It was too late to go into the office, and too early to grab a bite to eat. Besides, I wasn't hungry. But I had to do something to release this crazy energy. The gym? Nah. I was too tired from my sexual workout with Allee. I headed back upstairs. My short story was still lying on the bed. After putting on some sweats, I reread it. I hated to admit it, but Allee was right. It was good, but something was missing from it. Taking it with me, I crossed the room and sat down at my desk where my laptop faced me. I opened up the document on my desktop and began to type, forcing myself to really put my heart and soul into the two main characters. To really feel what they were experiencing. More show, less tell. An hour later, I came to the words THE END, and I reread the story. You know what, it was a hell of a lot better. Sadness washed over me. The father and the son had gone on an emotional journey that had brought them to a peaceful place even though their lives were both coming to an end. I couldn't wait to show it to Allee. Part of me wanted to call her, but damn it, I didn't have her cell phone number. And she was probably busy with her massage client. Besides, I shouldn't act too eager. My mother always said, "Absence makes the heart grow fonder." Perhaps, that's what kept her with my father.

Hungry now, I wound downstairs when my cell phone rang. I made a mad dash to the kitchen, where it was lying on the polished steel counter. I was hoping it was Allee and praying it wasn't Charlotte. It was neither. It was my father. Ryan Madewell III.

"Hello, Father."

"Ryan, I want you to meet me at the Four Seasons at six."

He ended the phone call before I could say, "Yes, sir."

His curtness unnerved me. What did he want? No one said no to my father, including me. Fuck. I had less than an hour to shower, shave, get dressed in full suit and tie, and get uptown in the middle of rush hour. Being late for my father came with repercussions. I was going to have to take the subway.

The Four Seasons bar was bustling. Well-dressed Fortune 500 executives were quietly mingling with each other, some with extremely attractive women beside them. Like my father, Charlotte hung out here too. Inwardly, I shuddered, hoping I wouldn't run into her.

I spotted my father right away, seated at the ample corner table that was permanently reserved for him. Clad in an expensive, custom-made gray suit and matching tie that went well with his slicked-back salt and pepper hair, he was already nursing his thirty-dollars-a-pop scotch. Women eyed me as I wove through the bar to his table.

"Have a seat, son." His eyes were steely, and his voice was cold.

I nervously sank into the plush leather club chair across from him.

His eyes stayed riveted on my face without blinking, and his mouth was pressed into a grim line. "Where were you this afternoon?"

"What do you mean?" I shot back, hoping a waiter would come by soon to take my drink order. I certainly wasn't going to tell him about my afternoon with Allee.

"You weren't at the shareholders' meeting."

Fuck! I had totally forgotten about that dreaded meeting. My father expected me to be there. No ifs or buts about it.

"I called your office. They said you weren't in."

I fumbled for an excuse. "Um, uh, I was sick."

His menacing eyes lanced into me. "Don't bullshit me, Ryan. And don't ever do it again. You will pay the price."

With that, he slapped a hundred dollar bill on the table and strode off, his gait a blend of grace and arrogance. I was too numb to move. My own father, that bastard, had threatened me. Maybe, he should pay the price. But deep inside, I knew I could never beat my father at his own game. Or win a place in his heart.

I needed a drink. Desperately. My eyes darted around the bar for a waiter and then they grew wide. Heading out of the bar, was someone who looked a lot like Allee. At least from the back. She had long, ebony hair that cascaded past her shoulders, well-toned calves, and slender ankles. And a perfect ass. Except it couldn't be Allee. She was wearing a tight, mid-thigh blue dress cut low in the back and matching six-inch stilettos. She walked seductively in them like she was born wearing them. No, it couldn't be Allee. I must just be fantasizing about her. Damn the effect she was having on me.

"Why, hello, Ryan." A too-familiar voice hurled me out of my fantasy. I looked up. It was Charlotte with a flute of champagne in her hand. She was dressed in a stunning tweed suit, Chanel I thought. "Do you mind if I join you?" She took the empty seat to the right of me. My stomach churned.

She took a sip of her champagne. "I'm sorry about the other night. I think I may have had too much to drink."

"There's nothing to apologize about," I said without a trace of emotion.

Her classically gorgeous WASP face brightened. "So we're back together." It was a statement, not a question.

"No." I was actually now glad I didn't have a drink because it might have blurred my thinking and made me say things I didn't really mean or want to say.

Her cat-green eyes narrowed, and her voice took on a snippy tone. "What do you mean?"

"I mean, it's over between us. I don't want to see you anymore, Charlotte."

Her face turned into a glacier. I thought she would throw the flute at me—just what I needed, another gash—but instead she slammed it onto the table. Inwardly, I sighed with relief as she leaped up from the chair. "Call me when you've come to your senses," she hissed before storming out of the bar.

I finally ordered a drink, pleased that I hadn't given Charlotte any hope for reconciliation. There was another girl working her way into my heart. The complicated, mysterious, and beautiful, Allee Adair.

# EIGHT

"What's she like?" Duffy asked me first thing in the morning before we sat down to review the upcoming edition of *Arts & Smarts*.

"A lot different from Charlotte. She has dark hair and lives in Queens."

"No, I mean in bed."

I rolled my eyes. Like I said, he thought with his dick. My silence gave him the answer he was seeking.

"Find out if she has a friend." Duffy never had any luck in the girlfriend department. The poor bastard needed to get laid before his dick withered away.

I thanked him for covering for me yesterday and then told him to get to work. The magazine was going to press on Friday. There were tight deadlines to meet.

As for me, getting into my work was easier said than done. I couldn't focus. All I could think about was Allee. I felt different about her than the other girls in my past, including Charlotte. There was something about her that made me feel connected to her despite our social and cultural differences. She challenged me. Made me think. Made me laugh. Made me take stock of myself. Made me feel alive. And made me fuck like I'd never fucked before. I hardly knew her, yet I was afraid of losing her.

With shaky fingers, I dialed the Met and, once again, asked my favorite operator to give her a message to call me back. The jovial operator, who was by now used to me calling, promised to get the message to her quickly. I hung up the phone.

All day I waited for her to return my call. She didn't. Damn it! Why didn't I take down her cell phone number? I had no other way to get in touch with her.

At six thirty, I had my work done for the day. I marched past Duffy's desk and asked him if he wanted to go for a drink.

"No action tonight?" he asked.

"You overestimate me, Duffster."

One hour later, I was drunk as hell. Damn that girl.

# NINE

T he week went from bad to worse. The printing press malfunctioned, shorting our circulation, ultimately costing Madewell Media a shitload of money. And me, a shitload of grief from my father. Worse, Allee didn't return my calls. No matter how many messages I'd left for her, including one that I had found her eyeglasses—she had left them behind in my loft when she'd rushed off to her massage client. Interestingly, when I had put them to my eyes to see how nearsighted she was, I'd discovered that they were pretend glasses; there was no prescription in the lenses. I was baffled by why she would wear such big, nerdy glasses when, in fact, she really didn't need them.

As the week progressed, a slew of negative thoughts passed through my head. They kept me distracted at work when I couldn't afford to be and tossing and turning until the wee hours of the morning, further affecting my ability to get anything done work wise. Maybe I was just a one-night stand. Or she thought I was a jerk (I'd been accused of that before). Or thought I had gone back to Charlotte. Or I wasn't her type. Maybe Sid was more than her other boss. Or she met someone new. Or something bad happened to her.

That was the last thought that crossed my mind on Friday. It was eight thirty in the evening; I had been working late the whole week to make up for lost time. Panic gripped me. Why hadn't I thought of that before? Grabbing my overcoat, I raced out of the office and asked Marcus to drive me as fast as he could to the Met. Thankfully, the Met was open until nine o'clock on Friday nights. I had to get there before it closed. To see if she was there.

The mid-November night was chilly, and storm clouds threatened. My heart beat a mile a minute as we inched uptown. The bumper-to-bumper Friday night traffic was miserable. At this rate, we'd never get there in time. At Forty-Second Street and Madison, I jumped out of the car and began to run uptown. A former track star and marathon runner, I could do it. I had to do it!

My heart raced, and my lungs burned as I charged up Fifth Avenue, weaving in and out of the swarms of pedestrians. If people were staring at this crazed runner, I was oblivious.

When I arrived at the Met, it was after nine. Hundreds of people were flocking out of the front doors. I was panting. My eyes searched the crowd in desperation for her. I hoped I wasn't too late. Finally, after the crowd had thinned, I spotted her. She was wearing a drab gray wool coat and a striped knit hat along with a new pair of eyeglasses that were almost identical to the ones she'd left at my loft. She looked worn-out as she trudged down the steps. Fuck. Maybe something was wrong with her. I mounted the steps two at time, hoping to meet her half way.

"Allee," I shouted out to her.

Her mouth dropped open when she saw me. She galloped down the steps, attempting to run past me, but I caught her and held her firmly in my arms. She squirmed, trying to break away, but she was no match for my strength. I studied her face. Her eyes were painfully sad and her cheeks were sallow. She had lost weight.

"Get away from me, Madewell," she begged. There were tears in her eyes.

I didn't let go of her and, in fact, squeezed her tighter. "Why haven't you returned my calls?"

"Madewell, please! Let go of me." Her voice was watery and desperate.

"No, you're not going anywhere until you answer my question."

"I don't belong with you. You're too good for me."

"No, baby, you're too good for me." I pressed her even tighter against me.

Thunder roared in the night sky.

"Please! I've gotta go home and get ready for a massage client."

Maybe she had just been overworking. Fuck her client. I tugged hard at her ponytail that hung out from under her funky hat. "You're coming home with me."

"I can't." She blinked back tears. "You don't understand—"

"Stop it!" I crushed my lips against hers, hushing her, and pulled her down to a sitting position on the step where we were sparring. She couldn't resist my assault. Her tongue hungrily met mine, and a hot bolt of energy surged through my body.

Lightening flashed, and another loud burst of thunder followed. The sky opened up, and torrential rain fell upon us. But it didn't stop us. Soaked, our embrace deepened, the warmth of it fending off the icy chill of the pounding drops. I don't know how long it lasted, but she was the first to pull away. Wet streaks rolled down her cheeks... tears, not the rain.

"Why me, Madewell?" she asked, her voice hoarse and strained.

"Because, Allee Adair, I'm suffocating without you. You're the air I need to breathe." Cradling her in my arms, I removed her rain-streaked glasses and brushed away the shimmering rivulets dripping down her face. Just the mere touch of her infused me with light.

She looked deep into my eyes, hers still watering. "Oh, Madewell, I'm so afraid."

"Afraid of what, baby?" I held her tear-drenched face in my hands.

Her lips quivered. "That I'll hurt you."

That wasn't possible, I thought as I swept her

into my arms and carried her down the rain-soaked steps, my lips never leaving hers.

I carried her straight into my bathroom steam room. She was shivering wet. I set her down and rapidly peeled off her drenched layers of clothing. I removed mine just as fast. She let me wrap my arms around her naked body and hold her close to me as a cloud of steam warmed us. Tears were still streaming down her beautiful face, mingling with the steamy mist. I sealed my mouth over hers and kissed her deeply and passionately. With my lips still covering hers, I lifted her up off the water-coated tiled floor.

"Wrap your legs around me, baby," I breathed into her ear.

She did as I asked, twisting her long limbs around my waist like a pretzel. I carried her to the edge of the steamy room and pressed her against the dripping wet back wall, just high enough so that my cock could shoot easily into her glorious pussy. Her arms wrapped around my shoulders.

"Baby, I've missed you so much." I studied her angelic face, made dreamy in the steamy haze. My lips latched onto hers and pressed into another deep, tongue-driven kiss. Her velvety breasts skimmed my chest. I groaned as my girth grew between my legs.

"Oh, Golden Boy," she rasped as my mouth

released hers. "Make me come."

I was going to make her come hard. With my hand, I angled my hungry cock and guided it inside her. Her inner muscles clenched around my hardness. Such a warm "welcome back!" We both moaned with pleasure.

I dragged my cock back down her own steamy, wet walls, and then pressing her tight against the tiles with my hips, I picked up my pace, grinding into her with ferocity and velocity. Her rhythmic moans let me know I was hitting all the right spots. Her legs squeezed tighter around me, and my hands moved to her hips to keep her steady against the wet, slippery wall as I pounded faster and harder. Panting now, she fisted my hair with one hand and raked my back with the other. My breathing grew ragged with hers. As I built toward climax, the steam hissed in my ears.

"Come for me, Allee," I cried, pining to feel her shudder around me before I came.

"Oh, Madewell!" she screamed out as her orgasm broke loose.

"Oh, baby!" I groaned back. With a final deep thrust that made her whimper, I exploded inside her as her waves of ecstasy rippled around me.

I held her up against the wall for several long minutes, my pulsing cock still inside her, and then set her down onto one of the seating banquets that lined the other walls.

"I'll be right back," I breathed. I ambled to the glass door, turning my head to glance at her before I exited. In the cloud of steam, she looked so ethereal leaning back against the wall, with her eyes closed and her long damp tresses falling loosely over her full breasts. The sight of her otherworldly beauty made my balls tingle.

I came back to fetch her, scooping her up in my arms to transport her to the hot bath I had drawn. I gently lowered her into the deep copper tub. The water rose to her buoyant breasts. Scattered scented candles threw off muted lighting, bathing her in a golden haze, and Jason Mraz's "I Won't Give Up" filtered softly through the built-in speakers.

"That's a beautiful song," she said softly, her soulful eyes gazing up to meet mine.

"Yeah. It reminds me of us." We still had much to learn, but what I did know is that she made me whole in a way no one ever had. There was no way I was going to let her go. Getting down on my knees, I threaded my fingers through her loose, damp hair and cherished the feel of her.

She shivered.

"Are you still cold, baby?"

"No," she rasped seductively. "I'm hot. Hot for you."

My cock twinged. It was aching again for her. Swelling and throbbing. I slid gracefully into the tub behind her. I lifted her buttocks onto my thighs and folded my arms around her taut torso. My hands groped her supple breasts, massaging and squeezing them. As her nipples hardened, she arched back her head and, with eyes closed, hummed to the melody of the song. Her sensual, husky hum tugged at my heartstrings. It came from somewhere deep inside her, a sad, distant place I didn't know or understand.

Leaving one hand on a tender breast, I sponged her back and neck, alternating the dabbing movements with flutter kisses. She tasted and smelled so delicious. I let the sponge fall into the water. Nibbling the nape of her neck and earlobes, I moved my hand to the soft folds between her legs. After stroking them, I rubbed her clit with the pad of my thumb. Around and around, in firm little circles, the way she liked it. Her nub hardened quickly. Her chest rose and fell as her breathing grew heavy. I just couldn't get enough of her.

"Are you ready for me again?" I breathed in her ear. I was a ready as ready could be. My cock, a pillar of hard flesh between my legs. A torpedo ready to be released.

"Take me, you fucking son-of-a-bitch."

Her dirty talk turned me on even more. I lifted her a few inches off me and spread her legs slightly, making way for my thick, hard, pulsating dick. With one forceful thrust, I dove into her from behind. The sudden deepness of me inside her made her yelp. I splayed my hands firmly over the haunches of her hips and ground up and down her warm, wet tunnel. Gripping the rim of the tub for support, she bounced up and down, meeting my every thrust, deepening the insatiable pleasure her exquisite pussy was giving me. I felt my cock swelling inside her as I drove toward another orgasm with single-minded fury. Our moans and groans washed out the music. She was riding me to heaven.

This time I wanted to come with her. "Now!" I growled.

"Oh, Golden Boy!"

As she came shuddering around me, spasms rocked my cock. My whole body shook as I bathed her blissfully with my molten release. It was the most mind-blowing orgasm I'd ever had.

I told her I loved her; I couldn't help it.

From that moment on, Allee Adair was officially my girlfriend.

# TEN

We fell into a routine. We got up together, had coffee, went for a jog, and then fucked our brains out, which could be anywhere from the elevator to the bed to the kitchen counter. Then we showered together, sometimes unable to resist each other, and got ready for work. I usually walked, dropping Allee at the local subway stop. I urged her to let Marcus drive her to the Met, but she refused, saying it would take too long and not look good among her fellow staffers.

Most nights, we went to my health club together and then came home and ordered in, Allee always paying for half. But at least once a week, Allee would make me dinner. She was a fantastic cook, having mastered Julia Childs's recipes to make her feel like Paris was at her fingertips. Usually, after dinner, Allee would read an art history book, curled up on a couch, and I would write. Not articles for *Arts & Smarts*, but rather short stories. I had shown Allee my revised story about the father and son, and it had brought tears to her eyes.

"That's the way, Madewell," she said to me.

"Do you really think it's good?" I responded in disbelief.

"No." She paused, making me quiver with doubt. "It's great. Now shut up and write another one before I change my mind." She poked her tongue out at me. I wanted to suck it. Man, she was infuriating. Such a tease!

And, of course, every night when we were together we would make glorious love. Usually more than once. Sometimes all night long. We couldn't get enough of each other, and I missed her every minute she was away from me. She was not allowed to text or make personal phone calls while at her job except during her short lunch break, so the days at work were particularly frustrating for me. It didn't stop me, however, from sending her sexy text messages. All day long, I longed to hold her and smother her with kisses. My mouth ached with desire and so did my dick. More than occasionally, I had to hide my boner under my desk or jerk off in the men's room. It was pretty amazing I got any work done at all.

Our life together was so different than the one I had with Charlotte, who had insisted on dining out seven times a week at some posh Upper East Side restaurant where she usually didn't eat a thing. She never wanted to eat downtown or stay at my place, as she couldn't stand to be away from "her people"—rich, snobby Upper East Siders. Sex with Charlotte was perfunctory. Get it in and get it out. She needed her beauty sleep. Most weeknights, we never had any.

Talking about my ex, we bumped into each other a couple of times, but each encounter was icy and uncomfortable. Though I had seen her linked with other eligible billionaire bachelors in various gossipy publications, my mother told me she was furious with me, but convinced I would come to my senses. Neither she nor my father was pleased that I had dropped her. Neither were Charlotte's hoity-toity parents who had already reserved The Pierre for a June wedding. My mother wanted to know if I was dating someone new. I told her I was. She was eager to meet her, and so was my father. Both hoped she came from as pedigreed a family as the Vanowens. The last thing I wanted to do was to introduce Allee to my drunken mother or subject her to my judgmental father. Unfortunately, at some point, that dreaded meeting would have to take place.

There was only one downside to living with Allee. She was still at Sid's beck and call. A few times a week, he would call, and she would have to go directly from her job at the Met to a massage client. Still suspicious of Sid, I wanted her to stop with the second job. It took her away from me and made both of us irritable.

"I can easily pay off your college loans and any other debts," I told her one night after a delicious session of making love.

"Madewell, I can't accept your money," replied Miss Feisty and Independent.

"Well, then, maybe you can work fewer hours at night."

"I'm trying to work it out with Sid. It's not that easy. Let's not talk about it anymore. Please."

Knowing I was never going to win this battle, I had no choice but to let her continue with the extra job. On those nights, she always went back to her apartment in Queens. I had only been there once—to help her pick up some clothes and bare necessities to keep at my loft. Located in an ethnically-mixed section of Forest Hills, it was a small, rundown flat but furnished with flea market finds that reflected Allee's quirky personality and gave it charm; posters of her favorite Impressionist paintings hung on the walls. I insisted that she let Marcus drive her there when she was done with her massage appointments. But again, she adamantly declined, preferring to take the subway. It made me sick with worry that she traveled there alone late at night. She told me to get over it. She was a big girl who had taken care of herself her entire life. The only thing I'd gotten her to agree to was giving me her cell phone number so that we could be in touch all the time. I begged for a set of her keys in case she ever lost them or in case of an emergency. But she refused.

We spent our first Christmas together. We both agreed to buy each other a present, but only under

Allee's stipulation that we not spend a lot of
money.

"Madewell, if you buy me something expensive,
I swear I'll return it and never speak to you again,"
she had threatened over dinner one night.

"Will you still let me make love to you?"

She did her infuriating eye roll. "I'll have to
spank you first."

A spanking from my girl sounded very
appealing. My cock tingled.

While I was dying to buy her something
super expensive like the vintage diamond watch
I'd seen in the window of a local antiques shop
to replace the shabby cloth band one she wore, I
ended up buying a beautiful, thick collectors' book
containing reproductions of all the paintings that
hung in the Musée D'Orsay.

"Oh, Madewell, I love it!" she beamed as she
unwrapped it under our tree Christmas morning.
Little did she know that it cost several hundred
dollars, even on eBay. She flung her arms around
me and initiated a deep passionate kiss. As my lips
melded against hers, my cock hardened, wanting
more.

My gift was a large heart-shaped chrome key
ring—something I desperately needed as I was
always misplacing or losing my keys. On it were
the keys to her apartment as well. It was about
time, and it made me feel better knowing I now
had easy access to her apartment in case of an
emergency. I returned the kiss.

I thanked my lucky stars that my parents had flown to their house in Aruba to escape the frigid winter weather. Allee prepared a delicious beouf bourguignon dinner, which we consumed in the late afternoon with a bottle of hearty Burgundy wine. Afterward, we retreated to my bed and fucked our brains out until we could fuck no more. We cuddled together and watched *Miracle on 34th Street*. I gazed up at my skylight. Snow was falling.

Allee Adair was my miracle. My angel. The best Christmas present I'd ever gotten. After one last orgasmic round of kissing, stroking, licking, and groping, we drifted off facing each other. Skin to skin. Organ to organ. Heart to heart.

Three months into our relationship, Allee came flying down the steps to the Met when I went to pick her up, something she rarely let me do. It was Valentine's Day, and she had reluctantly agreed to let me take her to dinner at the Café des Artistes, easily the most romantic restaurant in the city. Wearing a vintage faux-leopard coat that she had found at a local flea market, she looked radiant.

"Guess what!" she beamed as she climbed into the Escalade. "I'm going to Paris for a year!" She flung her arms around me.

My heart practically stopped. "What do you mean?"

"I won a fellowship to study art at the prestigious

École des Beaux Artes. I applied for it last year."

I grabbed her by her shoulders. "What am *I* going to do?"

"You can come with me. Write in the Café de Flore like Hemingway."

"It doesn't work that way. I've got a fucking job. I run a magazine." Rage was seeping through my veins.

"Then we'll go our separate ways." Her expression darkened. "Hey, Madewell, I know our relationship isn't going to last forever. You're a Fifth Avenue gazillionaire, and I'm a poor girl from Queens. It's just a matter of time until you find another Charlotte."

*So she thought she was some kind of Band-Aid?* I was hurt, not only by her lack of trust in me, but also by her own lack of self-esteem.

"But how will you support yourself?" My tone was resentful and challenging.

"It includes living expenses, and besides, I've saved some money from my other job."

*Damn that other job.*

"I don't want you to go." I was loud and clear about it.

"But I've waited my whole life to go to Paris."

"And I've waited my whole life for a girl like you. Allee Adair, will you marry me?"

It came out as simple as that. On Valentine's Day. Stuck in traffic at the corner of Fifth Avenue and Seventy-Ninth Street.

She gasped in shock. "You want to marry me?"

"Yes."

"Why me, Madewell?"

"Because I'm madly in love with you." I looked her straight at her. She didn't blink.

She stared at me blankly and made my heart thrum with one of her unreadable "hmms."

"Well…"

"Yeah."

I crushed my lips onto hers so that she couldn't say another word. Or change her mind.

# ELEVEN

Although I hadn't yet picked out a ring (I wanted it to be unique and special), Allee and I were officially engaged. On the first day she had off from the Met, I introduced her to everyone in my office. They all loved her. She was warm, affable, and funny. So different from stuck-up Charlotte who treated everyone like dirt.

"Dude, she's one hot babe," said Duffy, taking me aside. "Find me one like her." The fact that Allee was Irish like Duffy made them bond quickly. I couldn't be happier that I'd chosen her to be my wife.

The next in line to know about the news was my sister Mimi. She wanted to meet Allee right away and proposed flying down from Boston with her spouse, Beth, over the weekend. Before getting off the call, she asked me if I had told our parents about the engagement. I told her I hadn't. I wasn't ready. That I'd never be ready. She understood.

To celebrate our engagement, my sister made a reservation at a charming French restaurant that was within walking distance of my loft. Wrapped under my arm as we strolled, Allee confessed that she was nervous about meeting her.

"Stop worrying," I told her. "Mimi is nothing like my mother or father. You're going to love her and she's going to love you."

"As much as you love me, Madewell?" she asked teasingly.

"Baby, no one can love you as much as I do." That was the truth. I flipped her around and slammed my lips against her, deepening the bruising kiss with my tongue. She moaned into my mouth. If people were staring at us, I didn't give a damn. That's how much I loved her.

Mimi and Beth were already seated at a candlelit table when we arrived. I introduced Allee. They both gave her a warm embrace.

"She's gorgeous, little bro!" Mimi said. "If I wasn't already married, I might go after her myself."

I gave my sister a wry look. "She's *not* gay. Trust me."

"How do *you* know that, Madewell?" quipped Allee. Both Mimi and Beth laughed hard as I blushed with embarrassment. It was going to be a good night.

We ordered a bottle of Burgundy and eased into conversation. All of us had a glass, except Mimi who had ordered a Perrier. She was wearing a smart pantsuit, as was Beth, her spouse of five years. She'd taken Beth's last name, more than glad to be rid of the Madewell name after my father had disowned her. Unlike me, who resembled my mother, my sister had both the fortune and misfortune to resemble my father, right down to his steely gray eyes. Tall and fit, she was handsomely attractive and wore her prematurely graying hair in a flattering buzz cut. Beth, an ordained minister and activist for gay and lesbian rights, looked a lot like her. They could practically be sisters.

The conversation was lively. My sister told Allee that her real name was Meredith, but that I couldn't pronounce it as toddler and called her Mimi instead. The endearing name stuck forever.

Allee responded, "He still has problems with big words."

"Like what?" I quipped back.

"Like sex."

"Do not! And that's not even a big word!"

"Gotcha!" Allee said, bringing more laughter to the table.

My sister, a high-powered, family-law attorney in Boston, went on to share some of her recent cases. One of them involved a young girl in foster care who was suing her foster care parents for neglect and abuse. Allee listened intently and told my sister that she had been in the system and wished she'd done that. Over the past few months, I had learned about Allee's past in dribs and drabs. It was not something she enjoyed talking about. The abuse she'd suffered as a child ranged from beatings to attempted rapes. She was a survivor. I was sure that her defiant need to be in control stemmed from the abuse she'd experienced. I wanted to kill every son-of-a-bitch who had neglected and abused her.

Over a delicious cheese fondue that we shared, Mimi asked Allee a lot of questions. My sister-the-lawyer was the ultimate interrogator, subtle but sharp. I learned things about my wife-to-be that I hadn't known before... like the fact that her parents were hippies who had met at Woodstock. Though both were artists, her father was also a musician who dreamt about a recording career. She fumbled with her locket to open it and showed us a photograph of them holding her as a toddler. I had strangely never asked to see what was inside her locket, which she told us had belonged to her mother. I studied the photo. They were a young and beautiful couple, Allee being a cross between them. The vibrant expression on their faces told me they were in love, with everything to live for. Their tragic, premature death sent a pang of sadness through me, especially since it came with such unfortunate consequences for Allee.

Allee told my sister and Beth about her museum job, which segued into the story of how we met. Of course, wise-ass Allee claimed that she saw me first, but I wasn't going to fight a battle I couldn't win. She went on to share her dream of one day working at the Musée D'Orsay in Paris. My sister had taken several art history courses at Wellesley, and had spent her junior year abroad, so they had a lot in common. Allee sat googly eyed while Mimi talked about her year in Paris.

"Why didn't you go?" my sister asked her.

"I had to deal with some personal stuff." Basically, the same excuse she gave me. Her eyes grew forlorn. She was obviously regretful, and it made me feel bad for her. Maybe one day, I would take her to Paris.

Over decaf cappuccinos, Beth announced that she and Mimi also had some exciting news.

"I'm pregnant!" said Mimi, blushing. "And we're having twins—a boy and a girl. They're due in September."

Holy crap! I was going to be an uncle. "That's awesome! Does Mother know?"

"Yeah. She was mostly concerned about where I was registering for baby gifts. Target didn't go over well."

I rolled my eyes. That was my mother for you. "Do you think she'll tell Father?"

Darkness fell over Mimi's face. "I don't give a flying fuck if he ever knows. That bastard is never going to see his grandchildren."

I regretted that I'd asked the question. *Stupid me*. Allee squeezed my hand under the table, sensing my unease. My sister was stubborn—like my father. She could not, and would not, ever forgive him for disowning her.

Beth, coming to Mimi's rescue and mine, quickly changed the subject. She told us that they were staying at the London Hotel and about how gay friendly it was. Tomorrow they were going to take in a Broadway show and then they were flying back to Boston.

I was going to miss my sister, I thought, as the waiter brought the check. I insisted on picking up the tab despite Mimi's loud protest. For sure, I was going to see her more often once the babies came. Family was important to Mimi. It was a tragedy that my father had disowned her. Yes, he was a bastard.

"What did you think of my sister?" I asked Allee as we strolled arm-in-arm back to my loft.

"She's awesome. And Beth's great too."

I was thrilled she liked them both, and it was clearly mutual.

"What about us being Aunt Allee and Uncle Ryan?" I still couldn't get over the fact that my sister was having twins.

"It's pretty cool." Her voice wavered a little.

"You know, one day we may be called 'Mommy' and 'Daddy'." Under no circumstances would any kid of mine ever be forced to call me "Father."

Allee didn't respond. Then, I realized we'd never discussed the "baby issue." Maybe she didn't want to have kids, given her tragic childhood. I was cool with that; we'd have each other to cherish forever. Brushing a silky strand of hair out of her face, I decided not to pursue the sensitive subject right now, especially after such a great evening.

Allee remained unusually quiet for the rest of the walk home.

When we got back to my loft, I was beat and headed upstairs to the bedroom. Allee said she wanted to hang downstairs for a while, and that she'd be up later. Even short times away from her drove me crazy.

I woke up at half past one, and Allee was still not in bed. Concerned, I kicked off the covers and rolled off the mattress. Throwing on my robe, I trotted downstairs. In the darkness, I could hear her softly crying. My heartbeat accelerated as I hurried toward the sound of her sobs. She was huddled in a corner, her head buried in her arms.

"What's the matter, baby?" I asked, crouching down beside her.

She slowly lifted her head. The moonlight beaming through the skylight made her fair skin luminous. She turned to me, her eyes glazed with tears. "Madewell, I've gotta to tell you something. Something I should have told you a long time ago."

A secret? I thought we had none. "What is it, baby?" I asked, steeling myself.

"I can't bear children. I'm infertile."

It took me a few long moments to register the shock of her words. My knee-jerk reaction was to say, "Why didn't you tell me this earlier?" Instead, I folded my arm around her heaving shoulders and drew her close to me. I brushed away her tears with my other hand and smoothed her hair.

"So, we'll adopt. That's one lucky son-of-a-bitch who gets to be our child!"

Allee curled her mouth into a faint smile. "It could be a little girl, you know."

Whatever child would be ours was meant to be. It didn't matter to me if it was a boy or girl. What mattered was that Allee was going to be the mother of my children. Our children.

She rested her head on my shoulder, and we joked about baby names. While we couldn't come to any agreement, one thing was for sure. There was never going to be a Ryan Madewell V.

I swept Allee into my arms and carried her upstairs. Maybe we didn't make a baby, but we made sweet glorious love until the wee hours of the morning. We were all over each other, groping, grasping, stroking, kissing. Just as the sun came up, I finished her with a tenderness that made her orgasm roll over my exploding organ like a crashing wave, washing me in a sea of ecstasy. Oh, how I loved this girl!

# TWELVE

It was finally time to introduce Allee to my parents. My mother had told my father that I had a new girlfriend, and he was insistent on meeting her. What neither of them knew was that I planned to marry her.

Allee took a lot of care getting ready for our evening together with my parents—acting quite the opposite of her usual carefree self who casually threw on her museum uniform, sweats, or a pair of jeans. As cocky and confident as she was, she was very nervous about meeting my parents. I couldn't blame her. I was anxious too.

"How do I look?" she asked.

"Fuckable." I eyed her from head to foot and grinned sheepishly. She was wearing an elegant, sleeveless black dress that came just to her knees and showed off the defined curves of her toned body and long limbs. She bought it with her own money. At some point, she was going to have to get used to the idea that my money was her money and that I could buy her things. In fact, the entire third floor of Barneys if she wished. As she slipped on a pair of sexy, black suede peep-toe pumps that made her long, shapely legs even longer, the burning urge to rip off her dress and fuck her right on the floor surged inside me.

She rolled her eyes at me as though she was reading my mind. "What's your father's name?" she asked, catapulting me out of my fantasy.

"How could you forget? The same as mine minus one. Except I call him Bastard."

She rolled her eyes again. "I know a lot of people with that name."

"But you don't know one like my father."

"What do you mean?"

"You'll see."

I had given Allee some insight into my father, but nothing could prepare her for the reality of meeting him. If she was lucky, he'd shake her hand, test her on her knowledge of Ivy League schools, size her up, and then show her his collection of trophies—if she was worthy of such a treat. If she wasn't worthy, he would mentally throw her into a trash bin and ignore her.

I always hated the fact that I had to share his name. There was no way around it. There was another kid at Andover who shared his father's name—Maximillian Wentright III. But lucky him, he got to go by Max. I was happy that Allee always called me "Madewell" and not Ryan.

"What about Bastard's wife?" she asked.

"Eleanor." I could have said her name was "Pathetic," but I didn't want to perpetuate a sick joke. I felt sad for my mother that she had to endure my father. But it was her choice.

"That's a pretty name." Allee headed over to me, walking gracefully in the high heels as if she'd been born wearing them. I was wearing a suit to please my father—and a tie. She helped me finish knotting it—something she also did surprisingly well. Her skills never ceased to amaze me, from cooking to dressing—and undressing me—to fucking. Maybe she'd had a hot boyfriend in her past who'd taught her what do. The jealous streak I harbored kept me from asking. I didn't want to know about her past boyfriends. Or sexploits. I was that possessive. After she straightened my tie, I kissed her lightly on the lips. My stomach clenched with nerves. I was not looking forward to my dinner with my parents. Not one fucking bit.

At the last minute, Allee put on her eyeglasses. "You don't need them." I lifted them off her beautiful face and slipped them into my jacket pocket. I still hadn't asked her why she wore fake glasses. Once we got through this night, I was going to find out.

When Allee stepped into the elegantly appointed lobby of my parents' swank apartment building, with its white-gloved concierge service, she got cold feet. "Let's catch a foreign flick and split," she said, her eyes turbulent. "I'll even make you come over popcorn."

Part of me wanted to make a run for it too, and she sure made it tempting, but we had come this far. The longer I waited to introduce Allee to my parents, the harder it would be. I squeezed her clammy hand and reassured her how stunning she looked.

She was wearing her long, wavy hair loose, held back with a black velvet headband. Lightly dusted with makeup, she truly had never looked so breathtakingly beautiful.

"My parents will probably adore you," I told her with a kiss to her head.

She gave me the evil eye. "Don't bullshit me!" she rasped.

I quirked a lame smile. She was right. They never liked anyone west of Fifth Avenue or below Fifty-Seventh Street. I gave her hand another gentle squeeze.

After stepping out of the elevator, we were greeted immediately by Maria. As usual, she was thrilled to see me and wrapped her ample arms around me in a warm embrace. I introduced her to Allee.

Maria smiled brightly. *"Ella es muy linda."*

"What did she say about me?" Allee asked nervously.

She said, "You're fat and ugly. And that you should wear a bag over your head."

"That's not funny, Madewell." She nudged her elbow into my ribs as Maria led us into the expansive living room. My mother, elegantly dressed in beige pleated slacks and a matching silk blouse, was seated on a creamy damask couch. A half-drunk champagne flute was in her hand. With Allee's hand entwined in mine, I strode over to her and gave her my customary kiss. She gave Allee the once-over.

"So you must be Ryan's new girlfriend." There was a slight slur in her speech. I wondered how many glasses of champagne she'd already had.

"Yes, Mother. This is Allee Adair."

"You're not by chance related to the Adairs of Palm Beach?"

"No, ma'am, I'm not." Allee's voice quivered.

My mother took another sip of champagne. "Please, call me Eleanor."

Allee, relaxing a little, surveyed the room. Her eyes zeroed in on a small oil painting of a ballerina on the wall by the baby grand piano.

"Eleanor, is that a copy of a Degas by the piano?" she asked.

My mother's lips pursed as she shot Allee a condescending look. "Darling, reproductions are found in hotels. Everything you see here is an original."

I cringed. Allee gulped. "Ohmygod! Ryan didn't tell me that his family owned a real Degas. He's one of my favorite painters."

My mother took a swig of her champagne. "Ellie—"

"It's Allee, Mother," I intercepted. She

was sloshed all right. I supposed the buzz, or numbness, or whatever she felt was an antidote to the loneliness and pain caused by my father's indiscretions.

She continued. "You have such an unusual accent. Where are you from?"

"France," said Allee with a poker face.

I had to bite down on my lip not to laugh.

"That's a very unusual French accent."

"*Oui.* I come from a very unusual region of France. Not many people have heard about Reines." She spelled it out.

I almost peed in my pants. "Reines" in French meant "Queens." Allee asked my mother if she could look more closely at the painting. "Be my guest," she slurred, returning to her champagne. As Allee strode over to examine the Degas (Man, did she know how to move in those heels!), my father made his grand entrance. My brief moment of levity came to an abrupt halt.

"Allee, I'd like you to meet my father, Ryan Madewell III."

Allee pivoted around on her heels. She made eye contact with my father. Every ounce of color drained from her face. I seriously thought she might pass out.

My gaze darted back to my father. As blanched as her face was, his was reddened. The expression on his face was a mixture of shock and disdain. How could he be so judgmental so quickly? Wearing his classic uniform, a rich black cashmere blazer and tan slacks, he stiffly met her halfway.

"So, we at last formally meet, Miss—"

"Adair," Allee stuttered. She hesitantly offered him her hand. It was trembling.

He lifted it to his lips and kissed it. Allee didn't move a muscle.

"Let's eat, shall we?" said my father, his voice as frigid as a glacier.

We adjourned to the formal dining room. Tonight's meal was Cornish hens à l'orange. I think Allee may have enjoyed the French dish, had the tension in the air not been so thick. A knife couldn't cut through it.

Throughout the meal, my father's eyes alternately clashed with Allee's and mine. She barely touched her dinner. I didn't eat much either. Whenever I looked at Allee, she looked away from me. She hadn't regained her color.

"Are you okay, baby?" I asked her, wishing I could take her in my arms. Unfortunately, she was seated across from me.

"I'm sorry. I don't feel well." She excused herself from the table, asking Maria for the location of the nearest bathroom.

My mother, on her God-knows-what-number glass of champagne, was oblivious to the strained atmosphere and blabbered on about her recent philanthropic endeavors and the latest society gossip. Among her coterie of friends, she had gained the nickname "Loose Lips Eleanor" whenever she drank too much. By the end of dinner, we knew the dirt on every Botoxed socialite in New York. She even made a cutting remark about my sister and her pregnancy. My father's eyes narrowed, and his mouth pressed into an angry line. "That lesbian sister of yours is not fit to be a mother," he growled.

I cringed. He was not fit to be a father.

Before coffee and dessert were served, my father coldly asked to see me in his study. He took his scotch with him. Fuming inside, I followed him.

He sat down behind his antique desk and looked me straight in the eye.

"Son, I'm going to get straight to the point. I want you to stop seeing that low-life tramp."

My blood curdled. How dare he call her that? He spent all of one minute talking to her. I wasn't going to let him get away with it.

"Don't talk about her like that, sir."

"I'm your father and I can say what I want. She is not worthy of the Madewell name."

"Well, I think she is."

"What do you mean?"

"I'm going to marry her." The words shot of my mouth like bullets.

A fury fell over my father like I'd never seen. His face hardened, and his fists clenched until they turned white.

"Son, if you marry that woman, I will destroy your life. Starting by firing you from your job."

I met my father's fiery gaze head on. "No need, Father. I quit."

I stormed out of his office, without looking back to see his expression, and stomped back to the dining room. Fortunately, Allee was returning at the same time. She still looked terribly pale. Faint, in fact.

I grabbed her by the arm. "Baby, let's get the fuck out of this hellhole."

"Darling, so soon?" slurred my mother in her drunken stupor. Maria, clearing the table, looked my way with compassion.

Introducing Allee to my sicko parents was a bad idea. A really bad idea. Maybe we just should have eloped. And maybe that's just what we were going to do.

I cradled Allee in my arms in the backseat of the Escalade while Marcus drove us back to my loft downtown.

There was silence on her part. Her eyes looked glazed, though I knew she wasn't drunk; she hadn't even touched her wine. "What's the matter, baby?" I asked, stroking her silky hair.

"I told you; I don't feel good."

I pressed my lips to her forehead. It wasn't hot. No fever. "Do you have your period?" I ventured.

Charlotte was always sick when she had hers. I instantly regretted asking when I remembered she was infertile.

She simply shook her head. Closing her eyes, she sank deeper into my chest. Once we were back in my loft, we got ready for bed. Allee lethargically put on a pair of my sweats, saying she was cold. I held her in my bare arms. The burning urge to make love to her spread like a wildfire inside me. I nuzzled her neck.

"Not tonight, Madewell," she murmured, pushing me away.

This was the first time she had spurned my advances. I yearned to tell her about my decision to quit *Arts & Smarts*, but I couldn't penetrate the thick wall she'd put up. She slept on the other side of the bed, not letting me even snuggle her. In the middle of the night, she woke up shaking and screaming, "Get off me," over and over.

"What's the matter, baby?" I asked, comforting her in my arms.

She was damp with cold sweat. "I had a terrible dream. Your father was in it. He was a monster. And your mother was in it too. She watched him eat me alive."

I got it. My parents had sickened her. I knew because they sickened me.

I smoothed her hair and kissed her lightly on her head. "It's okay, baby. I'm here. No one's going to hurt you." *That bastard!*

Holding Allee in my arms, I thought about

tomorrow, when I would tell my staff that I was leaving *Arts & Smarts*. Words didn't sprint into my head, so I was going to have to wing it. Before I drifted off, the sleepy sandman from my childhood sprinkled me with sadness.

# THIRTEEN

After a restless night of sleep, I woke up at the crack of dawn. Allee was not beside me. And the smell of a delicious breakfast was not wafting up the stairs. I staggered out of bed and did my normal morning routines. Pulling out my jeans and a tee from my walk-in closet, I noticed that Allee's museum uniform was gone, along with her coat. Perhaps she had an early-morning meeting at the museum. I tried her on her cell. No answer. I left a message on her voice mail, asking to call me back right away. I desperately wanted to tell her that I was stepping down as Editor in Chief of *Arts & Smarts*. I needed her support. And I needed to hear her husky, sexy voice.

I got dressed quickly and made myself some coffee. I was not looking forward to going to my office. Allee's failure to return my calls didn't help.

Once I was there, I gathered my troops in the kitchen by the coffee machine.

I sucked in a deep breath. This was beyond hard. I'd been at *Arts & Smarts* for over five years, nurturing and watching it grow like a child. The staffers and I had grown close. They were like family.

"Guys, this is difficult." I inhaled another deep, anxious breath. "For personal reasons, I'm stepping down as Editor in Chief of *Arts & Smarts.*" Gasps filled the room.

Inhaling again, I continued. "In the transition period, until a new Editor in Chief is found, I'm appointing Duffy McDermitt as my successor. All of you know Duffy. He's talented, passionate, and committed. He will lead the way, and it wouldn't surprise me if he found his calling in this new role."

All eyes turned to Duffy. He was as humbled as he was shocked.

"*A 'n S*'ers, you don't know how hard this is for me." My voice grew watery. "You've been like family. In fact, the best and most talented family I could ever have."

There were tears and sniffles all around. It took all I had to stifle mine; Madewells were not allowed to cry. "All I can say is that I will miss you all and look forward to every edition of *Arts & Smarts.*"

Amidst tears and cheers, I humbly marched out of the room. Duffy followed me.

When I reached my desk and started packing up my personal belongings, Duffy asked me why I was doing this.

I answered with one word. "Allee."

He threw his arms around me. "Good luck, man."

"And good luck to you, Duffster." He was now the one who had to deal with my father, the bastard.

I was still in a state of shock when I returned to my loft. I had just stepped down as Editor in Chief of *Arts & Smarts*. I had never quit anything in my life. Madewells weren't allowed to be quitters. In a way, I should chalk this up as a victory. I had defied my father for once in my life.

I immediately tried calling Allee again on her cell; when she didn't answer it, I called the museum. I desperately needed to talk to her; she would make me feel better, make everything feel right. The jovial operator promised to give her a message. Rather than waiting for her to return my call, I decided to go for a jog around my neighborhood. Maybe a run would give me some clarity as to what I was going to do with the rest of my life. Unfortunately, it didn't help. My mind was too muddled with uncertainty, rage, and despair. Fuck my father.

When I got back from my run, there was a text message from Allee on my cell phone.

*I can't see u anymore.* My heart hammered. Was she breaking up with me because of my parents?

*What do u mean?* I immediately texted her back, hoping that she was on her lunch break and would reply.

*It can't work.*

*WTF?*

There was no further response. I tried calling her, but she wouldn't pick up. I tried again, leaving her a message to please call me back. That it was important. No response. I tried one more time and then I called the Met again to have them give her an urgent message to call me. The day turned into night. I didn't hear back from Allee. I was beginning to think it was futile. Fuck. I bet my father got to her. The fucking bastard. Not only was my career over; my relationship was over too.

# FOURTEEN

I tossed and turned all night. Allee never called me nor did she come home. Unable to sleep, I tried calling her several times on her cell phone, but it went straight to her voice mail. I was so pissed I almost tossed my phone across the room.

I finally drifted off, only to be awoken by the sound of my intercom buzzer. Who the hell could it be at eight o'clock in the morning? I knew it couldn't be Allee, as she had a key to my loft. Groggy, I staggered out of bed and checked my surveillance camera. My half-shut eyes grew wide. It was Charlotte. What the hell was she doing here? I hadn't seen or heard from her for over three months. And this early hour was a far cry from her usual ten o'clock wake-up time. Seriously, she was the last person I wanted to see, now or ever. With the exception of my father.

I buzzed her in. She sprightly bounced out of the elevator, wearing one of her Chanel suits and carrying a chic, colorful plastic folder under her arm.

"Hi," she said seductively.

"What's up, Charlotte?" My tone was terse.

"I thought you'd like to see these." She handed me the folder. "Open it."

Her green eyes stayed glued on me as I unwound the string that fastened the folder. A proud smirk spread across her lips.

"Your new girlfriend is a very hard worker." Her voice was dripping with sarcasm.

I removed the contents and froze in shock when my eyes met the first photo. It was a shot of well-dressed man in his sixties kissing a beautiful, sexy young woman—Allee! The imprinted date on the picture indicated that it had been taken earlier in the week. The night Allee had to accommodate one of her massage clients. Nausea rose to my chest. I wanted to throw up.

"Have a look-see at the rest of them at your leisure."

"Get the fuck out of here, Charlotte."

"Whatever. I'm off to the D&D building to meet a new client." She flashed a smug, toothy smile. "Feel free to call me when you're done."

She breezed over to the elevator and let herself out. I was shitting in my pants.

My hands trembling, I flipped through the stack of photos. Obviously, my ex had hired a private investigator to follow and spy on Allee. Each photo was more shocking than the one before. Here were shots of Allee kissing, undressing, teasing, and, damn it, fucking well-dressed—and undressed—older men in all kinds of positions. Her wardrobe ranged from tight short, low-cut dresses and stilettos to lacy black pushup bras and skimpy black panties with garters to absolutely nothing. She had on lots of makeup and wore her hair loose. With each photo, I grew sicker and sicker. So, this was Allee's real second job. God fucking damn it. She was a high-priced hooker.

I finally got to the last photo. I recognized the dress immediately. It was identical to that tight blue dress I'd seen on the woman leaving the Four Seasons bar the night I'd had drinks with my father. It *had* been Allee! Quivering, I studied the photo. Allee's back, draped with her long, dark hair, was to me, her body ensnarled in the arms of a man whose face I couldn't see because he was obviously kissing her. There was something familiar about his suit. I examined the photo more closely, zeroing in on the monogrammed gold and diamond cufflinks he was wearing. The initials inscribed in them brought a rush of bile to my mouth. R.M. It was my father.

Okay. I'll admit it. I puked my guts out. Nothing had prepared me for the shock of this discovery. Did Charlotte recognize my father? I didn't think so because she would have rubbed it in my face.

After cleaning up the mess I made in the living room, I took a long, hot shower. I was still sick to my stomach. It was hopeless. No amount of water could flush the photos out of my head or wash away my disgust and hurt. Fighting another bout of nausea, I slid down the travertine wall and let the steaming water pound onto my bowed head. I didn't know if I still loved Allee or despised her. Only one thing was for sure: I loathed my father.

My father's office building was located on the northeast corner of Park Avenue and Fifty-Eighth Street. I took the elevator to his thirty-fifth floor penthouse suite, my eyes focused on the panel of lit-up floor buttons. The passengers, who surrounded me, were a blur.

The elevator doors parted, and I stomped straight past the receptionist to my father's corner office. His attractive, blond secretary gazed up at me. "Ryan, do you have an appointment with Mr. Madewell?"

My eyes burned into hers. "Hazel, I don't need a fucking appointment. I'm his son." I marched straight into his office.

His office was enormous and furnished with the finest antiques money could buy. Floor-to-ceiling windows overlooked the city. One wall consisted solely of a bank of flat screen monitors that were streaming news channels from around the world. He was seated behind his imposing desk, on speakerphone.

"Father, get off the phone." My voice was

authoritative. It was the first time in my life I had ever told my father to do anything. To my surprise, he ended the call.

"What is it, son? Is there something urgent I should know about *Arts & Smarts?*" His voice was business-like and calm.

"No. It's something you should know about *you.*" I handed him the folder that was tucked under my arm. "Open it."

Fumbling, my father unwound the cord and pulled out the contents. His eyes grew wide and his hands shook. When he got to the last photo, his mouth dropped wide open with shock. He threw the contents onto his massive desk. All color drained from his face.

"Listen to me, Ryan. She's nothing to me. I only fucked her twice."

Twice? Once was too much. Rage was rushing through my bloodstream.

"And Father, was she as good for you as she is for me?"

My father lowered his head and didn't answer. "Please don't tell your mother."

Is that all he had to say? Didn't he care one bit about the fact that I was—or had been—in love with this woman? That she was *everything* to me?

With shaking hands, my father assembled the photos and put them back in the folder.

"Take them and get out of here." He rose and shoved the folder back into my hand.

"Don't you want to keep them, Father? You

can publish them in one of your tabloids. I'm sure they'll sell lots of copies and drive up the price of Madewell stock."

His eyes clashed with mine.

"There's something else I want to leave you with, Father."

With one seamless move, I did something I'd always wanted to do. I lifted my right hand, clenched my fist, and punched my father in the face. I hit him so hard, my knuckles stung.

My father, stunned, put his hand to the large red welt I had left on his cheek and rubbed it. Blood flowed from his nose. He couldn't get his mouth to close or spew a single a word.

"Bastard!" Without looking back, I stormed out of his office.

Instead of my father disowning me, I disowned him.

My next stop: The Met. I had to confront Allee. Marcus expertly wove in and out of the mid-day traffic, making excellent time uptown. I glanced down at the folder on my lap. My stomach clenched. My emotions teetered between extreme rage and extreme dread, though they were tipping on the side of dread. I had no idea of how I was going to feel when I saw Allee. Or what I was going to say. For a writer, my command of words often failed me.

The museum was bustling with visitors and tourists. I spotted the beautiful, blond, long-legged tour guide I had encountered when I first met Allee. I had learned from Allee that her name was Samantha, Sam for short, and that she had become Allee's best friend at the museum.

"Do you know where I can find Allee?" I asked her.

She gazed at me flirtatiously. She definitely was a looker, but I didn't have time for small talk. My nerves were like little electrical impulses, ready to explode.

"She's conducting a VIP visitors' tour of the Impressionist collection," she replied.

"What floor is that?"

"Second."

I dashed off without thanking her.

"Observe the way the colors dance in the light and..." Standing before a large painting of a Degas ballerina, a weary-looking Allee was giving a guided tour to a small group of well-dressed Japanese tourists. When she spotted me, she stopped in mid-sentence. Her jaw stayed open wide.

I grabbed her by the elbow and jerked her away. Stunned expressions washed over the faces of the tourists.

"What the fuck are you doing, Madewell?" The

Asian tourists oohed at the word "fuck."

"We need to talk." Clutching the folder with the photos, I dragged her over to a nearby observation bench. I shoved her down onto it. She defiantly stood up, only for me to shove her down again and hold her there forcefully with my free hand.

"Didn't you get my text? I don't want to see you anymore." She tried to squirm away from me, but it was futile.

"Madewell, let go of me. You're gonna make me lose my job."

"Then, we'll be even."

"What the hell are you talking about?"

"This." I flung the folder onto her lap. "Open it."

Slowly, she undid the fastener and removed the contents. She gasped and her face turned white as a ghost. Her hands trembling, she leafed through the photos. When she got to the last one of my father all over her, her body shook.

"Oh. My. God."

"When were you going to tell me?" Fury fueled my words.

She bit down on her quivering lip. "Oh, Madewell, I'm so sorry. So, so sorry." Under her spectacles, tears leaked out of her eyes. Normally, I would have lifted her eyeglasses onto her head and wiped them away, but today I didn't.

"I didn't know he was your father. You have to believe me."

"It doesn't fucking matter." My voice was

harsh. "Just tell me—why?"

"I tried to warn you," she sniffled. "I needed the money."

Rage was consuming me. Eating me alive. "Bullshit!"

She gazed up at me with her watering eyes. "I've tried to get out of the life, but it's not easy with Sid."

"Well, it won't be hard to get out of mine." I barked the words.

Her tears amplified until she was audibly crying. "I already am," she sobbed. "We should never see each other again."

I loosened my grip around her heaving shoulder. She remained seated, her now uncontrollable sobs holding her prisoner. Her tears fell, drop after drop, onto the photo with my father. The tear-stained photo made me feel worse than I already felt. I didn't want her to shed tears over my father in any way. I snatched the photo away from her and ripped it to pieces while she tearfully watched. I gazed down at the ragged shards on the floor. The photo was as torn apart as our lives.

Allee's flooding eyes stayed locked on me, and as much as I hated her at this moment, her beauty still touched me in a profound, bitter way. I needed to leave. Get away from her. As I pivoted on my heel, she choked, "Golden Boy, I wish we'd never met."

Her words burned through me like acid. She knew from the beginning our relationship was doomed. It just took my father to put it over the edge. The pain was too much. I wanted to rip out my heart and throw it at her.

Leaving the rest of the photos behind, she staggered to her feet. She managed to collect herself and drifted back to her tour group, never turning her head once to look at me. Shell-shocked, I slumped to the elevator, dumping the painful photos into a deep waste can along the way.

After four months of endless love, Allee Adair and I had just broken up.

# FIFTEEN

The next few weeks after my breakup with Allee were hell. Pure hell. I didn't sleep, didn't shave, and didn't write a word. I lived on junk food and beer and craved a cigarette. A phone call from my buddy Duffy got me out of my deep funk.

"Hey, dude, I haven't heard or seen you in ages. What's going on?"

"Are you free for a drink tonight?"

"Yeah. Meet me at our watering hole at six."

"Dude, you look like something the cat dragged in," said Duffy over beers.

Yeah, I looked like shit for sure. My face was scruffy, my hair disheveled, and I didn't even bother showering or getting dressed properly. I was wearing a flannel pajama top over a pair of unpressed jeans.

The buzz from the beer allowed me to open up slowly. I told Duffster about the photos, my encounter with my father, and my breakup with

Allee. He sat wide-eyed without interrupting me or even taking a swig of his beer.

"Holy guacamole!" said Duffy when I took a breather and guzzled my beer.

Setting the mug down, I said, "The sickest part of the whole story is that I miss her."

Duffy gazed into my eyes. He was almost like a brother to me. "That's because you're crazy in love with her. Man, if that babe was mine, I'd never leave her."

Damn him. He was right. I was still madly in love with Allee Adair. The memories of us filled every waking moment. And they didn't let me sleep. I couldn't live without her. I needed her as much as I needed air to breathe.

I chugged my beer. "She should have told me."

Duffy scrunched his face. "Come on, dude. Get real. Do you really think some chick, who's really into you, is going to come out and say, 'Hey, by the way, I'm a high priced call girl. Hope you don't mind.'"

Only Duffster could make me laugh while I was on an emotional road trip to Hell.

"How can I continue to see her after all that's gone down?"

"Hey, Rye-man, she had her reasons, but she didn't do it to hurt you. And she had no clue that was your father."

Over another gulp of beer, I imbibed Duffy's words. Balls! He was right again. Maybe I overreacted and didn't give Allee enough of a chance to explain her other life.

"Duffster, what should I do?" I didn't tell him that I'd tried to call her several times to no avail.

"Do what you do best. Write. Write her a letter and tell her how you feel." He gulped his beer. "Girls are suckers for letters. If it's meant to be, she'll come back to you."

I had no clue that Duffy McDermitt, who had never had a long-term relationship in his entire life, was a regular Ann Landers. I told him he should have his own advice column. "Dear Duffy." He snorted his beer.

The two of us each ordered another round from a passing waitress. When the bill came, I was feeling better than I'd felt in ages. "My treat," I told Duffy.

∞

*Dear Allee… My Dear Allee… My Dearest Allee.* Finally, after several unsuccessful attempts to write my letter, I slammed my laptop shut and tore out a sheet of paper from one of my notebooks. With my favorite black rolling writer pen, I wrote…

*Allee,*

*Ernest Hemingway once wrote: "I felt the Earth move out and away." When I met you, the Earth did exactly that. I felt a tremor all around me … and deep inside me.*

*Now, when I take a step, I no longer feel the Earth beneath the soles of my feet. All I feel is a painful emptiness in my heart. It's like I've stopped living.*

*I see you everywhere. But when I reach out to touch you, you're not there. It only makes the pain worse. Insufferable. Words don't exist to describe how much I miss you.*

*Despite all our differences, I fell in love with you the moment I set my eyes on you. There was something about you. I don't know if it was your beauty, your sass, or your passion, but whatever it was, the more I got to know you, the more I loved you. You made me feel like no other woman ever had. You brought me to a place I'd never been before. I've felt with you—emotions, dreams, and sensations—that I thought I'd never find with anyone. You've taught me who I really am.*

*Your breath breathes life into me, and your heartbeat soothes my soul. Quite simply, I cannot live without you. My life has no meaning. I wake up and want to go back to sleep. You are my essence. My raison d'être. The sun doesn't rise without you.*

*For whatever reasons you did what you did, it doesn't matter. I know now that you didn't intend to hurt me. There is no reason to apologize as I have nothing to forgive.*

*It's midnight. Outside my window, a church bell is ringing. For whom the bell tolls? It tolls for thee. Just come back into my arms and let me love you like before.*

*Ryan*

I carefully folded the letter and sealed it in an envelope. Tomorrow, I would send it with the most exquisite roses I could find. Then, wait to hear that rasp I loved.

# SIXTEEN

I had Marcus deliver the roses and the letter to Allee's apartment in Queens first thing in the morning. Sunrise. I wanted her have them when she woke up. A new day. A new beginning.

Marcus called me from her apartment to inform me that he had left them on her front stoop. She didn't answer the intercom, and unfortunately, in my haste to deliver my letter and the flowers, I'd forgotten to give Marcus Allee's spare set of keys in case he needed them. An uneasy thought darkened my mind. Maybe she had met someone new and had spent the night with him. *Don't go there, Madewell*, I told myself.

All day, I sat glued to my cell phone, waiting for some response. A call. A text. An email. Nothing. By three in the afternoon, I couldn't take it anymore. I tried calling Duffy for advice, but he was in a Madewell Media board meeting and unavailable. I almost felt as sorry for him as I did for myself.

Fraught with nervous energy, I went for a long run and then took a hot, steamy shower to clear my head. I donned a clean pair of jeans, a white tee, and my vintage leather motorcycle jacket. I had made a decision: I was going back to the Met and was going to get down on my knees, if had to, and win Allee back.

The Met was vast. Allee could be anywhere, so I went to the main office and asked one of her supervisors if they could direct me to her. To my surprise, the matronly woman told me that they hadn't seen or heard from Allee for two days. That was so unlike her. She loved her job and was very responsible. On the way out, I bumped into Sam. She, too, had not heard from Allee despite calling and texting her several times. An alarm button went off in my head.

I rushed back to the Escalade and asked Marcus to drive me to Allee's apartment as fast as he could. "Floor it!"

"Yes, sir." Strong and silent, he spoke only when spoken to.

We made great time getting out of Manhattan. Marcus was an expert driver, who could effortlessly weave in and out of traffic or follow another car in hot pursuit. He had driven once for CIA operatives. Now he was both my dutiful driver and armed bodyguard. Something that was a necessity because I was a Madewell, whether I liked it or not, in this dangerous world. He had been protecting me since I was a child. Over the years, we'd grown very close, and in some ways, he was the father I never had. Always looking out for my back. Being there when I needed him. Treating me with respect.

As we drove onto the Queensboro Bridge, the memory of Allee running up to me there during the marathon flashed into my head. I could picture her long, toned legs, perfect tits, flying ponytail, and her wicked grin. I was already in love with her. I had fallen in love with her the very minute my eyes set sight on her at the Met. Other memories whirled around in my head—from her quirky putdowns to our passionate and countless sessions of endless lovemaking. No matter what wrong she had done in her private life, I couldn't get her out of my head. I wanted her more than ever, and couldn't wait to see her. A nervous current coursed through my body. I just hoped she was okay.

A police barricade brought both my thoughts and the car to a sudden halt. "What's happening, Officer?" I heard Marcus ask.

"Bad accident ahead. No one can move until they clear it."

Marcus twisted his head back at me. "Hold on, Mr. M."

Without wasting a second, he floored the gas pedal, and we went crashing through the barricade. We zoomed past the accident. One of the vehicles was totaled; there were scattered car parts everywhere. Inside, I was an auto wreck too.

The jumble of emotions that pounded my head was giving me an excruciating headache.

Twenty minutes later, we pulled up to Allee's apartment building "Wait for me here," I told Marcus. I jumped out of the car before he could get out to open the passenger door.

My flowers and the letter were still on the stoop. I buzzed her apartment. No answer. I buzzed it again. No answer. My heart raced. I dug into my jeans pocket and pulled out the heart-shaped key ring that Allee had given me for Christmas. Her keys mingled with mine. After letting myself into the building, I bolted up the two flights of stairs to Allee's apartment, taking two rickety steps at a time. I rang her doorbell. Holding it down, I waited. No answer. I pounded on the flaking door and shouted, "Allee! Are you there? Let me in!" I shouted and pounded again. Still no answer. My fingers jittery, I jammed her apartment key into the keyhole. In one swift move, I unlocked the apartment door and kicked it open.

My eyes grew as round as saucers, and my heart skipped a beat. Something was wrong. Very wrong. Her whole apartment was turned upside down as if it had been vandalized. "Allee, are you here?" I yelled out frantically. "Are you okay?" No answer. Then I heard a faint sound coming from down the hall. Stepping over books, cushions, and broken pieces of glass, I sprinted to her bedroom. *Oh God! Please let her be all right!*

My heart almost stopped. She was there.

Sprawled naked on her bed, her mouth gagged and her hands tied by cord to the wrought iron headboard. Bruises marred her beautiful body; blood caked her face, and one of her eyes was swollen shut. She was shivering, and frightened whimpers escaped her throat.

"Jesus!" I choked as I rushed to her side. Using the Swiss Army knife (a gift from Marcus on my seventh birthday) that was attached to my keychain, I quickly cut through the cord, freeing her, and then undid the gag. Lowering myself to the bed, I gently cradled her battered body in my arms.

"Baby, tell me, what fucker did this to you?" I asked, brushing her matted hair out of her face.

"Sid," she stammered, her voice hoarse and tearful.

Fucking Sid. Her fucking pimp. He was going to pay!

"Baby, I need to get you to a hospital."

Her body convulsed. "Please, no hospital. Please!"

The terror etched deep on her face forced me to give in. I wrapped her in a warm blanket and carried her downstairs to the car. In my haste, I knocked over the vase with flowers, and from the corner of my eye, I watched the water saturate my letter and wash my words away. Marcus leaped out of the vehicle, and quickly opened the rear passenger door. Like a stoic soldier, he helped me get her into the car.

"Where to, sir?"

"My place." I didn't have to tell him step on it. With a loud screech, the SUV peeled away from the curve.

I continued to hold Allee in my arms like a baby and held some bottled water to her lips. As parched as she was, it was effort for her to sip it. Her eyes blinked tears.

"Don't cry, baby. It's all right now." I gently kissed her on the forehead.

"Oh, my Golden Boy, I don't deserve you."

"Shh." I stroked her hair. "We'll talk about it later."

She closed her eyes as we got onto the Long Island Expressway and sped back into Manhattan.

I gazed at her. Even this shattered state, she was still so beautiful. So, so beautiful. My fingers traced the outline of her lush lips, moist from the water. Then gently, I pressed mine to them. I loved her more than ever.

God help fucking Sid.

# SEVENTEEN

I immediately summoned our longtime family physician, Dr. Ned Goulding, to the loft. He was what is known as a concierge doctor—someone who, under our employ, made house calls at our disposal.

Dr. Goulding, with his medical bag, arrived within a half-hour. He was a short, scholarly-looking man with balding hair, wire-rimmed spectacles, and a warm twinkle in his forest-green eyes. He followed me upstairs to my bedroom. Allee was bundled up in my bed, under the covers, in a trance-like state. She looked so frail, so helpless. Sadness swept over me at the sight of her.

After carefully checking Allee over, he told me that she was badly bruised and in shock, but that she would be okay. There appeared to be no broken bones or head injury. The blood on her face was fortunately nothing more than a nosebleed, and the swelling of her eye would go away in a few days with the help of an icepack. He tactfully asked Allee if he could examine her privates. Allee weakly nodded. While he said there appeared to be no trauma there, he asked permission to swab her. Allee nodded again, tears brimming in her eyes. I knew why he was doing this; rage crescendoed in me at the thought of Sid violating my girl. Before leaving, he gave me a sedative to keep her calm and told me what she needed most was rest. Sensing my anxiousness, he swore he would keep everything confidential—even from my father.

After the good doctor left, Allee asked me to bathe her. Her voice was just above a whisper. I drew a hot bath and carried her to it. She wrapped her limp arms around me and leaned her head against my chest. I was worried about hurting her bruised body. I set her in the tub, supporting her with one arm. With a soapy sponge in the other, I skimmed over her bruises, hoping I was washing away her pain, and the memory of the scumbag who did this to her. Tears streamed from her eyes, even the one she could barely open, and a soft wail, like a siren, escaped her lips. Without warning, she slid under the water and stayed there. Holy fuck! She was drowning herself. Panicked, I fisted a clump of her long, thick hair to yank her out when her head torpedoed out of the sudsy water. She sucked in a large gulp of air and shook violently.

Perhaps, this was some form of cleansing for her. A washing away of the heartless fucks she wanted to leave behind.

"It's over," she said in hushed, monotone voice.

I hoped she meant the secret life she'd been

leading, and not us. Seeing her so close to death, I knew I could never leave her, or bear to lose her. I lifted her out of the tub, swaddled her in a large fluffy towel like a baby, and carried her back to my bed, holding her close to me.

For the next few days, she never strayed from my bed. She was too weak, so I carried her everywhere, even to the bathroom. Mostly, she slept. I never left her side. I ordered in chicken soup from the Jewish deli down the street, and fed it to her in the intervals she was awake. Sometimes, nightmares woke her, and I'd be there to comfort her and hold her trembling body in my arms. I wanted to turn into a superhero and squash the demons that plagued her.

I passed the time by writing. I worked on some of the stories I had written and started a new one. My writing was improving by leaps and bounds. I was really getting into letting my senses and heart rule my words. *See and feel the scene, then write it.* Allee would be proud of me.

I let the Met know that Allee was sick but would be returning soon. Within twenty-four hours, Dr. Goulding called me with good news. She hadn't been raped by Sid. That was a giant relief. And she was "clean." No STD's. Given that I had foolishly never used condoms with Allee, this was welcomed news as well.

By the end of the week, she was much stronger. She was sitting up in bed and eating on her own. Her appetite was coming back with the ferocity of an avalanche.

"Read me one of your stories," she begged.

I hemmed and hawed, but finally gave in and read the one I was working on. It was an allegory about a pedigreed Labrador who falls in love with a street mutt on his daily walk.

"It's about us." Allee smiled.

My sheepish eyes gave it away.

"It's so well-written, Madewell."

I was glowing. A compliment from Allee!

"Do they get their happily ever after?"

"I don't know. I haven't gotten to the end."

"Life has no outline, does it?"

Her profound words moved me. She was right, as always.

Over the course of the next two weeks, I learned more about Allee's secret life and came away with a newfound respect for her. She had fallen into it by way of a classmate at Parsons who, too, used it as a means to pay for her tuition and expenses. Plus, for Allee, the money enabled her to keep her dream of going to Paris alive. Servicing her wealthy clients was demeaning, and sometimes dangerous and perverted. She had thought often about giving it up, even before she'd met me. But once she was into it, there was no getting out of it. Sid threatened to expose everything if she didn't comply. When she told him she wanted out of the life, Sid went ballistic because she was his top earner. She was determined to give it up, regardless of the life-threatening consequences.

She deliberately missed a client appointment and that night Sid forced himself into her apartment and beat her up to send her a message. My poor baby! The more I learned about Sid, the more I hated the son-of-a-bitch. I was going to do him in. The only problem was that she didn't know where he lived. He was "invisible."

We never talked about her sexploits. Or about my father. For all intents and purposes, he was dead. In my life, and I hoped Allee's. My final encounter with my father nonetheless haunted me. I stayed away from the Upper East Side and his watering holes so that I wouldn't run into him.

The night before Allee was planning to go back to work, I came home with a shopping bag in my hand. Inside were several small containers and chopsticks.

"Chinese food!" exclaimed Allee, her appetite voracious.

I laid them out in a row on the dining table. Wearing my pajamas that hung sexily low on her hips, she opened the cartons one at a time, in perfect order. Chow Mein... Moo Shu Pork... white rice... and...

Her engagement ring. A sweet, turn-of-the-century diamond ring that came from an estate in France, so unlike the over-the-top Tiffany ring Charlotte had picked out. Allee gasped.

"Oh, Madewell, it's so beautiful!" *Like her*. Tears welled up in her loving eyes.

Before one escaped, I removed the delicate

ring from the carton. I needed to propose to her again. To let go of the past and do it right. Getting down on one knee, I gazed up into her eyes and asked, "Will you, Allee Adair, accept my hand in marriage?"

"Oh, Madewell! Yes! Yes! Yes!" Her breathy rasp deepened each time she said the word. She was almost orgasmic.

Enamored and aroused, I slid the ring on her finger and then lifted her hand to my lips and kissed the back of it. A tear rolled down her cheek.

I could wait no more. The tantalizing aroma of the Chinese food wafted into my nose, but what I was starving for was my Allee. Rising to my feet, I tore off my jeans and tee and then her PJ's. Her body had healed itself. Only a few traces of the bruises remained and she was a tad thin, but other than that, it was back to its former glory.

The sex that followed was beyond. Perhaps because we hadn't made love for almost two weeks.

I lifted her right there onto the table, laying her face up. Her glorious hair fanned across the glossy wood.

"Are you hungry, baby?" I asked.

"Yes," she said breathily.

With the chopsticks, I fed her a heaping portion of the Chow Mein. She swallowed hard.

A bit of it had fallen into her cleavage. Leaning over the table, I dipped my head and lapped up the noodles. My hands groped her sensuous breasts, and my mouth moved to her pink, puckered nipples.

I rolled my tongue around them and then sucked them, feeling them harden and elongate in my mouth. Oh, man, were they delicious! My erection pressed against the table, a tingling running up and down it.

"Can I have some more?" she rasped.

"Of the Chow Mein?"

"No, Madewell. Of you."

My stiff cock hardened even more at her words. I stood up. What a beautiful view I had of her quivering breasts and sensual face! I was going to watch her come. Drink in the expression on her face as I brought her to climax.

I began by fingering her clit, turning it into a hard nub. A long, pleasurable moan escaped her lush lips. Intermittently, I stroked her folds. She was wet with want. So, so deliciously wet. I sucked my fingers, glistening with her delicious juices, and, went back for more. Closing her eyes, she arched her head and moaned again.

"Open your eyes baby. Look at me."

She fluttered her eyes open and met my gaze.

"You're mine," I said, looking straight into her eyes.

"Only yours," she rasped back.

*Yes, only mine.* No other man could touch her. Ever. Not even a dead one. Anchoring my hands onto the smooth wood of the table, I buried my head into that warm space between her inner thighs. My eager tongue devoured her, flicking and licking the sweet, moist folds. She was mine.

All mine. I was never going to let any other man have her again.

I could wait no more. In a swift smooth move, I grabbed her by the ankles, slid her down to the edge of the table, and threw her legs over my shoulders. I reached for my erection and slid it into her pussy inch by thick inch. A bit of pre-cum and her slickness enabled it to glide inside with ease. Man, it felt good to be back inside her. She was so warm, wet, and tight. I started off slowly, with light, controlled strokes. I needed to know how much she could handle. The last thing I wanted was to hurt my baby.

"Go harder, Madewell," she said in that throaty voice. "Harder and faster. I'm not going to break."

A diabolical smile crossed my face. My girl was ready! I rammed my cock back into her drenched sex, amazed how deep I could penetrate her in this standing position. I picked up my pace and pumped harder. Intense, delectable pressure was building up along my shaft.

"Oh, oh, oh, oh!" she shrieked, meeting my every thrust.

"Am I hurting you, baby?" I asked, suddenly alarmed.

"You're killing me." But I could tell by her hooded eyes and parted lips that she was enjoying every minute as much as I was. I was hitting her magic spot, giving her extreme erogenous pleasure. My proud cock was screaming out, "Bull's-eye" each time, getting ready to climax in her hot juices. I watched her face contort with pleasure as she let me pummel her. All the while, my middle finger never stopped working her clit. Adding to her erotic pleasure, my other hand tweaked her perfect nipples. Her moans grew louder. She was on the edge.

I began to feel her waves of ecstasy spread around my hard thickness, bringing me to the place I wanted—no, needed—to be. I screamed out her name as my cock blasted a hot rush of my release. My juices joined hers as she cried out with pure joy. I brushed away the strands of hair that had fallen into her face so that I could see it. So beautiful! So sexy! So mine! Our eyes met.

"I love you, Ryan Madewell IV."

"I love you more."

"You're full of shit."

As I fingered her one more time and made her cry out with yet another burst of pleasure, I thought to myself: No, I'm not.

# EIGHTEEN

We got back into a routine, but it was slightly different than the one we had before the incident. I insisted that Marcus shadow Allee, just in case she ever ran into Sid again; he was lurking somewhere out there. Who knew what the low-life was capable of? After insisting that she could take care of herself, Allee finally gave in. She was slowly learning that she couldn't win every battle with me.

On weekdays, I walked Allee to the subway station with Marcus trailing close behind us. He traveled with her on the train to the Met every morning and back home in the evening. She still refused to take the Escalade to and from work.

After I would drop Allee off at the subway station, knowing that she would be safe under Marcus's watchful eye (she didn't know he carried a concealed weapon), I would go back to the loft to write. Allee couldn't be more thrilled that I'd quit my *Arts & Smarts* job. She was proud of me. "That took balls, Madewell," she had said.

I let Allee read everything I wrote. Most of the

time, she loved what she read, but occasionally she told me it was crap. I could always count on her for brutal honesty, whether I liked it or not. She encouraged me to send my short stories to a couple of literary magazines. "You're never going to be a professional writer if you don't get published." Allee, as usual, was right, but I was reluctant. I'll admit it—I was afraid of rejection. I had never gotten rejected in my life, if you didn't count my father's dismissal or Charlotte's breakup with me. I heard from my mother, who still called me regularly, that Charlotte had moved on to my old Andover classmate, Max Wentright III. His family had even more money than ours. I told my mother that he was perfect marriage material for Charlotte but not to bring up her name again. Fortunately, she knew better than to talk about my father. It was taboo.

Rejection after rejection came. I was downtrodden, thinking about a Plan B. Was it law school? Buy a restaurant and get some Cordon Bleu training? Start a blog about being an unemployed writer? Allee, however, never stopped being my cheerleader. "Remember, you just need one to sell," she said.

It happened at the end of April. On a gloomy, rainy day. When I opened my email, there was one waiting for me from the Acquisitions Editor of *The New Yorker.* My eyes grew wide as I read the words. They loved my story! I had sent them the one about the aging father and son. On top of wanting to publish it in the July edition of the magazine, they wanted to know if I would consider being a regular contributor. They were familiar with my *Arts & Smarts* articles and thought I had "a voice and perspective" that would fit well with their readers. Holy shit! The prestigious *New Yorker* wanted me! The one magazine my father revered and coveted but couldn't get his greedy hands on! I couldn't wait to tell Allee and called her right away on her cell. Fortunately, she was on her lunch break and picked up. "I'm coming home!" she squealed.

Thirty minutes later, Allee flew into the loft, holding a soaked umbrella in one hand and a bottle of expensive champagne in the other. She was beaming. She no longer wore her unnecessary eyeglasses, which I now understood she used to separate her daytime and nighttime personas and safeguard her identity when she was working for Sid.

"Congratulations, Madewell!" She wrapped her arms around me and crushed her lips into mine. "Let's celebrate." She popped the cork, and we guzzled the champagne straight from the bottle.

She then proceeded to tear off my jeans and tee and ravage me. Her work uniform came off too, along with the trench coat she was wearing over it. High from the afternoon champagne, we melted onto the cool hardwood floor, a tangle of arms and legs, unable to get enough of the other. We climaxed together, coming with reckless abandon. When I finally recovered, I sat up, stretching my long legs out in front of me, and positioned her naked body on my lap. She sat with one knee up and the other outstretched while I nibbled her ears and neck from behind, my arms folded around her full, heated breasts. The warmth of her buttocks on my swollen cock coursed through my body.

"Don't go back to work," I breathed in her ear.

Breaking away from me, she stood up and put her Met uniform back on. Even in that plain uniform, she was sexy and beautiful to me.

"Madewell, just because you've got a job again doesn't mean I can afford to lose mine."

I twisted my mouth in frustration. I suppose she had a point.

"You've never had to worry about money a day in your life." Her tone was snarky, and I wondered if we were verging on a fight.

What she said was true. I had never had to worry about getting food on my table, paying off student loans, or keeping a roof over my head. Sometimes I could be a self-centered jerk.

I loved that only Allee could do that... make me see the best and worst of me. Hoping to avoid a fight that I'd never win, I let it go.

Rising to my feet, I pulled her into my arms and covered her mouth with a final, passionate kiss.

"Keep writing, Madewell," she ordered as she let herself out of the loft. I shot her a wink. She was my lover, my muse, and the woman with whom I was going to spend the rest of my life. She was mine. As I started editing another story, I couldn't wait for her to come back home.

# NINETEEN

L ife was good. In fact, life couldn't be better. I enjoyed writing musings on the New York cultural scene for *The New Yorker* and sold several more short stories. One of them was even nominated for a literary prize. Allee, who was so proud of me, told me I should try my hand at writing a novel, but I wasn't there yet.

Good things happened to Allee too. She got a promotion at the Met and was now the Assistant Curator in the painting department. For her, it was a fantasy job, and one step closer to her dream of being a curator at The Musée D'Orsay. She no longer had to wear that uniform. I took her shopping at Barneys for a chic new wardrobe. I told her she had to look the part. I also told her that she had to stop equating me paying for stuff with taking money from her johns. It was a hard concept for her to get through her thick, stubborn skull, but ultimately, she acquiesced. When we got back to the loft, she gave me a fashion show, parading in front of me in all of her new outfits. Everything she put on looked great on her lean, curvaceous body. And everything she put on, I couldn't wait to tear off.

With our hectic work schedules, we kept putting off getting married. Finally, we set a date, but couldn't agree on where to hold our wedding. The one thing, however, where we were on the same page was that we both wanted a very small, intimate affair. Only a handful of our closest friends and family members. We knew exactly whom we wanted to invite. Still, we could not decide on a place. One night after marathon sex, it came to me. When I told Allee my idea, she said, "Madewell, sometimes you're fucking brilliant." Getting a compliment from her was like winning a big jackpot lottery. On the other hand, getting a mind-blowing blow job from her was like being handed an instant win. And that's what she gave me before we drifted off.

We decided to get married on the very spot in Central Park where we had completed the marathon together. The finishing line was going to be our starting line for our life together as husband and wife. It was a beautiful Sunday in early May, with spring in full fragrant bloom. Duffy, wearing a suit for the first time since I'd known him, was best man, and my sister, looking very pregnant, was maid of honor. Her partner, Beth, was going to officiate. We'd invited a handful of others...

Marcus, who had grown very close to Allee and was going to give the bride away since she had no father... my beloved nanny Maria...my mother who had not yet shown up...and Samantha, Allee's gorgeous blond friend from the Met. Chatting with her while I awaited Allee's arrival, I couldn't help wondering how my life would have turned out if I had asked her instead of Allee to show me the Picasso; fate is a strange bird. All the while, Duffy couldn't take his eyes off her. I swear he was getting a hard-on beneath his dress pants.

My heart did a flip-flop when I spotted Allee heading my way on Marcus's muscle-bound arm. Nothing could have prepared me for the intense emotion that swelled up inside me. She was wearing an antique ivory, mid-calf dress and a band of flowers around her head. Her dark, long hair hung loose, the shimmering curls cascading gloriously over her shoulders. She could have easily been mistaken for a belle époque beauty that had stepped out of Renoir painting. My bride was a work of art. I, in turn, was wearing a classic long-tailed morning suit, and definitely looked like a gentleman of that era.

Her eyes never left mine as we silently exchanged "I love you's." Her slow, steady progression toward me felt like an eternity. I couldn't wait to have her in my arms.

Finally, that moment came, and I swept her next to me. "Baby, you look beautiful," I said softly.

Her eyes twinkled as a warm smile flashed

across her face. "You don't look so bad yourself. Is everyone here?" She scanned the small group we'd invited. "Where's your mother?"

"I don't know," I murmured. "It's getting late. Maybe we should start without her."

A mixture of anger and disappointment coursed through me. What beauty appointment was holding her up? Or was she at some charity fundraiser? Or maybe she'd had one too many to drink? My heart numbed.

"We should wait for her. She's your mother. She couldn't possibly miss her only son's wedding," insisted Allee.

Sometimes I didn't know whose side Allee was on. At one point, she even thought we should invite my father. That was the only time we'd ever gotten into a major fight.

"After all he's done?" *The fucker.* There was no way I was going to reconcile with him after what he had done to me. And done to Allee. I was perplexed, in fact furious, that Allee would even consider sharing the same air with him. I couldn't even imagine the consequences. Except I knew they would be ugly.

"Stop being so hung up and egotistical," she chided. "At some point, you've got to let the past go. He's family."

She was pissing me off royally. "Yeah, and I suppose you think Sid's family too."

"Fuck you, Madewell!" she said hotly. Tears were brimming in her eyes.

I immediately regretted what I'd said, but not soon enough. She stormed out of the loft. I spent hours combing the streets frantically looking for her, my heart growing sick with worry by the minute. Did she hop on some Greyhound bus? Get hit by a car? Run into Sid? The possibility that something terrible had happened to her sent a wave of panic over me. Damn my big mouth! Finally, I spotted her at our local newsstand reading comic books. It was close to midnight. I sighed with relief.

She pretended she didn't see me and kept her head buried in the comic.

I sidled up to her and poked my head over shoulder to see what she was reading. *The Avengers.* "Why do you read superhero comics?" I ventured.

"Because they can wipe out the bad guys and save the world," she said, burying her nose deeper into the pages. "I've read them since I was a kid."

She had always been looking for someone to save her from her wretched, loveless childhood. I had to remember that beneath her tough-as-nails veneer, there was a thick layer of vulnerability. A soul that needed rescuing.

"Baby, look at me." I gripped her by the shoulders and spun her around to face me. Her watery eyes met mine.

"I'm sorry I said what I said. Sometimes I say things I don't mean."

"Shut up, Madewell." She slammed her lips against mine, then pulled away. "You are my

Superman."

I held her face in my hands and bore my eyes into hers. "Don't ever run away from me again, baby. You had me scared shitless."

When we got home, she gave me a blow job that made me fly.

And now, I was going to be her Superman for life.

The ceremony started without my mother. For whatever reason, damn her, she wasn't coming. My eyes met Maria's as a pang of sadness shot through me. *Mi pobrecito!* I heard her say silently.

The ceremony was short, but beautiful. Allee and I had each written our own special forever vows.

As I braced myself to recite mine, I saw my mother saunter up to us from the corner of my eye. She was chicly dressed in a pink, raw silk suit, but she looked older than the last time I'd seen her. Her lips pressed into a thin line, and fine wrinkles were etched around her mouth and eyes. Perhaps, she was in between injections. But the sadness in her eyes told me it was something more. She flashed a faint smile as I began my vow. Butterflies fluttered in my stomach even though I had practiced these words so many times before. A gentle squeeze of the hand from Allee and her loving gaze gave me the power to go forward. I began with a quote by Henry David Thoreau.

> "'It's not what you look at that matters;
> it's what you see.' When I first laid eyes
> on Allee Adair, what I saw transcended
> everything I had ever seen before. I saw
> a work of art that all the money in the
> world could not buy. And now I ask
> her to give me everything that she is in
> exchange for my love, and to share her
> life with me as long as we live."

Allee's tearful eyes stayed locked on me the whole time. Her lower lip quivered and then she bit down on it to stifle a sob. I could hear Maria positively bawling and was shocked to see my mother withdraw a lacy hanky from her clutch bag to dab her eyes. A small crowd of spectators, some dressed in jogging outfits, had joined our wedding party and watched the scene unfold with hushed, voyeuristic stares.

Now, it was Allee's turn. She took a deep breath and then broke into a dazzling smile. Her eyes never strayed from mine as she began with a quote from Picasso:

> "'Some painters transform the sun into
> a yellow spot; others transform a yellow
> spot into the sun.' Ryan Madewell, who
> paints with words, transformed me into
> the sun. I promise to rise with him and

set with him every day of my life... until
darkness prevails and death do us part."

With exception of the Picasso quote, she had
kept the rest of her vow secret; her words melted
my heart; it was if the noisy city had grown silent
because I could hear not a sound but her voice. I
battled tears. How much she loved me! How much
I loved her!

More sniffles, even among the unknown
onlookers. They were contagious. Marcus handed
me our wedding bands, two simple gold bands that
we had picked out together. Inscribed in each of
them was one word: *Toujours.* "Always" in French.

Following Beth's lead, Allee and I exchanged
I do's. There was no hesitancy or tremor in our
voices, just pure joy. With a warm smile, Beth
pronounced us man and wife. We were now Mr.
and Mrs. Ryan Madewell IV.

As cheers and applause broke out among
the spectators, I kissed my beautiful bride, so
passionately, so deeply. It was as if I'd never kiss
her again.

A celebration followed with a luncheon at Tavern
on the Green, a romantic restaurant located in
Central Park. It was a joyous celebration of our
union. In the elegant crystal-chandeliered room
we'd reserved, champagne and laughter flowed

before the meal was served. Duffy got to sit next to Samantha. She revealed she was from Southern California like him—and a surfer. Allee had tossed her small bouquet to her, and I swear it wouldn't be long before we would be attending my best friend's nuptials. When Sam excused herself to go the ladies' room, Duffy mouthed to me, "Dude, I'm in love." I gave him a thumbs-up. I had a hunch his dick was finally going to get some heavy-duty action before the day was over.

After downing her third glass of champagne, my mother excused herself from the table. She had a long-standing commitment with one of her charities. She was being honored and was expected to be there to give a speech. *Whatever.*

I excused myself from the table and escorted her to the entrance of the restaurant. I held her up by her bony arm. Having imbibed so much champagne in so short a time on an empty stomach, she was not walking in a straight line. I didn't want her to fall down.

"Thank you, Mother, for coming." I gave her a peck on her sallow cheek. "It meant a lot to Allee and me."

"She's not Charlotte, but I suppose she'll do." Her words stung me, but I held back a snake-tongued retort.

Before she parted, she reached into her pink clutch and handed me an envelope. "This is from your father. He wants you to have it." She averted looking me in the eyes.

I took the envelope from her and slashed it open. Inside was a check for one million dollars. You'd think my eyes would grow wide, but they didn't. Everything inside me clenched with anger. So he thought he could buy me back. Just like the way he bought conglomerates to add to his empire.

I thrust the check back into her hands. "Tell him, I don't need his money. Nor do I want it."

Wordlessly, my mother put the check back into her clutch. Her glazed, weary eyes met mine. "Your father misses you, Ryan." With that, she tipsied away, holding her head high as best as she could.

I couldn't wait to take Allee back to my loft. Rather, *our* loft. Unfortunately, we had to postpone a honeymoon to Paris. Allee was in the middle of a new Modigliani installation at the Met, and I was under deadline to get in my latest *New Yorker* piece. So, I had secretly decided to bring our honeymoon right to our bedroom.

When Marcus dropped us off, I scooped up Allee into my arms.

"What are you doing, Mr. Madewell?" she giggled.

"I am carrying Mrs. Madewell over the threshold." I replied as the electronic door to the loft lifted. "Close your eyes and promise not to open them until I say so."

Allee smacked my lips with hers. "Okay,

promise." She squeezed her eyes shut.

When the elevator door opened, I carried her straight up to our bedroom. "Cripes, how much do you weigh?" I asked jokingly.

"Fuck you." She pounded my chest, her eyes still glued shut.

"Okay, you can open your eyes now."

Allee blinked open her eyes, and her mouth dropped wide open with shock. Before us, smack in the middle of the space, was a magnificent antique four-poster bed. Allee had complained long enough about sleeping on my mattress on the floor and was always joking with me about not being able to afford a decent bed.

I had found this bed at a nearby antiques shop. When the proprietor had told me it was straight out of a grand Parisian *hôtel particulier* that had belonged to one of Picasso's muses, I knew I had to have it. The price was exorbitant, but I didn't care. I could afford it, and it was almost like owning a Picasso, which I couldn't afford. As I handed the dealer my credit card, I pictured ravaging Allee on it.

The dealer offered to arrange having a deluxe custom-made mattress made for the bed and delivering it on our wedding day. He also offered to have the bed made up perfectly if I picked out bedding and sent it to him.

Immediately after purchasing the bed, I scooted uptown to D. Porthault and picked out the finest Made-in-France bedding, including pillows, a duvet, sheets, and pillowcases. Unlike my former king-size mattress, this bed was only a double. Allee would have no choice but to cuddle with me in my arms every night.

"Wow!" exclaimed an overwhelmed Allee. "Did it come from some fancy hotel?"

The luxurious bed indeed looked like it belonged in the Ritz, where I had stayed several times on family trips to Paris. Propped on it, were a box of French chocolates, a bottle of chilled Cristal champagne, two fluted glasses, and my special little gift to Allee... a small needlepoint pillow that had the Eiffel Tower and the words "I'd rather be in Paris" woven into it. I had come upon the whimsical pillow at local tchotchke shop and knew it couldn't be more perfect. My dick hardened at the thought of making love to my beautiful new bride on the virgin mattress.

"Oh, Madewell," sighed Allee dreamily, still in my arms. "It must have cost a fucking fortune."

Funnily, this was exactly the kind of reaction I was expecting from her. By now, I had gotten used to her judging things by how much they cost. In the world I had grown up in, money had no meaning, except for the number of zeroes in your investment portfolio.

I told Allee about the provenance of the bed.

"You're bullshitting me!" she replied.

"I swear on my life I'm not."

"*Mon dieu!*" she gasped in her raspy voice. Her eyes watered. She was both awed and moved.

A smile danced across her face when she spotted the little needlepoint pillow.

"So, Mrs. Madewell, would you rather be in Paris?"

Allee thought for a minute, I'm sure just to taunt me. "Hmm… I'm not sure."

She was such a tease. My cock couldn't wait anymore. It was time to break in the mattress. After consuming her mouth with a delicious all-tongue French kiss, I gently lowered her to a standing position. Her eyes burnt into mine as I unfastened her delicate vintage wedding gown and let it fall to the floor. I was shocked that she was completely naked beneath it. Had I known that when we got married, I might have made love to her right in the middle of Central Park.

She stood before me and let me admire her magnificent, curvaceous body. My dick was swelling beneath my slacks, my balls tingling with desire. "Oh, my wife, you are so, so beautiful."

"You make me feel beautiful." With lust in her dark eyes, she moved into me. She undid my ascot and then removed my waistcoat and my trousers. I hurriedly stepped out of my boxers and my sockless shoes. My rigid rod was shooting at her like a missile.

I swept her into my arms again and laid her down on the bed. Her long curls spread across the plump pillows as she tipped her head to gaze up at me with her hooded eyes.

"What are you waiting for, Mr. Madewell?" she

rasped softly.

"I just want to look at you, Mrs. Madewell." Her breathtaking beauty mesmerized me. After several long minutes, I crawled into the bed, sprawling my body next to hers. Her silky flesh skimmed mine.

"Let's toast each other!"

Raising myself, I grabbed the bottle of champagne and popped it open. Usually, I did this expertly, but this time, the champagne exploded, splattering all over Allee's body. The shock of the cold spray made her jolt and yelp.

"I'm sorry, baby."

Allee was now laughing, that deep, sexy, contagious laugh that made me laugh too, and want to fuck her hard.

"Madewell, you've gotta learn to do that better," she managed between snorts.

I set the bottle on the floor. "Do I need to learn to do this better?" I asked, already lapping up the bubbly that glistened like dewdrops on her tender breasts. Her moan was my answer.

The combination of the champagne and her own sweet flavor sent a ripple to my hard as rock cock. After flicking her sensitive, rose-tipped nipples, my tongue slithered down her taut torso. It stopped to slurp up the little pool of champagne that filled her navel, and then glided down her abdomen in a straight line to her center. Beads of champagne sparkled like fairy dust on her silky sable triangle. I rubbed my nose against the soft, damp area, inhaling the delicious scent of her. She moaned again.

My champagne-laced tongue moved to her honeyed folds. Fuck, she tasted good. My hungry tongue rolled around her exquisite clit, hardening it and bringing her to cries of desire. I was ready. And so was she.

"Spread your legs, Mrs. Madewell." She eagerly did as she was asked.

I mounted her. It seemed fitting on our first night together as a married couple to take her this way. Primal. Raw. Basic. I pounded into her with no reserve, grunting with each deep, feral thrust. She moaned. I was hitting her hot spot and stimulating her clit. Our heartbeats drummed together, and our hipbones, like cymbals, crashed against each other. The flapping of our flesh was yet another percussion in this band of love. We sang along with our moans and groans.

Her breathing grew ragged and so did mine. I couldn't hold back. Harder! Faster! Holy fuck! She was bringing me to the edge. To the point of no return. Before I knew it, I was coming, showering her with my release, and shouting her name.

"Oh, Madewell!" she screamed out as she shuddered around me.

I stayed inside her, neither having the energy nor the desire to withdraw. She didn't move either. While my head nuzzled into the crook of her neck, she stroked my hair and hummed.

At last, I pulled my hot, slick cock out of her and rolled over so that our heads shared one of the pillows plumped up against the bed's headboard.

Parched from our heated round of sex, I grabbed the champagne and took a swig of it straight from the bottle.

"Give that to me," said Allee, her voice hoarse. Snagging the bottle out of my hand, she took not one swig, but two, and sighed loudly. "To us!"

I wrapped an arm around her, letting her head rest on my chest. We shared the remainder of the bottle, passing it back and forth, like it was soda pop.

"So, Mrs. Madewell, I ask you again. Would you rather be in Paris?" I playfully smacked her with the needlepoint pillow.

This time she didn't hesitate or play games with me. Turning her head, she gazed deep into my eyes. A sincere smile played across her face. "No, Mr. Madewell, I'd rather be here with you."

I crushed my lips into hers. Insatiable, Mr. and Mrs. Ryan Madewell IV rolled over to face each other and made delicious love three more times.

"I love you, Allee Adair Madewell," I whispered between flutter kisses.

"I love you more," Allee rasped, stroking my hair.

That wasn't possible, but I wasn't about to end our first night as a married couple with an argument.

Finally wasted, we drifted off in each other's arms. Our honeymoon had just begun.

# TWENTY

Every day of our married life together was a honeymoon. My days rose with Allee, and they set with her. She was *my* sun. I couldn't get enough of her and missed her every second she was away from me.

I was made Contributing Editor at *The New Yorker* and continued to write short stories whenever I had some free time. Allee couldn't be happier either. She loved her job. She loved her life. And she loved me.

After work, we often would go to my health club and work out until we both glistened with sweat. Usually, we would take a shower, but there were nights where we just couldn't wait to have each other and bask in each other's hot juices.

Most nights, we ordered in, but at least once a week, Allee would cook me a fabulous meal. I told her I was going to have to work out longer and harder because I feared her scrumptious French cooking was going to put on the pounds. "Ha, ha, Madewell." She laughed. "I'm gonna get you fat so no other girl will look at you."

After dinner, I would write, and Allee would do research for upcoming exhibitions or thumb through one of the magnificent art books in our growing collection. The way she sat cross-legged with her long legs folded in front of her was totally distracting. I kept imagining and wanting my cock in that triangle of space between them. Sometimes, I couldn't resist, and I would ravage her before we called it a night. "Madewell, you've gotta learn to keep your pants on," she'd always chide. I knew she secretly loved it as much as I did.

Weekends were always a lot of fun. Determined to run the entire marathon together next year, we went running for miles in Central Park on Saturday and Sunday mornings. In the afternoons, we went gallery hopping; Allee was convinced she was going to discover the next Picasso. When we got home, we would analyze some of the pieces we'd seen, usually getting into a major disagreement, and then we'd make everything okay again with a session of glorious lovemaking. On Saturday nights, we'd either go to a movie and dinner or double date with Duffy and Samantha. Just as I'd predicted, they'd become a couple. Duffy's life had finally turned around. He remained Editor in Chief of *Arts & Smarts*— and he was getting laid. Big time. It was just a matter of time before Duffy was going to ask Sam to marry him.

Allee and I both loved newsstands. With the growing popularity of online newspapers and magazines, many of them had sadly closed throughout the city. Fortunately, the one closest to us hadn't. Having grown up in the publishing business, I still loved the feel of paper beneath my fingertips and flipping from one page to the next. We always looked forward to buying the *Sunday New York Times* on Saturday evening. I couldn't wait to read the *Book Review*, and she gobbled up the *Arts & Leisure* section. Then, on Sunday mornings, usually after making love, we'd curl up on the bed over coffee, and read the rest of the paper.

I also always bought a copy of the latest *Arts & Smarts*. It made me feel attached in a bittersweet way to my old buds. Duffy, I had to say, was doing an amazing job. I was proud of him. While, at first, I had misgivings about leaving the magazine, which had been my life and baby for five years, I now no longer missed it. I couldn't be happier with the way things had turned out.

Allee would always come home with one other thing to read—a comic book. She was a total superhero fanatic. When she was little, she believed they could save the world. And save her. She was happy her name had double "L's" because Superman, her favorite superhero, was only attracted to women with them... Like *L*ois *L*ane and *L*ana *L*ang. I reminded her that Madewell had double L's too. She laughed. "Golden Boy, Superman is not gay."

One balmy Saturday night, as we strolled hand in hand to the stand after having dinner with Duffy and Sam, Allee's hand suddenly grew cold and clammy in mine. Marcus was trailing close behind us in the SUV.

"That's him!" Her body shook.

"Who?"

"Sid!"

Every nerve in my body became a sharp electrical impulse. He was much smaller than I'd imagined. Pimply and greasy. He was wearing a Fedora that complemented his white linen suit. A cigarette dangled from his mouth.

I signaled Marcus, who came to a screeching halt beside us.

"Baby, get into the car!" I yanked open the passenger door and shoved her inside. In a heartbeat, Marcus was by my side.

My blood curdled. The mother fucker's head was buried in a porn magazine. It was soon going to be buried in the cement. I looked at Marcus and jerked my head in Sid's direction. Marcus read my mind and nodded. The expression on his face grew fierce.

He took two giant steps, grabbed Sid by the shoulders, and spun him around. The scumbag didn't see it coming. Marcus punched him in the gut and then flipped him hard onto the pavement before he could say "Mommy." His obnoxious hat went flying, as did his cigarette. Clutching his stomach, he moaned in pain.

"Let me finish the son-of-a-bitch." With all I had, I kicked my shoe hard into his ugly face.

He writhed and groaned as blood poured out of his slimy mouth. Spectators gathered, but I didn't flinch.

His wretched eyes met mine. "If I you ever touch my wife Allee again, you'll be buried six feet under." I gave him another hard, ruthless kick where it really hurt. In his balls. He screamed out in pain, cupping his groin.

*Suffer, asswipe!* I crushed his cigarette with the sole of my shoe and then pivoted away from him, proud of my handiwork. Marcus high-fived me and escorted me back into the car.

"What did you to do him?" Allee asked anxiously as the car pulled away.

"I gave it to him and then told him I'd kill him if he ever came near you again."

Allee's eyes widened. "You'd kill for me?"

"Baby, I'd die for you."

"Oh, Madewell!"

A cheek-to-cheek smile spread across Allee's beautiful face. I was expecting a grateful kiss or a hug, but instead I got a question.

"Did you remember to get our *New York Times?*"

I was going fast from being a hero to a zero. "Damn it, I forgot it."

Allee gave me that maddening roll of her eyes and then tapped Marcus lightly on the shoulder. He gazed back at us through the rear view mirror.

"What can I do for you, Mrs. M.?" he asked, using her affectionate new name.

"Marcus, would you be kind enough to pull over and get us *The Times*. Mr. Madewell was too distracted."

"Not a problem." He quickly found a spot and hopped out of the car.

She was pissing me off. "Why did you ask Marcus to get the paper? I could have gotten it."

A diabolical smile flicked across Allee's face. "Because I want to properly thank you for being my hero."

Before I could say a word, she zipped down my fly and lowered her head to my lap. My little tease! So, this was how she was going to thank me. So very Allee!

Holding my balls in her palms, she wrapped her velvety lips around my cock. It immediately swelled in her warm, moist mouth, the pleasure insane. She ran her mouth down the shaft until the tip of my dick could feel her tonsils. Didn't she have a gag reflex? She came right back up and went right back down, repeating this movement until my cock was throbbing so badly I thought I'd pass out. For a moment, I forgot where I was. Arching my head against the headrest, I groaned loudly.

"My Superman," she squeezed in during a brief moment of respite.

After flicking the tip with her tongue, she went back down on me, taking me to the hilt. I roared her name as my cock exploded, sending blasts of hot semen down her throat. She swallowed hard.

Holy Mother of Jesus! Right there, in the back seat of my SUV, Allee Adair Madewell had just given me the best head I'd ever had.

She came back up and licked her lips, which were shimmering with my cum. I crushed my lips against them, tasting my sweet salty release. I deepened the kiss with my tongue. Even the jolt of the front door, signaling Marcus's return, didn't stop me. Finally, when Marcus pulled up to our loft, I released her.

Allee breathed into my ear. "Now, my superhero, I want you to fuck my brains out."

With that and the knowledge that Sid was out of our lives—forever—I couldn't have been a happier man.

# TWENTY-ONE

The only trouble with Allee was that she was working too hard. She loved her job and wanted to prove to the museum how capable and passionate she was. Often she worked long hours, coming home late at night. She sometimes skipped meals, and I noticed that she was fatigued and losing weight. I was worried about her.

At the beginning of June, Allee came down with the flu. She couldn't shake it. I fed her chicken soup from the neighborhood Jewish deli and gave her baths, but she remained listless and feverish. She stayed home from work for a week, but on the following Monday, she crawled out of bed and got dressed. She looked wan and gaunt. Her former body-hugging dress hung loosely on her.

"Baby, you can't go in," I protested.

"I have to. The Modigliani retrospective is opening next week, and there's so much to do." Despite the weariness in her eyes, she gave me that diabolical look that said, "Don't fuck with me." I had no choice but to let her go.

After a sip of coffee, she grabbed her bag and

shuffled to the elevator. As I was about to kiss her goodbye, her knees buckled. I caught her in my arms before she fell to the floor.

She was so light. So unexpectedly light. I carried her up to our luxurious bed and tucked her under the covers. "Baby, you're not going anywhere."

As she gazed up at me wordlessly, tears filled her feverish eyes. I stroked her hair and kissed her forehead.

While she was resting, I went back downstairs and immediately called Dr. Goulding. I deliberately didn't tell Allee I was summoning him because I knew she'd get mad at me. Making her angry would wear her out more.

∽

Dr. Goulding arrived within a half-hour. Carrying his medical bag, he followed me upstairs.

Allee made a face when she saw him, but remained on good behavior, which I knew was challenging for her.

"Let's see what's going on here," said the good doctor, sidling up to the bed. He went through the motions of listening to her heartbeat and breathing, taking her pulse and temperature, looking into her throat, and gently fingering her neck. Allee was admirably cooperative throughout the examination.

My heart pounded in anticipation. "Well,

Doctor?"

"Hmm. She has a low grade fever—nothing serious—and her glands are swollen."

I inwardly breathed a sigh of relief.

"There's been a strange flu going around, but just to play it safe, we should do a blood test."

Allee's deep brown eyes grew as round as saucers, and she bolted up from the bed. "Please, no. No blood test." Her whole body was shaking.

"Don't worry, my dear. It'll only take a minute, and it won't hurt." When Dr. Goulding pulled out a long needle from his bag, Allee's face blanched. I hadn't seen her turn so pale since her encounter with my father at that dinner.

"NO, please!" she screamed out. She was obviously terrified of needles.

I stroked her tumbled hair, trying to calm her. "Hold my hand, baby," I urged, offering it to her. Looking the other way, she acquiesced and squeezed my fingers as Dr. Goulding swabbed her veiny inner arm and then inserted the sharp sliver of metal. It was over before Allee could blink an eye.

"See, that wasn't too bad," said the doctor as he placed a sealed tube of her blood into his medical bag. "I'll try to have the results back to you tomorrow."

Nothing could put a smile on Allee's face.

"What should we do in the meantime?" I asked.

"Just rest and lots of liquids. My guess is that she'll be as good as new by the end of the week."

"I can't go to work?" Allee asked despairingly.

"No, my dear, it's out of the question."

So was making love. I just wanted my baby to get better.

⚮

The next day, while Allee was napping, I got a call from Dr. Goulding, as I was about to make a sandwich for lunch.

"Ryan, can you and Allee come by my office this afternoon?" I couldn't detect any emotion in his voice.

"Is there anything you can tell me on the phone?"

"We'll talk about it when you get here."

I ended the call, wondering what could be the matter with Allee. Dr. Goulding wanted to see both of us. A smile crossed my face as a remote thought popped into my head. Was Allee possibly pregnant?

⚮

Dr. Goulding's office was located on upper Fifth Avenue, not far from my parents' apartment. It was spacious yet homey, filled with a worn-out Chesterfield couch and several other unpretentious antiques. His degrees and numerous awards hung on the richly paneled walls.

Allee and I, holding hands, sat stiffly in two leather armchairs, facing him. Sitting behind his large antique desk, he lifted his glasses onto his balding head and gazed at us with forlorn eyes. While I had come to his office with optimism, I now braced myself for bad news. Allee's icy hand squeezed mine.

"Doctor, don't bullshit me. What's the matter?" Allee braved. Her voice was direct, devoid of emotion.

"Allee, you're sick."

I squirmed in my chair. "You mean like she's got Mono or that Epstein-Barr virus?"

The expression on his face was glum. "No, I'm sorry to have to tell you both this. She's much sicker than that. It's lymphoma."

Allee didn't say a word as my heart dropped to the floor. No, that wasn't possible. My beautiful girl had never been sick until last week. Never! Not one day! It had to be a screw-up.

"Are you sure?" My voice was shaking.

"Yes, Ryan, I'm sure. We ran her blood work three times."

Panic overtook me. "So, you're going to cure her. Right, Doc?"

Dr. Goulding took a deep breath. "It's a very aggressive type. I'm afraid there is no cure."

My mind was in thick fog. It took me several long minutes to register his words. Nausea rose to my chest. The rest of me was paralyzed.

"How long do I have?" Allee asked stoically

after several more long minutes of silence. Her face was as white as chalk.

Dr. Goulding pressed his lips into a thin, grim line. "We'll have to schedule a biopsy and bone marrow test. It could be a few months." He paused. "Or it could be a few weeks. I'm so sorry to have to tell you this."

Reality speared into me. Allee had cancer. She was going to die.

Her head against my chest, Allee sat cradled in my arms in the back seat of the Escalade. Despite the mild summer-like weather, her body was as cold as ice. We were steeped in silence and sorrow. From the blank expressions on our faces, Marcus knew something was wrong but dared not to say a word.

I stroked Allee's hair and kept my lips glued to her head. I couldn't understand why my baby hadn't shed a tear. Perhaps like me, the heart-breaking, gut-wrenching pain had made her numb. My eyes and ears shut out the world around me. The rush of midday traffic and sights of the city were just a blur. Why was this happening? Allee didn't deserve this. Christ. She wasn't even twenty-five yet—that birthday just a few weeks away. Why was God taking her away from me? Why did bad things happen to good people? Allee was good. Too good. Was the fault on her shoulders, something she'd done or not done? Or was it mine?

The doctor had explained to us that there was not much that could done at this late stage of the disease. Any therapy was purely palliative—it could relieve pain, but it couldn't stop the progression. The end. It would be up to us—to her—what we wanted to do.

When we reached the loft, Allee broke away from me and barreled out of the elevator. I watched with wide-eyed shock as she bolted to the bookshelf where she kept all her treasured art books. One by one, she tore them out and madly hurled them across the room.

"Allee, what are you doing?" I cried out. I ran up to her and tried to stop her.

"Leave me alone!" she screamed back at me, twisting her arms free of my grip.

She yanked out the thick book of Musée D'Orsay paintings that I'd given her for Christmas. Expecting to see it go flying across the room, I was surprised when she held it to her heart and fell to her knees. The dam of tears she'd been holding back broke, and she began to sob uncontrollably.

"God dammit. I was supposed to be in remission."

I instantly stooped down and wrapped my arms around her frail, trembling body. She was still clutching the oversized book like a pillow.

"Baby, what do you mean?"

Her tear-soaked eyes met mine. "Oh, my Superman," she bawled. "I had lymphoma my junior year in college. They said they got it. They said I was cured. That it wouldn't come back. The fucking liars!"

It hit me then why she couldn't go to Paris that year. Why she was infertile and couldn't conceive. And why she had to do that other job—to pay off medical bills in addition to her college loans.

"Oh, my baby. Why didn't you tell me?"

"I thought that—"

"Shh." I put a finger to her lips, soaked and swollen from her runny nose and tears. "I don't want to know."

She gazed up me and sniffled, "Can you forgive me, Madewell?"

I brushed away her tears. "Baby, there's nothing to forgive. I would have fallen in love with you and married you no matter what." The truth. That's how much I loved her.

"Tell me, you're not bullshitting me, Madewell," she stammered through her tears.

I framed her face in my hands and looked straight at her. "Allee Adair Madewell, I can't bullshit you. You know that." I was close to shedding tears of my own. So damn close it hurt. *Don't cry, Ryan. Madewells don't cry.*

Not letting go of my gaze, she slowly lowered the Musée D'Orsay book to the floor, setting it beside her. She wrapped her thin arms around my neck and buried her head against my chest. I just let her cry. For as hard and long as she needed. I stroked her tousled hair, relishing the silkiness of each strand. Finally, her sobbing let up a little, dissolving into hoarse, erratic whimpers.

"What do you want to do, Allee?" I asked softly.

She gazed up at me, tears streaming from her eyes. "I want to dance with you, Ryan Madewell IV."

For the first time that day, a ghost of a smile flickered on my face. It dawned on me that we had never danced together before. It was odd but true. Lifting her into my arms as I rose, I crossed the room to the coffee table between the leather couches. Reaching for the remote, I clicked a button, and "I Won't Give Up," our favorite song, filtered into the room. I tenderly set Allee down and pressed her close to me. She rested her head on my shoulder and let me lead the way. She followed me with ease—as if we had danced this way forever. We were again chest to chest, organ to organ, heart to heart. The mound of flesh between my legs wedged into her warm center while her breasts crushed against my pecs. We took small steps, swaying from side to side as if were sewn together. As if we were one.

Outside, thunder clapped, and rain began to pound on the skylight above us. We had weathered rough skies before and had gotten through. Now, our love was all we had to get us through the fatal storm we faced ahead.

She gazed up at me with those soulful espresso eyes. I warmed her lips with mine and closed my eyes with hers. The song played on. No, Allee Adair Madewell, I wasn't about to give up on us.

That night, we never stopped making slow passionate love—our own form of palliative therapy. It was all we could do to keep the pain away. Maybe I couldn't prolong her life, but I could prolong our love.

We were worth it.

# TWENTY-TWO

T he next morning I was up before the sun rose. After making myself a cup of coffee, I scoured the Internet and then made a couple of phone calls. In the middle of the night, while Allee had briefly fallen asleep in my arms, it came to me what we had to do. Maybe it wouldn't cure her disease, but it would make it more bearable. For both of us. With Allee still sleeping, I stealthily left the loft.

When I returned a few hours later, Allee was awake. She was sitting at the dining table, nursing some tea. She actually looked a little better than she had in a while. There was a twinkle in her eyes, and color rose to her sallow cheeks.

"Pack your bags," I told her.

She leaped up from the table. A mixture of terror and rage filled her eyes. "I'm not going to the hospital yet, Madewell!"

I didn't expect her to have this reaction, and I immediately felt terrible. I ran over to her and cradled her in my arms. "No, no, baby, of course not."

I pulled out an envelope from my back jeans

pocket and slapped it onto the table. "Open it, baby."

Perplexed, Allee reached for the envelope and lifted up the unsealed flap. She removed the contents and gasped.

Inside were two first-class, round-trip tickets to Paris.

Tears flooded her eyes. "Oh, Madewell, you shouldn't have."

I squeezed her frail body. Allee Adair Madewell was going to have her Paris. I owed her that. Life owed her that. Our flight was departing in the early evening after her other medical tests. Tomorrow morning, we would be in the City of Light.

While I spent a good deal of the flight writing on my laptop, Allee spent most of it dozing with her head on my shoulder. Every few hours she would wake up and ask me with the eagerness of a child, "Are we there yet?" Finally, just after the sun rose, one of the flight attendants gave her "final destination" speech, in both French and English, as we were about to land at Paris's Charles De Gaulle Airport. I gently woke Allee up. This was Allee's first plane trip. A little nervous, she squeezed my hand, keeping her face literally glued to the window.

"I don't see Paris," she said, her voice a little despondent.

I kissed her lightly on her head. "Don't worry, baby. You will soon."

∞

We passed through customs quickly. Both of us marked "pleasure" on our customs forms in response to the question about the nature of our trip. Deep in my heart, I prayed that this trip would give Allee the most pleasure she'd ever had.

Marcus met us at the arrivals gate. Allee was both shocked and overjoyed to see him. I had purchased a roundtrip ticket that had gotten him to Paris six hours earlier. I needed Marcus to be here for me. For us. When I broke down and told him about Allee's condition, I swear, beneath his shades, he shed tears. Allee had become as close to him as a daughter.

"I'm sorry, Mr. M," he'd choked. "Is there anything I can do?"

"Pray," I'd simply told him. *Yes, pray.*

Taking our bags, Marcus escorted us to the limo he'd rented. Though Paris was more of a walking city, I had a feeling we would need the limo more often than not, due to Allee's health. I helped her fasten her seatbelt, and in no time, we were speeding down the A1 en route to Paris.

I kept my arm wrapped around Allee as she kept her face glued to the tinted window. I knew her heart was racing. Mine was too. Thirty minutes into the ride, Paris came into view. "Oh my God!!

Paris!" she screamed out. She turned her head and smacked a wet, delicious kiss on my lips.

I'll never forget the expression on her face as our limo cruised through the streets of Paris en route to our hotel. She was speechless and wide-eyed, like a child in a candy store. When she finally saw the Eiffel Tower, she shrieked and bounced up and down on the car seat as though it was a trampoline.

I had told our family travel agent, who arranged the entire last-minute trip, that there was only one hotel I wanted to stay at—the Hôtel Ritz on the Place Vendôme. While my parents now always stayed at the swanky Crillon, I preferred The Ritz because of its location between Paris's Left and Right Banks; it was walking distance to everything. And, because this is where my literary hero, Ernest Hemingway, had hung out. When I told Allee that this is where he held court with all the famous artists of the 20's including Picasso, she freaked out.

Allee's eyes widened again when we checked into the hotel. I knew she had never seen such grandeur in her life. She studied it like it was a painting, taking in and analyzing every fine detail—from the gilded wall fixtures to the silk-fringed rugs. When I told her I had booked a suite where supposedly Picasso and one of his muses took refuge, she practically had a fit right in front of the check-in clerk.

The amused clerk smiled as he handed me our

key. "Enjoy your stay, Monsieur and Madame Madewell." His words sent a chill down my spine. Our time as "Mr. and Mrs." was finite. The reality that Allee might die right here in Paris set in. I tried not to think about it.

To say our room was luxurious was an understatement. The hotel, which was about to undergo a multi-million renovation, was nonetheless in top form. A Louis XIV four-poster bed occupied our suite along with many other fine antique furnishings. While she was in awe, Allee was more taken with the fact that Picasso, her idol, had slept here.

"Let's go to the Musée D'Orsay!" Allee said eagerly after unpacking her bag.

Though neither of us was particularly jet-lagged, I told Allee that we should take a nap, thinking only of her best interest. "We can go there tomorrow."

"No fucking way, Madewell," she snapped. "We're in Paris. We're going there *tout de suite! Maintenant!*"

The fiery look in her eyes kept me from saying no. It also reminded me that tomorrow was promised to no one. Especially her.

The Orsay was just a short walk from The Ritz. After fortifying ourselves with double espressos at a nearby café, we strolled there hand-in-hand.

Allee's eyes kept darting around so as not to miss anything. I hadn't seen her so happy or energetic in a long, long time. Maybe Paris was just the medicine she needed.

While I had been to the Orsay, an architecturally magnificent former Beaux Arts train station, several times before with my family, I had never seen its Impressionist and post-Impressionist masterpieces through the eyes of Allee. It was a whole different experience, one I would never forget. She was a walking encyclopedia, able to rattle off details about each painting from the inspiration behind it and the year it was painted, to the significance of a particular color or paint stroke. Every fiber in her being came alive as she made me see what she saw and love what she loved.

Late afternoon, we stood before Seurat's masterpiece, *Le Cirque*. Allee's voice suddenly grew weary, and she faltered on her feet. "Are you okay, baby?" I asked, steadying her.

She studied the painting, composed of countless dots in a style called "pointillism." She sighed, "I wish I had as many days left as there are dots in this painting."

Ironically, Seurat's premature death at the age of thirty-two had prevented him from completing the painting. A chill ran through me. I hugged Allee closer to me. Her dream of one day being a curator here was not going to happen. Her days were numbered.

We dined that night at a small, charming bistro on
Rue du Four on the Left Bank. We shared a delicious
pot au feu and a bottle of hearty Bordeaux. We
talked non-stop about all the other things we were
going to do in Paris and both laughed over the
question: Why does the French food and wine in
Paris taste so much better than it did in New York?
Before we could order dessert, Allee's eyes grew
heavy. "I think I need to get back to the hotel," she
said forlornly. My heart sank. I wanted so badly
to believe she was getting better, but, in truth, she
wasn't. It was only a matter of time, but I was
going to make that time the best time of her life.

Every day in Paris was a new adventure. Another
gift from God. We did everything from walking
along the Seine to visiting other famous sites
and museums, including The Louvre, The Jeu de
Paume, the Rodin, and the Picasso. As we stepped
out of the Panthéon, a street vendor handed us
a flyer for a discounted tour of the famous Père
Lachaise Cemetery where some of Allee's favorite
Impressionist painters, including Seurat, were
buried along with Proust, one of my favorite
writers. Tears welled up in Allee's eyes. Having
gotten back the results of Allee's medical tests,

that was one place we weren't going to visit. Death was just around the corner.

Given Allee's prognosis, we tried to make each day better than the one before and live our lives as if there was no tomorrow. We took photos everywhere we went. In each, we looked like perfectly happy newlyweds who had everything to look forward to in life. When I would later look back at these photos, I would discover the sadness hidden in Allee's eyes and mine. It was most evident in the caricatures we had done by a street artist in the artists' quarter known as Montparnasse. When I studied the one of Allee, I noticed the artist had not put highlights in her dark-as-night pupils. There was no glimmer of life in her eyes. He unknowingly—or knowingly—had captured death's presence.

Every day, Allee grew weaker. She was eating less and less, and she was growing thinner and thinner. When we went to Notre Dame and climbed the steps up to the roof to see the famous gargoyles, she almost collapsed midway. I carried her up the rest of the dark medieval steps piggyback style and carried her back down in my arms. She was light. So, so light.

One evening, I took her on a romantic Bâton Mouche dinner cruise along the Seine. After dinner, which she barely touched, we stood arm-in-arm along the railings and watched the City of Light pass by us. We faced the truth.

"I'm going to miss you, Allee," I said, stifling

tears.

She turned to me and looked me straight in the eye. Her face was stoic. "Stop it, Madewell. With love, there are no goodbyes."

I crushed my lips into hers and felt her scalding tears against my cheeks. This wasn't easy. To be dead honest, it sucked.

The next day, I took Allee to my favorite childhood memory of Paris—the carousel in the Jardin des Tuileries, the magnificent garden across the Seine, facing the Musée D'Orsay.

"Oh, Madewell! It's so charming! It's like a work of art!" she exclaimed, admiring the hand-painted horses and panels that depicted Paris.

As we stood in line with a group of adorable children, Allee told me she'd never been on a merry-go-round. My poor baby had never had a real childhood! It made me feel good that I could give her this experience.

When the spinning ride came to a halt, we boarded. Allee went for a beautiful horse with a red saddle. I helped her mount it, and instead of getting my own horse, I straddled it behind her. I wrapped my arms around her waist. My shaft pressed against her backside. The carousel began to spin, and as the horse moved up and down, I posted a little, rubbing my cock up and down against her. Holy shit! I was getting hard! Allee spun her ahead around and grinned wickedly, knowing the effect the ride was having me on me. Still holding her with one arm, I discreetly slipped my other hand through the loose waistband of her skirt and then slid it under her panties. Moisture spread on my fingers. My girl was wet! As I continued to ride, my fingers rubbed her clit vigorously. Holding onto the pole, she arched her head back and moaned. If it wasn't for all children around us, I swear I would have fucked her right there on the horse. I came first and then she shuddered around me. Oh, God, I needed that release, and I think she did too. For the rest of the ride, I nuzzled her neck, "I love you, Allee Adair Madewell," I whispered in her ear. She turned her head again, and her lips met mine; we kissed passionately. I was only slightly aware of youngsters giggling at us.

Afterward, I bought us ice cream cones. Sitting down on a nearby bench, I marveled at the way her tongue flicked and swirled around the creamy gelato. I wanted that tongue back in my mouth, and that's exactly where it went after she devoured the cone.

My tongue could have danced in her sweet mouth all afternoon. Finally, after many long minutes, I slowly pulled away. There was something I wanted to ask her. Something I needed to know.

"Allee, what is it like for you?"

"My cancer? It doesn't hurt—"

I immediately cut her off. "No, I mean sex. Sex with me."

A wistful smile ghosted across her face. "Always a little different. But always beautiful and intense."

"What did I feel like inside you?"

"You mean, 'do.'"

My nerve endings scrunched. I felt bad—beyond bad—that I'd used the past tense. My Allee's life wasn't over... yet.

She sucked in a breath of the fragrant spring air. "Oh, Madewell, you fill me. From my core to my heart. And when you make me come with you, you take me to a place outside my body where I'm flying in your arms watching a beautiful sunrise."

Her words moved me. Christ, I was going to miss her. I thought about asking her what it felt like when I came before her, but I wanted to hang onto the sensual image she'd created in my head. Squinting, I gazed up at the sun-kissed sky and yearned to make love to her right here on this bench so that we could soar together into the heavens. She squeezed my hand, and I knew she was thinking the same thing. My cock throbbed beneath my jeans, but not as much as my heavy heart.

We spent the rest of the afternoon holding hands and silently watching rosy-cheeked children at play. That was something we were never going to have. A pang of sadness swept through me.

Allee broke our silence. "Madewell, I need to tell you something."

The quiver in her voice made my heart race.

Had she taken a turn for the worse? "What is it, baby?" I held my breath waiting for a response.

"Maybe, we could have had a child."

My eyes grew wide. "What do you mean?"

"Before I had chemo in college, I had my eggs harvested."

"Meaning..."

"Meaning that some gynecologist extracted eggs from my ovaries and froze them at the City Center for Reproductive Medicine. In case, I ever wanted to have children. It was a long shot, but still..."

"Baby, I thought you said you couldn't have children."

"I can't now, can I?" There was sadness in her voice as she stared blankly at the Musée D'Orsay in the near distance.

"Why didn't you tell me this before?" Tenderness, not anger, colored my voice.

Allee lowered her head. "I thought if I told you this, you'd ask why I did it, and I would've had to tell you about my cancer. And then you wouldn't have..."

I stopped her mid-sentence and kissed her again. Nothing would have gotten in the way of me loving her or asking her to marry me. *No, nothing.*

While I held her in my arms, all the breakthroughs in reproductive medicine I'd read about flashed through my head. I was eager to get back to the hotel. Allee, fatigued, was ready. Marcus got us back there quickly, despite the crazy Paris traffic. While Allee napped in our room, I went down to the Hemingway Bar and made a series of phone calls, beginning with Dr. Goulding. By five p.m., I had an appointment with Dr. Ethan Moore, the head of the City Center for Reproductive Medicine, on the afternoon of our return to New York. It was worth a shot.

# TWENTY-THREE

On our last night in Paris, I wanted to take Allee for a dining experience she'd never forget. While she rested in the hotel room most of the day, I went to the landmark department store, Galeries Lafayette and picked out a chic little black dress for her to wear. Though since I'd known her she'd always worn a Size 6, I went with a four because of all the weight she'd lost. I hoped it wouldn't be too big.

When I returned to the hotel, Allee was propped up in bed, thumbing through a book about Picasso that we had purchased from one of the *bouquinistes* along the Seine. She looked very pale. Like all the blood inside her had drained.

"What's that?" she asked when she saw me holding a huge gift-wrapped box with a giant red bow.

"A present."

Her brows furrowed. She gazed at me sheepishly. She still didn't like it when I bought her things.

"Open it." I placed the box on the bed.

She carefully undid the wrapping and the ribbon and lifted off the top lid. When she found the dress beneath layers of delicate tissue paper, her mouth dropped wide open. It was a Lanvin. "Madewell, this must have cost a fortune!"

That translated as "I love it." "I want you to wear it tonight. I'm taking you to Le Jules Verne for dinner." It was a fine French restaurant located almost at the top of the Eiffel Tower.

"Will you help me get ready?"

I read into her words. Fifteen minutes later, we were chest-deep in our luxurious jacuzzi tub, soaking in the warm bubbly water. Allee was seated in front of me, her long, now thin legs outstretched with mine. The lights were dim, and I had lit several fragrant candles. The room smelled divine. We hadn't been intimate like this for a while. She bowed her head as I held up her glorious hair and smothered the back of her neck with kisses. Oh, how I would miss the sweet taste of her! I wished I could bottle it in a jar.

Using the jasmine-scented soap, I lathered up her back and arms and her still full breasts. Letting the bar of soap fall into the water, I groped the soft mounds in my hands, massaging and gently squeezing them. I rubbed her puckered rosebuds in circles with the pads of my thumbs and then pinched them between my thumb and index fingers, feeling them grow into pointed crowns. I closed my eyes, memorizing the feel of them. She let out a soft moan.

Beneath her buttocks, my cock grew hard and hungry. I wanted desperately to be inside her but wasn't sure she could handle my drive in her frail state.

"Rub my clit," she begged.

She wanted me. Still playing with her left breast, I moved my other hand below the water to her velvety folds. I caressed them, wishing she was facing forward so that I could bathe her with my tongue. I thought about turning her to face me, but she did it herself, as if reading my mind. My head dipped beneath the water, and I let my tongue stroke and dip into every hill and vale. Savoring them. The tip circled around her clit, and when I could no longer hold my breath underwater and had to come up for air, my middle finger seamlessly took over.

Clutching my biceps, Allee arched back her head and moaned. Her long dark hair fell gloriously down her back. My eyes, half-moons, stayed riveted on her. Her sunken face had an ethereal quality—a unique beauty—that tugged at my heart.

"You're so beautiful" I managed between mouthfuls of her ripe nipples. I sucked them tenderly and then trailed kisses down her torso. I could feel every bone of her rib cage against my lips but nothing could stop me. I couldn't get enough of her. Paris was for lovers. I told her again how beautiful she was.

"You're so full of shit. I look like crap."

Even in the shadow of death, she was still the wicked, wisecracking Allee I loved so much. The truth was, she was beautiful to me, and I told it to her yet again.

"Shut up, Madewell. Just make love to me."

I gazed into her eyes. "Are you sure?"

"Yeah, I'm sure."

Splaying her thin, but still muscular, legs, she helped me insert my girth inside her. I pulled her closer to me as she used her hand to edge it in, inch by thick inch. We moaned together. Reaching the hilt, my cock had found its home sweet home. The only place on earth where it belonged. "Oh baby," I cried out.

Holding onto her bony haunches, I glided in and out of her. Slowly and steadily. She held onto my biceps and arched her back. Whimpers escaped her lips. I hoped she wasn't crying.

"Are you okay, baby?" I asked, worried again that I was hurting her.

"Yeah, you feel so good," she said breathily.

"Tell me if it's too much for you. Or if I hurt you."

"You could never hurt me, Madewell."

My cock continued to swell inside her warm cavity, bathed by her own hot juices.

A rapturous feeling overcame me as my throbbing cock cried out for release. My lips consumed hers, our tongues probing and exploring as if they never had.

Her cries of ecstasy told me she was close to

climaxing.

"Come with me," she pleaded. Closing her eyes, she arched her back and dropped open her mouth as she breathed my first name—for the first time—upon reaching orgasm. I watched her come in all her glory as she convulsed around my exploding rod. "Oh, Ryan," she moaned again. The way she said my name drawing out the first syllable with a deep sexy lilt, made me burst inside her, coating her walls with my release. "Don't leave me, baby," I cried out, my voice caught between rapture and despair.

She wrapped her arms around my neck, leaning her head in until our foreheads touched. She nuzzled my lips. "Shh," she said softly. "I'm still here."

Our reservation at Le Jules Verne was for six o'clock. Because Allee fatigued easily, I deliberately made it early. Even at this unpopular dining hour, the posh restaurant was booked. When I told them my name, a window table for two opened up. The Madewell name came with its benefits.

The all-window, sky-high restaurant overlooked all of Paris. From our table, we could see The Arc de Triomphe, Eiffel Tower, Sacre Coeur, and numerous other sparkling monuments. The view was truly spectacular.

In contrast, the view of Allee was less than spectacular. Her brief after-sex afterglow had faded, and now her skin was pale again, almost ashen. Maybe our lovemaking session in the tub had worn her out. Or set her back. A pang of guilt stabbed me.

I ordered the exorbitant, prix fixe multi-course dinner for each of us along with an expensive bottle of Pouilly-Fuisé wine. Attentive white-gloved waiters brought the elaborate meal to our table, one dish at time. They also made sure our wine glasses were constantly filled. Allee hardly ate or drank a thing.

By the third course, a palate-cleansing sorbet, Allee looked faint. "Baby, you don't feel well, do you?"

She shook her head.

"We don't have to stay here. Do you want to go back to the hotel?"

Her pained eyes met mine. "No... a hospital."

Reality stabbed at my heart. *This was it.*

She tried to push herself away from the table but didn't have the strength. I leaped to my feet and scooped her into my arms. Panic gripped me.

"Someone, call for an ambulance," I yelled at the of top of my lungs.

"No, Madewell, please. No ambulance."

I had Marcus take us to the American Hospital of

Paris. Familiar with Paris, having once driven for the Ambassador to France, he wove swiftly through the maze of Paris traffic and got us there in no time; he knew what was happening and remained stoically silent. In the back seat, I cuddled Allee. Her breathing was labored, and she was trembling.

"I'm scared, Madewell," she whispered.

"It's okay, baby. I'm here." I smoothed her hair and kissed her forehead. Truthfully, I was scared shitless too.

Located in Neuilly-sur-Seine, a wealthy suburb not far from the Eiffel Tower, The American Hospital was a venerable private institution with a hundred year history. I had been there once myself as child after breaking an arm while playing soccer in the Jardin des Tuileries. Needless to say, my father was not pleased with having a sports-injured son to deal with while on vacation.

Being a Madewell once again had its perks. My parents were major contributors to the hospital, and my mother sat on the American Hospital of Paris Foundation Board. Holding Allee in my arms, I told the nurses at the front desk my name—Madewell, as in the son of Mr. and Mrs. Ryan Madewell III—and that I wanted the very best room they had for my wife. *Please*. No expense spared. With one look at Allee, lying limp in my arms like a wilted flower, they knew it was very serious. They moved quickly to get her checked in.

Twenty minutes later, Allee was in a hospital bed in a large private suite on the hospital's top floor. A team of doctors had contacted Dr. Goulding, who immediately faxed them her charts and made them aware of her end-of-life situation. My poor baby looked so tiny and frail hooked up to so many tubes, wires, and machines. They had her on her morphine drip to keep her pain to a minimum and some kind of sedative to keep her calm. She was also getting white cells and platelets to prevent infection. I sat in an armchair close to her side.

"Hi," she said weakly. "Sorry to ruin dinner. I'll pay you back for it."

I smiled. Lying near death, she still had that wicked sense of humor and that self-deprecating need to take care of herself.

"Shh," I said, taking the hand that didn't have an intravenous tube attached to it into mine. "Save your strength."

"No, Madewell. I want *you* to be strong for me."

I gazed at her. Even so close to death, she was so, so, beautiful. Her weight loss had hollowed her cheeks, making her extraordinary high cheekbones even more visible and breathtaking. They brought attention to her other beautiful features—those espresso bean eyes that still had a glimmer of life, her perky upturned nose, and her sensuous full lips. Her skin, now ashen, reminded me of a Picasso portrait.

"Is there anything else you want, baby?"

"Yeah. I want you."

Fighting back tears, I said nothing.

"Come into bed with me, Madewell."

Was she kidding? She wanted me to get into that narrow bed with her hooked up to all those tubes and gizmos?

"I'm skinny." She flashed a faint smile. "There's room for you. You won't hurt me... you never have."

Hesitantly, I rose from the chair and made my way to the bed.

"No, Madewell." Her voice was weak, just a little above a whisper. "Take off your clothes. I want to feel your raw body next to mine."

Wordlessly, as she watched, her eyes never leaving me, I peeled off my suit, my shirt and tie, my boxers, and lastly my loafers. I wasn't wearing socks.

All 6'2" of me stood before her, naked to the bone. Her eyes roved up and down my chiseled body. They lingered on the heavy package between my legs before returning to my face.

Her lips curled into that sexy, dimpled smile. "Hey, did I ever tell you that you're beautiful?"

I thought about it for a minute. Honestly, I couldn't recall her ever telling me that. She once said I had a body worth painting, but that was about it. "No," I said.

"Well, I'm telling it to you now. You're beautiful, Ryan Madewell IV."

The ache of the flesh between my thighs paled to the ache in my heart. The effect she had on me was close to being unbearable. *My* Camille, my fallen angel. I damned her and so adored her at the same time. *Be strong for her, Madewell. Don't cry.*

"Now, Golden Boy, get your rich tight ass in bed with me."

I didn't hesitate. I carefully slipped under the fluffy duvet, anchoring my naked body next to hers. To my surprise, my flesh brushed against hers. Beneath the covers, she was stark naked. Had my feisty beauty refused her hospital gown or shed it? Neither possibility shocked me. That was my Allee.

With a struggle, she rolled onto her side. "Face me, Madewell." I did as she asked, so that we were face to face, heart to heart, organ to organ. I studied her beautiful face, memorizing every detail as my body warmed hers. Our breaths mingled and her faint heartbeat beat against mine. With one hand, she slid my organ inside her. It felt warm and beautiful, as if we were one. Wrapping our arms around each other, we were positioned just like that hidden Picasso painting she had shown me the first time we'd met. She knew it too and, one more time, broke into that dimpled smile I would always remember.

Though her lids were heavy, her eyes burned into mine. "Madewell, there's one last thing I want to tell you." Her voice was barely audible.

"What's that?"

"That was a damn good article you wrote on that Picasso painting."

"Thanks," I said humbly. "I love you, Allee Adair Madewell."

I waited for her to say "I love you" back. It never came. She was fast asleep.

In the morning, she was gone.

# TWENTY-FOUR

I f death was a living thing, I was it. It was hard to believe my Allee was gone.

Before leaving the hospital, an administrator asked me about Allee's funeral arrangements. The query sent shockwaves through my numbed body. Allee and I had never discussed them. It wasn't what young married couples with everything to live for did. Despite her imminent death, I think we both secretly believed that a miracle would happen. That she would live, and we'd get our happily ever after.

Stunned into deep thought, I searched my mind and my soul for what I thought Allee would want. The thought of transporting her body back to New York sickened me. Then it just hit me. I knew what would make Allee happy. I asked the kind hospital staff to handle the arrangements.

A weary Marcus was waiting for me outside. I don't think he ever left the grounds or slept. The solemn expression on my face told him the words he didn't want to hear.

"I'm so sorry, Mr. M." A fat tear rolled down

the stoic man's face. Before opening the passenger door, he did something he hadn't done since I was kid. He hugged me. I so needed that, and was grateful that Marcus was part of my life.

The ride back to the Ritz was uneventful. I could have been anywhere in the world, because everything was a blur to me. Marcus respected my grief with utter silence.

I staggered into the Ritz exhausted, carrying a small bag of Allee's possessions. I had told the hospital to keep her clothing, including the black dress I'd bought her, and give it all away to a women's shelter. Allee would have liked that. All that was in the bag were her treasured locket, my antique engagement ring, her gold wedding band, and a letter that the nurses had found folded up in her purse.

Unshaven and unkempt, I stumbled into the Hemingway Bar. It was seven o'clock in the morning; no one else was there but me. I slumped into an armchair, the first one I came upon. I didn't know if I needed a drink or an espresso. I ordered both from the only waiter working the early morning shift. After I drained the drink, a whiskey straight up, I emptied the contents of the bag onto the table facing me. I ran my fingers over the jewelry and had the burning desire to see that photo of Allee as a toddler that was encased in the locket. I flicked it open. To my surprise, a tiny photo of Allee and me embracing on our wedding day had been placed over the other photo.

Memories of that unforgettable day whirled in my head and then others came back to me with the force of a rockslide. Each one hurt more than the one before. Our time together had been so short, yet it felt like a lifetime. I held her wedding ring and band in the palm of my hand and glared at them in a trance. The word *"toujours"* flickered in my eyes. "*Toujours*"... some bullshit French word for "always."

"Ryan."

A familiar voice catapulted me back into the moment. I looked up, and my heart skipped a beat. It was my father. What the hell was he doing here? Only three people in the world knew about Allee's condition and our trip to Paris other than Marcus—Duffy, a lapsed Catholic, who was heartbroken over the news and promised to go to Church to pray for her, and my sister Mimi and her partner Beth, who were equally stunned and saddened.

I stood up and faced him squarely. "How did you find me?"

"Your sister told your mother what was going on. The minute I heard about Allee's condition, I hopped on the corporate jet."

Fatigue sent a chill through me. Or was it grief? Or my father's presence?

"Ryan, I want to see her." There was compassion in his voice and steely eyes.

"Allee's gone."

"I'm sorry," he stammered. "I should go back. Would you like to fly back with me, son?"

I shook my head. "I have things to take care of here."

"Then I'll say goodbye."

I don't know what made me do it, but I repeated what my beautiful Allee had told me the other night on the Bâton Mouche. "Father, with love, there are no goodbyes."

He did something a Madewell was never allowed to do. He cried.

And in his arms, I cried too.

Alone again, I sat down to read Allee's letter, careful not to let tears spill onto the ink. She must have written it while I was away from her; the words were sprawled on The Ritz's elegant ivory stationary. Her penmanship was just like her—quirky, curvaceous, and beautiful.

*Madewell~*

*By the time you read this letter, I will be gone. I have no clue where I'm going or why this is happening to me. I only know I will miss you.*

*Your name, Ryan, comes from the French word "roi" which means "king." My name Allee is almost identical to the French word "allée" which means "gone." LOL. When I am gone, Madewell, I want you to rule with your heart and live your life. You have so much potential, so much to live for—with or without me.*

*Please don't mope around mourning me. Why mourn what you can't have? One day you will fall in love again. I know you don't think you can, but I'm counting on it. So, do it for me. I'm sure whomever you meet will be someone I'd like.*

*There's one other thing I want you to do. Make up with your father. He is the only father you will ever have. We've all erred in our lives, but we all deserve the chance to be forgiven. I hope you will forgive me for leaving you too soon. It's not your fault, my Superman, I could not be saved.*

*Go on living, my sweet superhero. Although our time together was so short, it was the best time I ever had. You gave me everything—love, laughter, Paris, and all of you. Just because I've stopped living my life, don't stop living yours.*

*One last thing... Write, Madewell, write. Write for me. I'll be reading every word from wherever I am. Always remember...*

*I love you more~*

*Allee*

I folded up the letter and let my tears fall.

# TWENTY-FIVE

In the morning, I steeled myself to pick up Allee's ashes from the Père Lachaise crematorium. The bitter irony that we'd both ended up here despite not wanting to visit this Paris landmark was not lost on me. It sent a shiver down my spine as I collected her remains. They were sealed in a small, elegant urn that reminded me of her once curvaceous body. I had thought about leaving them here, but this was not their final destination. They belonged somewhere else.

Marcus drove me back to the Ritz to pick up my laptop. Then by foot, I headed over to the Jardin des Tuileries where Allee and I had sat watching children play.

The magnificent gardens, though across the Seine, faced the Musée D'Orsay. Clutching the urn, I came upon a beautiful patch of French lilies that reminded me of flowers in one of the Monet paintings we had admired at the Orsay. While the day had started out sunny—the kind that defined springtime in Paris—storm clouds now threatened. Taking a deep breath, I removed the lid and scattered the ashes among the flowers. A clap of thunder... and the sky began to weep with me. I was reminded of that night I had kissed Allee in the pouring rain on the steps of the Met. I squatted down and pressed my lips to her wet ashes, sealing them with my tears to the earth. Wherever she was going, my Allee would always have this final kiss... and her dream of becoming a curator at the Musée D'Orsay in sight.

The pouring rain reduced to a fine drizzle. And soon, the sun again began to shine. Collecting myself, I walked slowly along the Seine over to the Café de Flore on the Boulevard Saint-Germain. It was one of the few places Allee and I missed going to.

The place was bustling, filled with all types— from attractive fashion models, whose stares I ignored, to old men wearing berets. I took a seat at one of the bistro tables. Dozens of great American writers had probably sat in this very chair... including Fitzgerald, Stein, Joyce, and my favorite of all, Hemingway, who wrote much of his first novel here.

After ordering a cappuccino, I pulled out my laptop. I closed my eyes.

*She was sexy and sassy. And had the voice of a goddess.*

*She loved Degas, Seurat, Picasso, and me...*

*Not necessarily in that order.*

*She also loved superheroes. She believed they could save the world.*

*I asked her once if she loved me more than she loved Superman.*

*She zipped down my fly and blew me so hard I was flying.*

*"You, Ryan Madewell, are my Superman."*

*Except I couldn't save her.*

What do you write...?

I didn't need an outline. Just my heart.

A tear spilled onto my keyboard as I typed the first word...

# EPILOGUE

*Three Months Later...*

I fidgeted with my hands as I sat in the sleek waiting room of Dr. Ethan Moore's world-renowned fertility clinic. Ethnically diverse, young couples, all longing and desperate for a child, surrounded me. Most were reading a magazine or watching the "Story of My Baby" video that played on the flat screen monitor on the wall above the reception window. I was too anxious to do either. Butterflies swarmed my stomach.

As it did often, my mind flashed back to that unforgettable day in Paris when Allee revealed that she had harvested her eggs before undergoing chemotherapy in college. I wished I'd known that earlier. I would have attempted the experiment I was doing now while she was still alive. How I wished I could have told the love of my life that we might have a child of our own. Whether she was with me. Or without me. On second thought, perhaps it was for the best. Maybe the sadness of knowing she would never have the chance to see or love this child would have been unbearable. Or even worse, knowing that the experiment had failed. I sucked in a deep breath. I was about to find out.

This was my fourth visit to Dr. Moore's fertility clinic since Allee's passing. The first took place upon my return from Paris. I learned that Allee had left me custody of her frozen eggs soon after we'd gotten married. It made me wonder if Allee had foreseen her destiny, and that in leaving me her eggs, she was asking me to perpetuate her life in some way. They were mine to do whatever I wanted. Dr. Moore, a warm, ruggedly handsome man in his early forties, spent an hour with me, discussing the options, including the viability of fertilizing them with my sperm.

Though sensitive to my grief-stricken state, Dr. Moore was honest with me. It was risky. The success rate of fertilizing frozen eggs wasn't high, but the good news was that it was doable, and babies born from this process had no risk for increased birth defects. I just had to prepare myself for the consequences: was I ready to be a single father if the procedure worked, and would I be able to deal with disappointment if it failed? Even though Allee had harvested many eggs that had been frozen in batches, allowing the option of trying again, Dr. Moore warned me that, for some people, the grief that followed failure was too much to bear. He told me to go home and think things over and to make another appointment with him when I had come to a decision.

I had been an utter zombie since Allee's death. I forgot to eat; I didn't want to wake up in the morning; I didn't want to leave my loft or see a soul. The only thing that helped me was my writing. Within my own written words, I found myself reliving my life with her. Her breathtaking face, that raspy voice, the memories of us filled my head every waking moment of the day. Even when I slept, I dreamt of her. Of us. And of our baby. I never knew if it was a boy or girl. I saw only a beautiful face. A rosy-cheeked, tiny face that resembled Allee's with twinkling espresso eyes and a tuft of ebony hair.

I decided to go forward with the procedure, blocking out the additional grief that might ensue if it didn't work. I owed it to her to try; I owed it to us. One month later, I met with Dr. Moore again to tell him my decision.

"Have you arranged for a surrogate?" he asked.

My heart skipped a beat. I hadn't given that much thought. When Dr. Moore told me that the process of securing a surrogate could take from six months to a year, I asked him if there was any alternative. For my own survival, I needed to go through the procedure as soon as possible. He told me that he could he freeze any resulting embryos while I searched for a surrogate and mentally readied myself for fatherhood. To my relief, the pregnancy success rate with frozen embryos was approximately the same as non-frozen embryos.

Two weeks later, I was back at Dr. Moore's clinic. A batch of Allee's eggs had been thawed. A bittersweet smile spread across my face when one of his nurses told me that they were of superior "A" quality. "Magnificent!" she exclaimed. *Just like my Allee.*

The smiley, buxom woman escorted me down a hallway, lined with adorable photos of "success story" babies, to a small, sterile room. Besides a sink and disinfectant, there was a rack of plastic cups and test-tubes labeled "Lubricant" as well as a rack of men's magazines, featuring seductive, big-breasted, naked models on the covers. There was also a flat screen TV.

"You may want to read one of these to help you," said the nurse with a wink. "Or watch the DVD."

I didn't need a porn magazine or video to help me jerk off. Closing my eyes, I wrapped my as-instructed, washed hand around my scrubbed cock, sliding it up and down with single-minded intensity; it swelled and stiffened quickly. All I had to do was think of my Allee. "Come for me, Madewell," I heard her rasp as my hard, thick organ exploded. I watched as my release trickled into the plastic cup I was holding in my other hand. Tears of relief and remorse snaked down my face. Sealing the cup with a lid, I slumped back down the hall and handed it to the nurse. She grinned ear to ear when she saw my specimen.

Now, it was just a waiting game. Two anxious

days later I got a call from a nurse at the fertility clinic, asking me to come by in the afternoon. Dr. Moore wanted to speak with me. Every muscle in my body tensed. The memory of rushing to Dr. Goulding's office to receive Allee's prognosis flashed in and out of my head. My stomach clenching, I braced myself for bad news as I sat in the waiting room of the fertility clinic.

"Is your wife trying to have a baby?" asked the attractive redhead sitting next to me. A chill crept down my spine; I was taken aback. Before my mouth could move, the nurse who had collected my sperm stepped into the waiting room. My already rapid heartbeat accelerated.

A wide smile spread across her face. I couldn't tell if it was genuine or put on. "Follow me, Mr. Madewell. Dr. Moore would like to talk to you in his office."

My hair stood on edge. This was definitely the beginning of bad news. I hesitantly rose from the comfortable couch and trailed behind the nurse down the hallway, passing the jerk-off room. My heart was thudding. Three doors down, she dropped me off in Dr. Moore's office, a cozy room filled with medical degrees, reference books, and family photos. He was seated behind his large desk.

"Make yourself comfortable, Ryan," he said as I nervously sunk into one of the armchairs facing him.

"I have something to show you," he continued, handing me a photo from a folder on his impeccably neat and organized desk.

With jittery fingers, I examined the black and white photo. Before me was the image of a quarter-size cluster of intersecting round shapes; it resembled a small blooming flower that a child might draw.

"What is this?" I asked, still peering at it.

"That's an embryo."

I gasped. Holy shit! It worked! One of my sperm fell in love with one of Allee's eggs and fertilized it. Just like I had with her...love at first sight!

"Ryan, there are actually three altogether. The chances of having Allee's child are excellent." He handed me another photo displaying all three embryos.

My vision stayed fixed on the burgeoning life forms. I was in awe. Three miracles!

The words of Allee's farewell letter danced in my head. *"Madewell... you have so much to live for..."*

Now, I did. Tears I'd been holding back leaked out of the corners of my eyes.

Allee Adair Madewell, I'm looking up...

*~THE END~*

Dear Reader~

You're probably sobbing. I know because I wept, too, as I wrote *Undying Love* and every time I reread it. While I originally didn't intend to write a sequel, one needed to be told. Ryan and Allee deserved more. In the sequel coming soon, Ryan gets his happily ever after and the spirit of Allee lives on! Willow's story is as moving and as special as Allee's. It will leave you yet again in tears. But tears of joy and a big smile. I promise!

Here is an excerpt from the sequel: *Endless Love.*

Love~ Nelle

SNEAK PEEK

# ONE

## Willow

I bawled until there were no more tears to shed. The last page of the book was soaked. Ready to fall apart like me. I slammed the book closed and gazed at the cover. A beautiful young couple in love. But in her dark, soulful eyes, I could now see death. Yes, Allee Adair knew she was going to die. That was her destiny. But the love she felt for Ryan Madewell would never die.

I had experienced my own *Undying Love*. When I was sixteen, a cab hit my mother, Belinda. Instant death upon impact. I'll never forget the day I came home from school, and my father sat me down at one of the tables in his deli. It was the very one I was sitting at today.

"What would you say if I told you Mom is dead?" he asked stoically.

Confusion sent a chill deep through me. "What do you mean, Pops?"

And then he told me. The tears just poured

and poured. Enough to make brine in a barrel of pickles. I never got to tell her "I love you." Those words, during my tumultuous teenage years, always stayed prisoners in my heart, though often they wanted to escape. Now it was too late. I never got to say goodbye. But love, according to Allee Adair, meant never having to say that word.

Pops and I went on with life without mom. His deli, Mel's Famous, was kind of a landmark on New York's Lower East Side, and regular customers kept him busy. As for me, I threw myself into my dancing at Julliard. An aspiring ballerina, my dancing kept the pain away. My father was concerned about my obsessive-compulsive behavior and made me see a shrink. Dr. Jules Goodman saved my life.

Dr. Goodman was now saving my life again. I was on sabbatical from The Latvia Ballet Company. A prima ballerina, I had collapsed on stage while performing *Sleeping Beauty* in Vienna. The in-house doctor said I was exhausted and malnourished. That's what my dad was told. What he didn't know was that I was suffering from another disease. A broken heart. Only Dr. Goodman knew what brought me almost to utter destruction. Physical and emotional. The real extent of the damage. For now, as I healed, that secret needed to stay between us.

Being back home in New York, living with my dad, was good for me. Afraid of losing the other great love of his life, he took care of me, feeding me lots of homemade chicken soup—the soup that made Mel's Famous famous. Slowly, I put back on the weight I had lost, even though I was still very thin by most standards. It felt good to be in comfy shoes and jeans although I was aching to put on a leotard and my toe shoes. To dance for *him*.

Gustav had been my cocaine. I could never get enough of him. He would be showing me how he wanted my leg to extend, and before I knew it, my legs were extended around him and we'd be fucking our brains out. It was like that. We would fuck anywhere, anytime we could. Between acts. During intermission. In my dressing room. Behind the curtain. On the stage floor after the lights had gone off. He knew how to arouse me like no other man could. Orgasms pirouetted throughout my body. One after another after another.

But now, Gustav was back with his wife Marguerite. He couldn't leave her. She was worth 1.5 billion dollars; the lifestyle and connections she afforded him could not be passed up. Despite his indiscretions, she always took him back. His beauty and sexuality were irresistible. I knew that for a fact. I hated him. Hated her more. But hated myself the most for letting myself believe that he loved me.

*Don't go there.*

"What's the matter, babykins?"

The warm voice stopped me before I could descend into darkness. I looked up. My father. In his perpetually stained, floor-length deli apron over his ill-fitting baggy pants and Mel's Famous t-shirt. There was alarm in his husky voice and his warm chocolate brown eyes. His bushy brows furrowed.

"Oh, Pops! I just read the saddest book ever." I showed him the cover.

My burly father smiled a smile of relief, and wiped away my tears with the edge of his apron. "The author's a regular; he comes here from time to time."

*Ryan Madewell?* "Really?" My tears subsided. "Do you think he'd be willing to sign my book next time he comes in?"

My father's smile broadened. "It doesn't hurt to ask."

"And, Pops, it doesn't hurt to lose weight."

Ryan Madewell showed up at my father's deli exactly one week later. I recognized him immediately because I had spent the whole week Googling him.

With a laid back style, he strode up to the well-stocked deli case, deciding what he wanted to order for takeout. He was wearing tight faded jeans, a creamy cotton tee and a baby blue cable knit sweater wrapped over his shoulders. God, he was gorgeous. Tousled sandy hair, misty blue eyes, a slight six-o'clock shadow over his movie-star handsome face, and a six foot-plus buff body that screamed, "I work out." In his Google images, he was gorgeous too. Just not this heart-stoppingly gorgeous.

I was minding the store while my father was at the bank making a deposit. Almost three in the afternoon, it wasn't very busy. In fact, he was the sole customer.

My eyes and body followed him while he lingered in front of the meat counter. Finally, he said, "I'll have my regular—a pastrami sandwich to go with a side of slaw."

"Would you like it hot?" I asked, my eyes meeting his.

There was a short stretch of silence before he said anything. "Yeah, I like it hot."

His soft, raspy voice was so damn sexy. I swear, my temperature rose ten degrees.

"What kind of bread?"

"Rye, please."

Rye bread for Ry-an. I wondered what it would feel like to be sandwiched between him and a yummy mattress. Oh God. This guy was making my mind travel to places it hadn't been for a long time.

I prepared the sandwich for him. I was good at this, having made deli sandwiches ever since I could remember. I picked prime, fat-free pieces of meat, microwaved them, and then piled them high between two slices of fresh rye.

"Would you like mustard?"

"Mayo, please."

I squirted mayonnaise from a pointed plastic

tube onto the sandwich meat, imagining it was cum. *Huh! What was I thinking?*

"That looks delicious," he said.

*So do you.*

I wrapped up the sandwich with the slaw and threw it into a paper bag.

"Would you like anything else?" I managed.

"A cream soda would be great."

Yes, a cream soda. I craved one too—personally delivered by his cock. My core was heating up and tingles spread between my legs. *Stop it, Willow!* Unable to compose myself, I pulled a soda bottle out from the cooler.

"I'll have that now, please," he said.

I handed him the soda, my fingers brushing against his. They were long, strong, and purposeful. The fingers of a writer. I watched as he wrapped his lush lips around the rim of the glass bottle and tilted his head slightly backward. His eyes closed as he savored the cold, refreshing beverage. I imagined this is what he would look like after having an orgasm. In my head, I unzipped his fly and gave him a hand job that made him explode and shout my name. *Holy fuck!*

"How much do I owe?" he asked, bringing me back to my senses.

"It's on the house, if you sign my book."

His beautiful squiggle of a brow arched and then he quirked a smile, made sexy by the way the left corner curled upward. "So, you know who I am."

I smiled shyly. "Yeah. I loved your book. Will you sign it?"

"Sure."

I was taken aback. I suddenly realized that the book was upstairs in our apartment above the deli. "I have to get it. Would you mind minding the store for just a few minutes?"

"Not a problem."

I hurried to the back of the restaurant and raced up the flight of stairs to the apartment my dad and I shared. The book was on my nightstand in the bedroom I had slept in as a child. I had reread passages of the book every night before I went to sleep. I think it helped me from having the nightmares that haunted me.

When I jogged downstairs, book in hand, he was behind the counter, attempting to cater to a twitchy elderly man. I had to bite down on my lip to stifle my laughter. The customer, one of our pickiest, was asking for an extra lean roast beef sandwich, dressing on the side, and French fries well done. Poor Ryan. No matter how many pieces of meat he cut, it was never lean enough for Mr. Picky.

Scurrying behind the counter, I said, "I'll handle this while you sign my book." He let out a loud sigh of relief.

"What's your name?" he asked, taking the book from me.

"Willow."

"That's a beautiful name." He smiled—this

time a dimpled smile that rendered me breathless. It stretched across his beautiful face as he pulled out a black pen from his back jeans pocket. Being a writer, I guess he always carried one with him. You could never tell when or where inspiration would hit.

I took care of the curmudgeon while watching Ryan sign my book from the corner of my eye. I had mechanically signed numerous ballet programs for fervent fans, but I hadn't been on the other side of the table for a long time. It was simultaneously nerve-racking and exhilarating. Stopping midstream, he glanced at me, his brows knitted together as if not knowing what to write.

After I got rid of Mr. Picky, I handed Ryan the bag with his sandwich. He, in turn, gave me back the book.

"Thanks," we said in unison, our eyes never straying from one and other.

A saucy grin spread across his lips as he strode to the front door with his sandwich bag in hand.

When he was gone, I eagerly flipped open my book. On the inscription page were these words:

*Willow~*

*I look forward to seeing you again.*

*~Ryan*

What did that mean? Did he want to go out

with me? Or was he talking about coming back for another sandwich? My heart pounded with anticipation and anxiousness. The truth was, I couldn't wait to see him again.

# TWO

## Ryan

There was something about her, I thought as I briskly walked to the pub where I was meeting my best bud, Duffy McDermitt. We had a standing boys' night out every Tuesday. It was a way of staying in touch and keeping up with what was going on with *Arts & Smarts* of which he was now Editor in Chief. He had replaced me after I quit following a major and painful blow up with the publisher—my father—one I tried not to dredge up since my father and I were making amends. Slowly but surely with the help of a top Manhattan shrink. Duffy, just as I predicted, was doing a great job with the magazine. Advertising sales were at an all-time high, and on the online "zine" was flourishing.

It had been a long time since some girl had an effect on me. With the success of my memoir, *Undying Love*, and my family name, I was, like it or not, one of New York's most eligible bachelors.

A minor celebrity. Everyone—from my editor to my drycleaner— was trying to fix me up. Without meaning to sound boastful, I could have my pick of any girl in the city. Even top supermodels. There were drinks and scattered dates, but nothing beyond that. The bottom line, I wasn't ready. I still couldn't get the love of my life, Allee Adair, out of my head.

But there was something about this girl Willow that got under my skin. Her unruly, waist-long, fiery hair. The sparkle in her olive green eyes. And that compact, ripped body that peeked through her long deli apron. I couldn't take my eyes off her tight heart-shaped ass as she sprinted up the stairs to retrieve my book. She moved with the grace of a dancer. The fact that she really loved my book and wanted me to sign it was a turn on too. And, boy, she sure knew how to make a man a sandwich. Why the hell didn't I ask her out?

The pub was dark and crowded, especially at the bar which was famous for being a hot pick-up spot. Elbowing my way through the wall-to-wall crowd of eager-to-meet singles, I spotted Duffy at our usual booth toward the back. He already had a beer.

"Yo, dude," said Duffy as I took a seat opposite him. An attractive blond waitress came by and I ordered what Duffy was drinking. A Guinness on tap. She eyed me flirtatiously before disappearing into the crowd.

"That babe has the hots for you," said Duffy.

Ignoring his comment, I said, "The last issue of *Arts & Smarts* was the bomb." I still regularly read the magazine even though I was no longer editor or had any desire to be associated it with again.

"Thanks, dude." Beaming, Duffy gave me an affectionate punch to the chest and took a gulp of his beer.

"How's my old man treating you?"

"He leaves me alone. I think he's just gotten used to the idea that *A&S* is his rebellious child."

My father, Ryan Madewell III, was the founder and CEO of Madewell Media, a Forbes 500 company that controlled broadcast outlets and publishing entities around the world. He was worth 3.8 billion dollars the last time I checked. *Arts & Smarts* was just a small cog in his vast media empire.

"How are things with you and Sam?" I asked as the flirty waitress lowered my mug of beer onto the distressed wood table. Sam, short for Samantha, was his beautiful fiancée. Like Duffy, she came from Southern California and loved to surf. He had met her at my wedding to Allee. She was Allee's friend and colleague at The Met. It was love at first sight for Duffy who had never managed to score in the girlfriend department. Ironically, had I chosen her to show me a hidden treasure at the museum, I may have never married Allee. Sometimes, I secretly wished I had so that I wouldn't have had to endure the tragedy of Allee dying so young. Life could be just so fucking unfair.

"She's great, man. She's starting to show. She's nervous that she'll be as fat as a cow at the wedding."

Duffy had been living with Sam for almost two years. When she discovered she was pregnant a couple of months ago, they finally decided to tie the knot. They were getting married in a few weeks in Malibu, where Sam's parents had a beach house. Duffy had asked me to be his best man, and I had agreed.

I took a swig of my beer. "Sam's going to be a beautiful bride," I told Duffy. "How's the wedding stuff going?"

"Bitchin'. Sam's got it under control. But the daddy thing is already freaking me out."

"You're going to do great." Inside, a pang of envy shot through me. A baby with Allee had not been in our cards. Or should I say, raising one with her. I had kept the success of my fertility experiment secret from Duffy. In fact, everyone.

"So, Ry-man, what's up with you?"

I told him how the movie version of *Undying Love* was moving along. They'd approved my screenplay and had already selected a director. Ryan Gosling was being considered to play me. Anne Hathaway had already committed to the role of Allee. As much as I was pleased with this casting decision, no one could be my Allee.

"Man, that movie is going to be blockbuster. Every girl in America is going to be in love with

Ryan Madewell."

I rolled my eyes at him. "Nah, they're going to be in love with Ryan Gosling or whoever plays the part."

Duffy snorted. "So, dude, what's going on with the rest of your life? You get laid yet?" Duffster was constantly telling me that I needed to start seriously dating again. It had been over two years since Allee had passed away, and I wasn't getting younger. He was convinced my dick was going to grow old and fall off.

I took a big gulp of my beer and then I said it. "I met someone." I came to a sharp pause and took several more swigs of the cold frothy beverage.

"Hey, man, don't go AWOL on me. Talk to me."

I reluctantly told him all about Willow and our encounter. In the end, it actually felt good to confide in him.

"Seriously, dude, I can't believe you wrote in her book you wanted to see her again and you didn't ask her out. Or write down your phone number or email address. What a doof!"

Maybe I blew it. Maybe I just wasn't ready. Maybe I really didn't want to. Maybe, maybe, maybe, maybe. I drained my beer.

"Madewell, get your fucking dick back to that deli before it withers away and ask that babe out."

"Okay, okay."

"And buy yourself a pack of condoms."

Duffy ordered another round of beers. I guzzled mine. The cold beverage seeped through my veins

while the image of a girl named Willow danced
through my head.

∽

My downtown loft wasn't far from the pub. I
walked home. The buzz I got from the beer mixed
nicely with the crisp autumn air. I wrapped my
cashmere scarf, a gift from Allee, around my neck
to shield myself from the wind.

When I got home, it was always the same. I
came home to the ghost of Allee. As soon as I
stepped out from the freight elevator that took
me to my loft, I saw her curled up on the leather
couch she favored, reading one of her treasured
art books. She gazed up at me. Her dark wavy hair
cascaded over her shoulders, and her espresso bean
eyes twinkled, already undressing me. I always
imagined her beautiful and radiant, not the faded
beauty she had become when she got sick. There
were photographs of her everywhere.

"Hi, baby."

"Hi, Madewell. I missed you. Where were
you?"

"Having some beers with Duffy at our favorite
watering hole."

"Have you eaten it yet?"

"Nope." I thought about the deli sandwich
I had stored in the fridge. I forced the image of
Willow out of my head.

"Then, why don't you have me instead?" So

Allee-like.

My cock stiffened. My balls ached. Fuck. When was it going to stop? I could taste her, smell her, feel her. My shrink told me I needed to move. Get a new apartment. A new bed. A new life. I just couldn't bring myself to do it. I needed to stay connected to her in any way I could.

I checked my phone messages and then wound up the spiral of polished metal stairs to *our* bedroom. I quickly shucked my clothes and put on my pajama bottoms and a tee. I did my normal bathroom routine and then hopped into bed. Into the beautiful, antique four-poster bed that I shared with the love of my life. Tomorrow morning I had an interview on *Good Morning America,* so I had to be up bright and early.

I couldn't fall asleep. My cock was throbbing. I needed relief. Closing my eyes, I slipped my hand under the duvet and began jerking myself off. Harder. Faster. I imagined her long, limber fingers around my shaft, her warm breath heating my cheeks, her dancing eyes. I was heading fast and furiously toward an explosion. In an instant, a burst of hot semen covered my hand. My heated body relaxed, and I opened my eyes halfway. Facing me was the image of a beautiful girl. She had wild flaming red hair and glittering green eyes. Willow!

# ACKNOWLEDGMENTS

I want to thank my husband and children who put up with me as I plowed through this novel and made countless revisions. I wrote *Undying Love* as part of a challenge to write a complete novel in the month of November. I know…nuts.

I am also indebted to my formatter and cover designer Glendon Haddix of Streetlight Graphics, my proofreader, Kathie Middlemiss of Kat's Eye Editing, and my beta readers— my dear friend, "Smiles," and my fellow writer and friend, Mallory Love, author of *Sunset Motel*.

A special thanks also goes to Dr. Clement Yang and Dr. Eliron Mor for advising me on medical ethics, cancer treatments, and fertility breakthroughs.

Finally, a shout-out goes to my dear readers. I love you all!

# ABOUT THE AUTHOR

Nelle L'Amour is a former executive in the entertainment and toy industries. While she gave up playing with Barbies a long time ago, she still enjoys playing with toys with her two children... and husband. She aspires to write juicy stories with characters that will both make you laugh and cry and stay in your heart forever.

She is the author of the three-part bestselling erotic romance series, *Seduced by the Park Avenue Billionaire*. Writing under another pen name, she is also the author of the critically acclaimed fantasy/romance series: *DEWITCHED: The Untold Story of the Evil Queen.*

Nelle loves to hear from her readers. Connect to her at:

http://www.facebook.com/pages/Nelle-Lamour/185733381565323

http://twitter.com/nellelamour

nellelamour@gmail.com

# BONUS MATERIAL

## AN EXCERPT FROM SEDUCED BY THE PARK AVENUE BILLIONAIRE

## PART 1: STRANGERS ON A TRAIN
### By Nelle L'Amour

# 1

I'm going to miss my train! That was all I could think of as I dashed through the stately entrance to Philadelphia's majestic 30th Street Station. My best friend Lauren, with all her connections, had scored a bunch of coveted tickets to the Black Eyed Peas concert in Central Park and I was among those she had chosen to be among her entourage …so I had to be home by seven, shower, and get dressed. I rushed past the tempting food court toward the information center. The old fashion flip-letter Amtrak Train Information board made a ticking sound as it updated arrivals and departures. I glanced up. Shit! My train to Penn Station was leaving in five minutes from Gate 5. My eyes darted around the elegant, high ceiling, art-deco station, for the escalator leading down to the train platform. Despite how many times I had been in this vast station over the past few months, I never knew where I was going. My sense of direction was nothing to be proud of.

My eyes bounced from the famous Angel of the Resurrection statue to another bronzed statue. A god. A 6'2" golden-haired Adonis perched on the VIP mezzanine. Even from this distant vantage point, I could I could tell he was wearing one of those super expensive custom- tailored beige suits that New York's tycoons donned once Spring hit. It made a stunning contrast with his St. Tropez tan, the kind wealthy Manhattanites sported all year round. With his expensive designer glasses perched on his perfectly blown flaxen hair, he looked like he was right out of *GQ*.

I couldn't get my eyes off him. The sight of him made my knees weak and my heart hammer. I had dreamt of men like this, but the reality of ever meeting one was way out of my league. I was a geeky, recent college who, after several false starts, had finally landed an entry-level job at Ike's Tikes, an established New York City toy company, and was struggling to make ends meet. Beautiful men were just not in my cards. They never had been. But my mom had always told me it was okay to dream. And for a minute, as Adonis pivoted his head in my direction, I imagined his eyes burning across the station into mine.

A booming voice put an end to my reverie— and the pulsating I felt between my legs. "Last call for Amtrak 148 to Penn Station boarding at Gate 5." In a blink of an eye, Adonis was gone. Out of my life and dreams forever. My pulse accelerated as my eyes flickered around the vast station for the gate sign. Finally, I found it and began to run, my messenger-style leather bag flying behind me. The escalator descending to the train platform was out of order. Thank goodness, I was wearing my trusty combat boots. At breakneck speed, I clambered down the daunting three flights of stairs, praying that the train would not leave without me.

"Wait!" I screamed as the automatic doors of the sleek silver train were closing. I skimmed through one of them, narrowly missing being a smooshed sardine.

Breathing heavy, I staggered through the car, desperately searching for a seat. Nothing. It was rush hour and every seat was taken. Maybe I would have better luck in the next car, I thought as I wobbled across the connecting bridge, the train rolling into motion. I so needed to sit down, catch my breath, and relax. I was exhausted and rundown. Not just from my sprint to the train, but from months of juggling my Manhattan-based job as the assistant to a demanding female executive with visits to my ailing mother who was receiving experimental cancer treatments at the world-renowned Hospital of the University of Pennsylvania. Seeing my mother in her weakened state, all hooked up to IV's and machines, never helped no matter how cheery she was when I came to see her.

As the train picked up speed, I struggled to keep my balance and open the sliding door to the next car. Sparing all the muscle power I could, I finally yanked it open and tumbled into the cabin. This car was different than the one before. It was far more spacious and deluxe. Roomy pairs of rich brown leather scats lined the aisles, and the well-dressed occupants were sipping cocktails in real glasses and toying with the latest electronic gadgets. This was obviously business-class. I sure as hell did not belong here wearing my T.J. Maxx midi skirt and Fruit of the Loom t-shirt. Oh yeah, and my worn out combat boots which I had found at a flea market. This was the cabin where Louis Vuittons, Jimmy Choos, and Chanels mingled with other LVs, Jimmies, and Cocos. No, I didn't belong here. Not one bit.

Fighting the speed of the train and my embarrassment, I clumsily zigzagged down the aisle, occasionally grabbing onto the corner of a seat for balance. Like the previous cabin, every seat was taken. No one seemed to notice me, but truthfully, I wanted to get out of here as quickly as possible. As I neared the rear end of the car, the train jerked, lurching me forward and then flying into the lap of a *Wall Street Journal*-reading commuter to my left.

"I'm so sorry," I squeaked at my victim whose face was still buried in his *WSJ*.

He flexed his leg muscles under my muscular butt, signaling me to get up and then slowly lowered his newspaper. A smirk curled on his lips. *Those lips!*

My heart leaped into my throat. Adonis!

"Sit," he said, motioning to the empty window seat next to his.

"Um, uh, I'm in economy," I stuttered, my eyes unable to leave his face no matter how humiliated I felt. Up close, he was even more beautiful than I imagined with his chiseled nose, strong angular jaw line, and piercing eyes, the color of sapphires.

"Don't worry; I'll handle it," he said with a wink.

Holy shit! Adonis had just winked at me!

"Sit," he growled, this time as if it were an order.

With a powerful heave of his knees, he bounced me to my feet, forcing me to plop down next to him.

Holy shit again! I was going to spend the next hour and a half sitting next to this gorgeous man—a man that existed in my dreams—and now I had no idea what to say. My heart pounded.

"What's your name?" he asked, in a coy tone that suggested he was daring me to answer.

"Sarah," I replied, pulling myself together in time to reply in a very business-like voice.

"Saarah," he repeated, his voice deep and sexy.

The way he said my name drawing out the first syllable with breathiness—sent a chill down my spine. I could not help thinking of my favorite song from one of my favorite movies, *West Side Story*. "Say it soft and it's almost like praying."

"Ari," he said next, not giving me time to ask the obvious.

A fitting name. Almost like Ares, the Greek God of War. This man was a warrior. A beautiful warrior. And I was soon to find out that conquest was his middle name.

I held out my slender hand to shake his. Truthfully, I didn't know what else to do. His long, tan fingers entwined mine. His grip was strong. Powerful. Slowly, he raised my hand to his lush lips. Blood rushed to my head as they pressed ever so gently against the back of my palm. One by one, he unfolded my fingers, sucking each one as if they were candy sticks. The wetness of his warm saliva glistened on my fingertips. Butterflies fluttered in my stomach, and moisture pooled between my legs. *What the hell was he doing? And what the hell was I?*

My heart was racing as fast as the Amtrak. I needed to stop this. Move to another seat. My eyes darted around the cabin, but still there were none to be had. No one seemed to notice what was going on; they either had their face buried in a newspaper or book or were occupied with their cell phones, iPads, or Kindles.

This was just not right. I was sitting next to a complete stranger and letting him suck my fingers. He could be a total whack job… a molester… or serial killer. Who knew? Though my fear was fleeting, I made up a desperate clichéd excuse. "Um, uh excuse me. I need to use the restroom." Actually, I really did. I needed to get away from this mysterious, seductive stranger and get a grip.

"It's right behind us," said Adonis dryly, returning to his newspaper.

I leaped up from my seat. Tripping over my bag, I caught a glimpse of Trainman's bemused expression. He refused to move his long legs, forcing my butt to brush against them as I made my escape.

The door to the unisex restroom located at the back of the cabin was locked. That meant someone was inside. I tapped my foot impatiently, my head filling with the image of the blond, blue-eyed Adonis sitting next to me. Why couldn't I stop thinking about him? These kinds of things never happened to geeky me. They were the stuff of novels and movies. Not my boring all-work-no-play life.

"Hi." A familiar velvety voice catapulted me out of my thoughts, and a waft of warm breath blew across the nape of my neck. I spun around.

My mysterious stranger. His crisp blue eyes burned into mine, making my temperature soar, and my legs turn to jelly. What was he doing here? I suppose he had to go. I couldn't stop that.

I turned my head away and stared squarely at the bathroom door, praying silently that whoever was in there would hurry up. He blew hot air on my neck again and wrapped his arms around my waist, pulling me tight against his rock-hard body. A bulge pressed against my buttocks. I was getting sick to my stomach and might need the bathroom more than I originally thought.

Finally, the door burst open in my face; a sour-faced, overweight matron barged out. Calling on every muscle in my body, I broke free of Trainman's grip and hastily dashed into the stall and the stench she left behind. My hands shaky, I fumbled to slide the latch, but before I could get it through the lock, the door forcefully swung open.

"I couldn't wait," Trainman growled, pushing me against the cold metal sink basin. He thrust his hips tight against mine. I was trapped.

He leaned in close to me. A mix of his warm minty breath and expensive cologne rushed into my nostrils, eradicating all traces of the fetid odor. His eyes narrowed, turning into collectible slivers of blue sand glass. His mouth descended onto the right side of my neck then slowly trailed upward to my earlobe. He clamped his warm, moist lips on the cartilage, alternating between nipping and sucking it. Oh my God! I didn't know my earlobes could feel so much. The last time they felt anything was when I got them pierced in eighth grade. And that was pain. Pure pain. Now what I was feeling was joy. Pure tingly joy…and the sensation was coursing through my entire body.

Still pressing me hard against the sink with his hipbones, he pinched my dime-size nipples between his thumb and index fingers and then began massaging them in small counter clockwise circles, each rotation harder than the one before. Magically, the buds elongated and hardened beneath my navy cotton t-shirt. A new I-want-to-burst-out of my skin sensation gathered in the triangle between my legs. I moaned softly.

"You don't wear a bra," he murmured in my ear.

I rarely wore a bra because I really didn't need one. My boobs never got past a small A-cup, the size of old-fashioned champagne saucers. Before I could say a word, that is if I could utter a word, he whispered, "Sexy."

*Moi,* Sarah plain and tall, sexy? And this coming from this gorgeous beast? Pinch me. I must be dreaming this entire fantasy. As if on cue, he pinched one of my nipples again. My crotch roared silently in delight. No, this was real okay. And it was happening to me. Sarah Greene. Art school graduate. Aspiring toy designer. Twenty-five-year-old virgin.

I stared at his beautiful face. His eyes were tilted downward. A sly smile tipped to the left made me nervous. In a good way.

While one hand continued to twirl a nipple, the other slid down my torso past by tight, twisted abdomen and under the waistbands of both my skirt and pantyhose. His hands felt like hot velvet as they explored my inner thighs.

"Hmm," he moaned. "No panties?"

I never wore panties with pantyhose. Why bother? They were called pantyhose for a reason. And I confess, not buying expensive panties—and bras—saved me a lot of money—money I needed desperately to visit my sick mother.

"Very sexy," he said, enunciating each syllable, as his fingertips made their way to the triangle between my legs. They stopped to caress my patch of hair, stroking it as if were a beloved pussy... cat.

"So soft and silky," Trainman pronounced as

if I were auditioning for one of those look-at-my-gorgeous-hair product commercials.

After a tug of a curled clump, his fingers plunged lower to the smooth folds between my legs. They explored this new territory eagerly like someone who was searching for gold. And then he discovered it. The nugget. Greedily, he rubbed the pad of this thumb around his discovery with intense little circles that were driving me insane. A loud moan escaped my lips.

"You're so wet," he crooned.

That was an understatement. I was swimming in my own juices. My eyes caught a glimpse of him. A wicked smile crossed his face, and his blue eyes glistened.

He squeezed the folds of my labial lips together and then used his fingers to spread them apart.

"I want you," he moaned, his voice all hot and breathy.

And despite myself, I wanted him. More than anyone or anything. Well, except for my mother getting well again.

Still massaging my nub with his thumb, he plunged his long middle finger into the cavity between the folds. I gasped, not prepared for the shock of penetration. Shockwaves spread through out my body as his finger glided up and down the soaked, spongy walls, in and out, each thrust deeper than the one before.

"Baby," he moaned. "You're so hot."

I gasped again, still not sure this was really

happening. My core was aching for more. Desperate for it. Why wasn't I resisting?

"I'm going to take you now," he growled.

Take me where? I didn't want to be anywhere, any place but here in this cramped bathroom with this mysterious sorcerer who was doing his magic on me.

Using his free hand, he yanked down both my skirt and hose. He must have popped the side button to my skirt because there's no way it would have slid down my hips, no matter how boyishly narrow they were. My eyes glanced down at my skirt puddled on the floor and my pantyhose scrunched up above my combat boots. As they made their way back upward, I heard him unzip his fly. My gaze stopped short at a massive hunk of pink, veined flesh that was aimed at my crotch. I was ready to surrender. Yes, take me now.

"Sit on the sink," he ordered.

I was in no condition to argue. I plunked my buttocks down on the edge of the steely basin. The cold metal gave me goose bumps all over. He pulled off my boots and the hose.

"Now, spread your legs."

*Yes, sir.*

An intensity washed over his face. Like an artist who was contemplating painting his masterpiece. He placed both hands on my hips to anchor me.

"Now, take me and insert me where you want me."

Holy shit! He wanted me to touch that

monstrosity? Cradle it in my hands? Our eyes met, mine wide-eyed with fear and excitement, his hooded with determination and desire.

Hesitantly, I wrapped my slender fingers around the pillar of flesh, surprised that they could circle around it despite its diameter. I'd never felt a man's penis before. The touch beneath my fingers was hot, velvety, and pulsating. I knew exactly where I wanted it. The hollowness inside me was crying out for it. I need to be sated by him. Totally consumed.

Gently, I angled it upward toward the opening between my legs. I slid the tip inside. He gave it a sharp thrust, jettisoning his member deep inside me. The initial pain and shock of the hard fullness was enough to make me almost fall off the sink or into it, but as my muscles relaxed, it felt good. Like it belonged and had found its home sweet home.

"Oh baby, you're so tight." Rolling his tongue over his lips, he gripped my hips and lifted me off the sink basin so that we were almost face to face. My feet dangled like a rag doll's, not touching the floor below.

"Wrap your legs around me," he ordered, pressing his hard body close to mine.

In no condition to argue, I did what he said, wrapping my long legs around his lean, torso like a pretzel, causing the crotch of my hose to split apart. He gripped my thighs. My arms swung around his neck, and I squeezed him tightly, clasping the rich fabric of his suit jacket between my fingers. This was one ride I did not want to fall off.

Pressing me firmly against the bathroom wall, he thrust his stone-hard member deeper into me, and I gasped with a mixture of shock and ecstasy as the tip rammed against a hypersensitive spot. He groaned. He slid his rod down and then thrust it upward again, this time even harder against the bull's-eye. I moaned. He groaned louder. He repeated the pattern, speeding it up with every in and out. How could that giant thing between his legs fit so easily and comfortably inside me? Every thrust elicited a moan from me louder than the one before and a groan from him, deeper than the previous. I moved my arms to his buttocks, folding them firmly around the rock-hard cheeks under his trousers and fell into the rhythm of his in-and-out movements. Our breathing grew ragged.

"Oh baby, what you do to me," he groaned, his voice an octave deeper and sexier beyond belief.

"Don't stop," I pleaded, my voice breathy, my mouth dry.

"Don't worry."

He planted his thumb back on my clit and massaged it vigorously as his member glided up and down my flooded tunnel, hitting that mega-spot again and again. My temperature was rising. Sweat was pouring out of every crevice of my body. Squeezing my legs tighter around him, I closed my eyes to savor the unbearable pleasure this gorgeous beast was giving me.

"Are you on birth control?" The words drifted through my head, not expecting them. I managed a throaty "yeah" as he thrust his member once again into my tunnel of joy. I had been on the pill for several years due to my irregular cycle.

"Good, baby," he murmured in my ear. He yanked back my head by my ponytail and rolled his hot, velvety tongue up my neck. So, this was my reward for the right answer. The sensation drove me crazy. I felt like a puppy being scratched in her favorite spot.

He accelerated his pace, of both the banging and massaging. Whimpering, I didn't think I could take it any more. My sex throbbed as a wildfire raced through my body, shamelessly kindling every nerve inside me, from my head to my toes. I was about to implode.

Without warning, I felt him exploding. "Oh, Saarah," he groaned, drawing out my name. I convulsed around him, my own deep explosion sending shockwaves through out me. *Oh my God. Oh my God. Oh my God.* I wasn't sure if I was saying the words aloud or screaming them silently in my head. What was happening to me? I had never had such a mind-blowing experience.

Slowly, he pulled out of me. I was surprised at how big and rigid his now glistening member still was. He grabbed a paper towel from the dispenser, cleaned himself up and then adjusted his pants over his thick length. I don't think he was wearing underwear either.

"Sarah," he said as he zipped up his fly, "do you still have to pee?"

"Yes," I stammered, as I pulled up the remains of my pantyhose and slipped on my skirt. I was shaking, dazed and drained from his plundering.

Trainman rolled his eyes and then let me pee in peace. And privacy.

After latching the door, I got back dressed and sat on the toilet longer than I needed to. Tremors tearing through me, I gazed down at the big rip in my pantyhose, in the so-called "reinforced" crotch area. A translucent, creamy substance coated my inner thighs. The events that had just happened reeled around in my head while orgasmic vibrations were still coming at me with recklessness of a rockslide. Why did I let myself do this? Why? Neediness? Insecurity? Maybe a desperate escape from the anguish my dying mother was causing? Or just because this man was the sexiest member of the opposite sex I'd ever laid my eyes on? Finally, I tore off a generous piece of toilet paper and wiped by bottom from front to back just like my mother had taught me. A translucent layer of ruby-veined semen clustered on the soft white paper. I was bleeding. Reality hit me like a brick. I had just lost my virginity to a stranger on a train.

In a state of mild shock, I slowly raised myself from the toilet, pulled up my damp, crotchless hose, and washed my hands in the sink that now held so many memories for me. I splattered a little of the cold water on my face and sipped some from my hands to quench my parched mouth. For the first time, I looked at myself in the mirror. My reflection startled me. My hair was disheveled; my big brown eyes half moons, and my full-lipped mouth locked in a parted pout. I was no longer the girl who only minutes ago had almost been squished by a pair of automatic train doors. I looked like a woman. A woman who had just been fucked. Big time.

Hastily, I fixed my ponytail and threw some more water on my face. I glimpsed myself again in the mirror. Not too much better but, at least, better. Taking a deep breath, I unlatched the door and made my way back to my seat. My body was quivering. Especially the part between my inner thighs.

Trainman smiled when he saw me. I was shocked how put together he looked, his golden hair neatly back in place and his blue eyes twinkling. Maybe he was a pro at having some nice innocent girl as a ride home meal ticket.

This time, in true gentleman fashion, he rose from his seat and let me sidle to mine with a modicum of grace. We were back to sitting side by side.

As the speeding train passed through different neighborhoods, from the poorest to the tawniest, we shared a self-imposed silence. Whatever we were thinking in our heads was enough to keep us entertained. I wondered—who was this man?... what did he do?...why did he choose me?

Words stayed trapped in my throat. I swiveled my head sideways and stared at his gorgeous, high-cheekboned profile that showed off his long eyelashes, strong chin, and fine Roman nose. What was he thinking? The impassive look on his face made his thoughts unreadable, and it frustrated me.

The delicious, constant throbbing inside me would not die down, and in fact, intensified with the friction of the zooming train over the tracks. Overwhelmed with a mixture of confusion, bewilderment, awe, and a touch of guilt, my eyelids grew heavy. I set my comfy leather chair into a reclining position while Trainman pulled out his iPhone from his briefcase and caught up on emails. His skilled hands moved quickly on the touch screen keyboard. God, he was good with those fingers! Unable to read what he was writing, I peered out the window and soaked in the scenery. Before long, I could no longer keep my eyes open and drifted off.

"Last stop, New York Penn Station." The loud announcement woke me with a startle. I blinked open my eyes, to find my head resting on Trainman's broad shoulder.

"I'm sorry," I said, collecting myself.

"Don't be." He gave me a quick dimpled smile that rendered me breathless.

He helped me to my feet. "Ladies, first."

As I side-stepped past him and made my way to the automatic sliding doors, the sinking feeling that I might never see him again set in.

Penn Station was stinking hot and bustling with commuters and tourists, and it wasn't even summer yet. It tasted, smelled, and sounded like 30th Street Station's ugly stepsister. Trainman clasped my hand as we wove our way in and out of the bustling crowd of rush hour commuters and ubiquitous homeless. His hand was warm, the grip demonstrative but not too tight. I quickened my pace to keep up with him, his stride a blend of grace and arrogance. He was clearly an expert on manipulating this oppressive swarm of people. Despite having lived in the City for almost a year and taking my share of subways, I had yet to master the ruthless New Yorkers always in a hurry to get where they were going.

Half way through the station, a sharp tug from behind me followed by a forceful shove sent me crashing to the filthy Penn Station floor. Dazed, I caught my assailant, a skinny Latino youth, running through the crowd with my bag! My life! My cell phone! My wallet! My identity! And the cash I needed to get through the weekend.

"LITTLE FUCKER!" yelled Trainman, taking off in hot pursuit.

Staggering to my feet, my eyes could not believe the speed with which his long legs carried him. It was like watching a scene from *Mission*

*Impossible* with Tom Cruise or some stunt double running after the bad guy. My assailant glanced back at Trainman, panic washing over his face as he saw my action hero gaining ground. Even as the bad guy picked up speed, the gap narrowed until Trainman pounced him, sending him crashing to the floor. He lay sprawled on the floor, between Trainman's powerful steepled knees, his face frozen with fear.

I hurried toward them. Gripping the lad by a clump of his greasy ebony hair, Trainman yanked him to his feet. The boy was shaking and near tears, and I was taken by how slight he was compared with my tall, mighty, broad-shouldered hero. The boy surrendered my bag and defensively raised both hands, clearly afraid that his captor might strike him. Still clasping his hair, Trainman lifted the youth until his Nikes no longer touched the ground. The boy grimaced in pain. And then Trainman lowered him. I was close enough to hear Trainman growl, "Now, get the fuck out here." He released the boy, who, wasting no time, sprinted through the crowd without looking back.

Trainman wheeled around, his eyes searching the crowd until they landed on me. I stopped dead in my tracks. I was shaking—unsure if it was from the shock of being violated or the shock that this gorgeous man had risked his life for me—I mean, the kid could have had a knife—was striding my way.

"You okay?" he asked, his blue eyes surveying

every inch of my body.

"Yeah," I managed. Glancing down, I noticed that there were patches of gray dust on my calf-length beige skirt. My right knee hurt from the fall. I lifted up the hem of the skirt to check it out. No blood. Just a large hole in my pantyhose— though it was a mere fraction of the hole between my crotch. Embarrassment crept through me.

Ari handed me my bag, intact and in one piece. "Hold on to this," he said, his frown curling into a wry, but oh so sexy smile.

I flashed a quick smile back. My gaze met his once again, and I was immediately aware again of the waves of ecstasy crashing again my pelvis. My heart thudded. Thank goodness the hum of the crowded station drowned out the sound.

"I'm having drinks with someone," he said.

He needed to say no more. He was meeting some gorgeous super-model. The type of woman he belonged with. My heart sunk. It was time for my exit line.

"Um, okay," I spluttered. "Thanks for everything." *Yes, everything.*

Without saying goodbye, I hastily headed toward a sign that said Exit. I walked blindly through the throng of rush-hour commuters and homeless, brushing up against more than I wanted. It was over. My scenes from a movie were over. I didn't even know a thing about him. His last name. Where he lived. What he did. What did it matter? I'd probably never see him again. It was just a fluke thing that wasn't supposed to happen to me. I shrugged my shoulders and inwardly sighed. Yet, there was so much of me that kept hoping I would feel his strong hands on my shoulders, stopping me dead in my tracks. Spinning me around. Pulling my head back with a yank of my ponytail. Sinking his lips into mine and then parting them with his tongue, inviting me for a smoochy dance right in the middle of Penn Station. That's what happened in movies. With wishful thinking, I stole a glance backward. Trainman was hugging a tall, shapely, drop-dead gorgeous redhead in a chic suit. Just his type. I hastily pivoted around and quickened my pace. Why was I fooling myself? My *West Side Story* was a dream. My life was a reality show. A really lame reality show.

# 2

I decided to walk home from Penn Station. The furnished apartment I was subletting on West 45th Street between Eighth and Ninth Avenues on the edge of the theater district was not far. Besides, it was a warm May night, and I needed the air to clear my head. Unfortunately, the intense throbbing in my groin area kept me in a fog. Trainman's beautiful face filled my mind while his beautiful dick filled every other part of me. And then the image of that beautiful redhead made it all go away faster than I had lost my virginity. The reality that I was no longer "the twenty-five year old virgin" as Lauren sarcastically called me made me shudder with disbelief. It had to happen sometime, but now I had mixed feelings that it had happened with that Adonis. A stranger on a train.

Mounting the five-step landing that led to my brownstone apartment, I dug deep into my messenger bag in search of my keys and sighed with relief when I found them. Had it not been for Trainman, I would have had no bag or keys. For all I know, that kid, having access to my identity and address, might have vandalized my apartment and wiped out everything. And if I happened to be home at the time, who knows what else might have happened. I shuddered thinking about the possibilities.

I jiggled the keys into the double metal locks, one after another. It was a royal pain in the butt to open the front door, but one could never be too safe in this big city, especially in my neighborhood which was still considered a little seedy.

Once inside, I used a tiny a key attached to the chain to open one of three tarnished metal mailboxes that lined the chipped entryway. Two other tenants lived in the building—Mrs. Blumberg, on the second floor, a retired Broadway actress who always had a story about her song and dance days to tell me and was convinced she was related to the mayor, and Mr. Costanzo, on the ground floor, who owned a pizzeria and was always trying to feed me. My apartment, identical to theirs, was located on the third floor.

Bills. Bills. And more bills. And a letter from The Hospital of the University of Pennsylvania. I would deal with all of them later. Right now, I had to hurry and get myself ready for the Black Eyed Peas concert in Central Park. Perhaps some good music and food would get my mind off my sick mother and the sick feeling I had about never seeing Trainman again.

Usually the trek up the steep three flights of stairs was effortless for me, but this evening it was challenging. I was worn out, my insides torn both physically and emotionally. As I mounted each step, the image of my mother, wan and frail, life ebbing out of her alternated with the image of Ari, tan and fit, putting life into me. I could still feel his hot pulsing member deep inside me.

Breathing heavily, I unlocked the double locks of my apartment door after several attempts. Jo-Jo, short for Josephine, the sweet black cat I was caring for while his (her?—I wasn't sure) true owner, a flamboyant singing-dancing transsexual, partook in year-long tour of *La Cage Aux Folles,* immediately brushed up against my ankles and meowed.

The flat, a railroad apartment, was small but pleasant. I was lucky to have found it on Craig's List. It was rent-controlled, so I was not paying much, and the tenant even gave me a small break for looking after Jo-Jo. The only thing odd about the apartment was that the walls were painted hot pink, and there was a large framed photo of Josephine Baker (obviously the inspiration for kitty's name) above the pseudo-Victorian sofa. The other flea market finds that filled the apartment gave it a *je ne sais quoi* charm that appealed to me.

Jo-Jo followed me into the small galley kitchen, where I proceeded to open a can of Fancy Feast and put it into his special bowl on the Formica counter. I'd better check my phone messages; it had been a while.

I pushed play on the answering machine that sat on the other end of the counter. Lauren: "Where are you?" CLICK. Lauren: "What are you wearing? Remember, my cotillion friends are coming." CLICK. Lauren: "Where are you?"

CLICK. Lauren: "Guess what! Taylor is taking me to the Hamptons." CLICK. Lauren: "Call me!" CLICK. Lauren: "FYI, your cell phone is turned off."

No more messages. My heart sunk. So much of me wanted to hear Trainman's sultry voice. "Saarah. Call me. I want to make you wet and fuck your brains out."

*Stop it, Sarah!* I silently chided. He was probably already bedding that beautiful redhead. And he had no idea where I lived or how to get in touch with me. Chances were I'd never see or hear from him again. Yet, the raw aching I felt for this man continued to consume me.

Enough. I'd better call Lauren and let her know that I was back in town and that I would meet her at her at the 72nd Street entrance to the park at 7:30. As I reached for my phone, the buzzer on my intercom sounded. Lately, any time it did, my heart dropped to the floor, thinking it might be some messenger with the news of my mother's passing. Nervously, I pressed the button and talked into the intercom. "Yes?" My voice trailed off.

"Delivery for you," said a male voice with a heavy New York accent.

That was strange. I wasn't expecting anything. Unless my new evil boss had decided to send a stack of her expenses to take care of over the weekend. I had taken the day off to visit my mother, and she was not one bit happy about it. So, this was her revenge.

I pushed the button on the intercom that unlocked the front door. "Just leave it on the stairs."

"You need to sign for it," said the invisible voice.

"Fine. I'll be right down."

Grabbing one of the loose pens that I kept in a tin can on the counter, I galloped down the three flights of stairs. The aftershocks of my orgasm measured 6.0 on the "I can come" scale.

Waiting for me at the base of the staircase was a twitchy man holding a box that must have measured five feet in length. It was magnificently wrapped in violet paper and topped off with a white bow the size of a basketball. This could not possibly be for me.

"Sign this," said the man, handing me a receipt. Sure enough my name, Sarah Greene, was printed on the paper along with my address and apartment number. Huh? And then it hit me. Of course, it was a gift from my mega-wealthy debutante friend Lauren, who probably sent me something nice to wear to the concert tonight so I wouldn't be an embarrassment in front of all her high society friends. She had threatened to burn my entire wardrobe once, and now this was her way of sending me a message.

Grabbing the receipt, I plastered it against the hallway wall and signed my name. The deliveryman promptly left, and I humped the stairs with the large package in my arms. What did Lauren pick out for me? Knowing her over-the-top expensive taste, I'm sure it was something like Seven for Mankind tight ass jeans and some Roberto Cavalli bold print halter-top cut so low you could see my navel. Trendy things that flat-chested, straight-as-an-arrow, bohemian me had no right wearing. And would not look good in.

Once back inside my apartment, I gently laid the massive package on the couch and carefully unwrapped it. I'd never seen such a meticulously wrapped present, and the dazzling bow must have cost a small fortune. Lauren could afford it. Her father, Randolph Hoffmeier, was a major Wall Street CEO, and she already had a substantial trust fund from her Mayflower-descended family.

The box was from Bergdorf's. Wow! The only time I'd ever set foot inside that store was the one time my new bitch boss sent me there at lunch to pick up a tube of her favorite Chanel red lipstick. Dressed in my cheap version of bohemian whatever, I stuck out like a sore thumb among all the expensively dressed and scented women and couldn't wait to get out of the place. I spent the rest of my lunch break down the street consoling myself at T.J. Maxx.

I carefully removed the box top. Layers of delicate tissue paper lined the interior of the other half. I peeled them away and then I gasped. Facing me was a beautifully folded black silk dress with two sparkling spaghetti straps. A tag hung off one of them. Marc Jacobs. Size 6. No price. I lifted the dress by the straps and held it up in front of me. It was gorgeous. Simple but elegant. But certainly not the kind of thing one would wear to a rock concert in Central Park. What was Lauren thinking?

My eyes returned to the box and came upon a small white envelope with my name printed on it. Draping the dress over an arm, I reached for it and pulled out the contents from under the unsealed flap. My eyes grew big as I read the note and so did the explosions that were rocking my body.

> *Ms. Greene~ Please wear this tonight. I shall collect you at 8 p.m. Please be downstairs.~Trainman*
>
> *PS Please do not wear pantyhose*

A mixture of holy cow and damn him took saturated my brain. How the heck did he know where I lived? Wait. Of course, the stalker must have gone through my messenger bag while I was waiting to use the restroom on that damn train. He got my address from my driver's license. He must know everything about me. My height. My weight. My checking account number with my home phone number. My social security number. What kind of gum I chewed (Big Red). Crap. I bet he even thumbed through my sketchpad and read the journal I kept with my favorite sayings.

One of them flashed into my head. "*When in*

*doubt, leave it out.*" Damn it! I should have never let him sink his cock inside me. None of this would have happened. None of it. Except… there was no doubt. I had wanted him as much as he had wanted me.

And now there was another problem. I couldn't see him tonight. I had plans with Lauren. Trust me, she rubbed it my face that she was able to get those reserved-seating Black Eyed Peas tickets because her father's investment company managed Fergie's assets and that I was lucky that she counted me as one of her best friends.

The shrill ring of my phone hurled me out of my thoughts. It must be Lauren. I dreaded answering it because she got super mad if I didn't call her back right away. For a friend, she was very high maintenance.

Finally, after the fifth ring, just before the call went to my answering machine, I ran over to it and picked up the receiver.

"Saarah, do you like your dress?"

Fuck. It was him. The temperature in the kitchen suddenly rose ten degrees.

"It's very nice." Who was I kidding? It was the most fabulous dress I'd ever owned. And the most expensive.

"I'm looking forward to seeing you in it."

Shit! How the hell was I going to tell him that I had plans? That I couldn't see him tonight.

CLICK.

I wasn't. I immediately dialed Lauren's number.

Her answering machine was on. *Beep.*

"Lauren, something's come up. I can't go to the concert tonight. I'll explain tomorrow. Have fun."

CLICK. Phew! That saved me from having a nasty, drawn out conversation with her. I suppose I could also try her on her cell, but truthfully, I didn't want to. And I wasn't feeling that guilty. She had her entourage. I'd still pay the consequences tomorrow, but right now, I had to get ready for my date with Trainman.

Taking my new dress with me, I headed toward the bedroom that was adjacent to the living room. A loud knock at my door stopped me in the hallway. Retracing my steps, I peered through the peephole. Mrs. Blumberg. She was rather entertaining, but quite frankly, I had no time for her right now.

I unbolted the door.

Chewing a big wad of gum, she said in her thick "New Yawk" accent, "I was just on my way to shul when this came for you." She handed me a shopping bag. Inside was another gift- wrapped package, this one significantly smaller, maybe a foot long by six inches. My heart fluttered. Now what?

Mrs. Blumberg's crinkly eyes fixated on the black dress that was still folded over my arm. "Hot date tonight? I hope he's Jewish."

God, she was nosy. And so annoying. I didn't respond.

"So, how's your mother doing?"

Sadness swept over me. After I left the hospital, my mother was scheduled for another treatment. They always made her feel sicker than she already was. I fought back tears.

"She's hanging in there."

"Oy!" She shook her head, a bright-orange ball of frizz. "I'll say a prayer for her tonight."

"Thanks." Mrs. Blumberg meant well. It was hard not to like her even though she could be annoying.

"So, what are you waiting for? You gonna show me whatch'ya got?"

God, she was being difficult.

"Mrs. Blumberg, I'd love to spend time with you but—"

"I know. I know. It's okay to hurt an old lady's feelings. You gotta a hot date."

Her voice trailed off as she shuffled to the door to my apartment. Closing it behind her, she got in her last two cents. "Make sure you wear clean underwear. And don't let him touch you there."

I sighed; if she only knew. "There" tingled with the thought of being touched by "him" again. Wasting no time, I reached into the shopping bag and tore the package open with the hunger of a starving wolf. Two words on the lid of the shiny white box blazed in my eyes: JIMMY CHOO. I lifted the lid to find another note, the sexy, bold handwriting identical to that of the note that accompanied the black dress.

*Wear these tonight. Remember, no pantyhose.*—TM

Holy cow! He bought me shoes? The kind you see in *Vogue* and the copy says: "Price on Request." A creamy white duster bag encased the shoes. My heart pounding, I removed the shoes. I gasped. A pair of six-inch high black satin peep-toe pumps. Size 9.5AA. How the hell did he know my crazy shoe size? Did he remove my two sizes too wide combat boots stuffed with inner soul pads to make them fit while I was dozing on the train?

A horrifying thought crossed my mind. I was born wearing combat boots. How was I going to manage to walk in these sexy beasts? I took off my boots and placed the high heels side by side on the floor. Placing one hand flat against the wall, I stepped into them, right foot, then left. Sarah, plain and tall, was suddenly taller. Six inches taller. A 6'2" pillar.

I let go of the wall. Okay, I could balance in them. But could I walk in them? I was going to do my trial runway walk down the hallway to my bedroom. Still carrying the little black dress, I took my first step, then my next. My ankles wobbled, and the intense throbbing inside me was not doing anything to help my balance. *Focus, Sarah. Focus.* Pausing for a deep breath, I took another step and then another…I was getting it down. My bedroom was just an arm's length away. Victoriously, I stumbled inside it. Jo-Jo, whom I'd honestly forgotten about, followed right behind me.

My shoebox size bedroom, painted in another shade of hot pink, consisted of a queen-size bed that took up most of the space, faux-French mirrored armoire, matching nightstand and a sliver of a closet. Jo-Jo jumped up on the bed and curled up on the garish leopard-print satin sheets left behind by the transsexual. Not wanting the dress near the furry cat, I draped it over my closet door. I glanced at the alarm clock on my nightstand. 7:15 p.m. I had less than an hour to get ready for my date. Quickly, I slipped out of my peasant skirt, letting it fall to the floor. As I pulled my t-shirt over my head, a waft of his cologne drifted into my nose. God, he smelled so divine. Maybe, I should never wash this t-shirt. Hold on to it as keepsakes. A souvenir of losing my virginity.

Wearing my torn pantyhose and my six-inch Jimmy's, I stood before the armoire and gazed at my reflection in the mirror. My normally long legs seemed to go on for miles. The heels accentuated my calf muscles and toned thighs, both gifts of having been a tomboy my whole life. I ran my palms over my pert champagne-cup breasts, aware of the hardening and soreness of my small nipples. The memory of Trainman nipping and tugging them filled my head. An electric current surged through my body.

Holding onto the armoire, I removed my new shoes and slid down my pantyhose. I had the urge to hold them to my nose, but I let them scrunch on the floor. Maybe, I should put them in a zip lock baggie and hide them in the armoire. The scene from an episode of *Law and Order* popped into my head, as if losing your virginity to a stranger on a train was a crime. Jack McCoy: "Your honor, I present to the court Exhibit A: Defendant's Cum-Soaked Pantyhose."

Inwardly chuckling, I headed, naked, to the hole in the wall bathroom located off the small hallway that connected the living room and bedroom. I turned on the water and hopped into the narrow, tiled stall shower and, with misgivings, let the warm water wash away the residue of my Trainman encounter. I lathered my hair with shampoo and rubbed my soapy hand between my legs, surprised that the bud between it was so sensitive and engorged.

After conditioning my mid-back length hair, I stepped out of the shower and wrapped a towel around me. A leopard print one that matched the satin sheets on the bed. I glanced at my reflection in the medicine cabinet mirror. My too-big-for-my-face chocolate eyes were a little bloodshot from my lack of sleep, but my skin was glowing, and I thanked my lucky stars for the zillionth time that I had been blessed with good skin. The genes of my mother. My heart grew heavy again—the image of her once radiant face, now sunken and sallow, filled my mind. I wondered how her treatment went. I so badly wanted to call her, but usually after one of them, she was weak and nauseated and preferred to talk to no one. Not even me, her only daughter. Best friend and confidant. How I missed my mother!

With a weighty sigh, I threw my soaked chestnut hair into a ponytail and dabbed on some berry-flavored lip-gloss, something I rarely did. The thought of Trainman licking it off my lips made me tingle. I hadn't been kissed by him. Fucked. But not kissed. What would that feel like? At last minute—thank you, Mrs. Blumberg—I spritzed myself with perfume. Sarah Jessica Parker's Lovely, a birthday present from Lauren.

I headed back to my bedroom and beheld the little black dress, waiting for my body to claim it. Careful not to get my lip-gloss on it, I slipped it over my head, squeezed my arms under the spaghetti straps and pulled it down. It stopped mid thigh and fit my body like a glove, giving me little curves I never thought I had. The silky satin was cool and soothing against my skin. I pulled off the tag and tossed it into the waste can. Jo-Jo gave me the cat's meow. Marc Jacobs and I were now one.

*"Don't wear pantyhose."* I could hear his sexy voice saying the words. Okay, so panties it would be. I opened the door to my armoire and pulled out a pair from the narrow drawer where I kept my collection of Fruit of the Looms. Cheap, comfy white panties I bought on sale at the downtown Target. I slipped my feet into the leg openings and slid them up under my dress. I stared at myself in the mirror. Damn! I had panty lines. Ugly panty

lines.

"*Remember, no pantyhose.*" Fine. I'd live with the lines, but silently I cursed my Fruit of the Looms, wishing that I had a single pair of those obnoxious butt-floss thongs. I slipped my bare feet back into my black satin Jimmy's and gave a final look at myself in the mirror.

Sarah, plain and tall in her little black dress and grown-up high heels, no longer looked plain but instead borderline elegant. More *West Side Story* lyrics floated in my head. "See the pretty girl in the mirror there." But, damn, damn, damn, those panty lines. They were ruining everything. Impulsively, I reached my under my dress and yanked the panties down, letting them slide down to my ankles. I kicked them off, almost losing my balance.

The phone in the kitchen rang. My answering machine picked up. I could faintly hear Lauren's voice, The Black Eyed Peas singing, "Tonight's the Night" in the background. "Sarah, what the fuck is going on? Call me immediately." CLICK.

I glanced again at my alarm clock. 7:55 p.m. Lauren would have to wait. Pantyless, I, Sarah Greene, was ready for my next encounter with her mysterious trainman.

8:00 p.m. I stood anxiously on the landing of my apartment. My eyes darted east and west, searching for a tall, golden-haired Adonis that stood out from the crowd. A melting pot of New Yorkers passed me by, several pausing to stare at me. A silver-haired businessman gave me a wink and a rapper type gave me a thumbs-up wolf whistle. I wasn't used to being noticed, let alone winked and whistled at. It was as empowering as it was embarrassing.

My nerves grew edgier by the minute. What if he was going to stand me up? The image of the beautiful redhead flickered once more in my head. I always said, *"The grass can't* compete *with the trees,"* and I was just a blade of grass in a big city filled with beautiful women.

My heart was sinking, and my inner vibrations were ticking like a countdown clock. And then as I was about to lose all hope, my eyes caught sight of my long-legged Trainman running down the street in my direction. He loped up the landing, taking two steps at a time. He grinned mischievously.

The sight of him shocked me. He was dressed in jeans—the expensive, premium denim kind—and a black cotton tee—the expensive, yummy kind. I immediately felt overdressed in his LBD and uncomfortable.

"Hi," I said nervously. I hated myself for my banality.

In my six-inch heels, we were practically the same height. His piercing blue eyes burned into mine and then traveled down my body, lingering on places he had no right to be. "The dress suits you," he said at last with a glimmer of approval.

He offered me his arm, and my eyes fixed on his biceps. Perfect, not too big to shout professional weight lifter but enough to let me know that he worked out. The rest of his body was equally sculpted to perfection. The outline of his muscled thighs and calves was visible through the denim, and I could see the ripple of his abs beneath his fine cotton tee.

I hooked my arm in his, glad to have someone help me down the steps in these mile-high heels. *Please don't let me trip. Please!* I prayed silently.

I made it to the street. A small victory. I suppose we were walking somewhere—there were lots of good restaurants in the theater district—but truthfully, I was not looking forward to walking more than a block in my Jimmy's. My feet were already beginning to ache, and I still did not trust myself in them.

"My driver will be here any second," said Trainman.

Driver? What was he talking about? In a heartbeat, a sleek black limo slithered up to us. Trainman motioned with his finger to it and helped me step off the curb.

A tall uniformed man with rich ebony skin and the intimidating build of Mr. Clean immediately came around the car and opened the backdoor.

"After you," said Trainman.

I looked at him with hesitancy and then with as much grace as I could muster in my tight black dress and six-inch high Jimmy's, I slid into the car. Trainman climbed in after me. The passenger door closed, and I was sitting once again next to my mysterious stranger-on-a-train.

The posh, spacious interior felt alien to me. Rich black leather seats, plush carpeting, dark tinted windows, plus a dark glass partition separating the two of us from the driver. There was also a well-stocked bar. I'd never been in a limo before. Obviously, Trainman was rich. *Very* rich. Again the question: What was he doing with me?

He stretched his long, taut legs out in front of him, and I noticed he was wearing expensive black loafers, with no socks. I impulsively crossed mine—acutely aware that I was not wearing underwear. The thought made me press by legs tighter together; I wondered—was this some kind of defense mechanism?

Trainman glanced down at my crotch—holy shit, did he know? —and then subtly down at my feet. A sly smile flickered on his tanned face. Was it the beautiful shoes or the fact that I was not wearing pantyhose that pleased him? I dared not to ask.

The scent of his expensive cologne, mixed with that of the car's rich leather, wafted up my nose, making me feel light-headed. Butterflies fluttered in my stomach, and the throbbing in my groin kicked up a notch with the movement of the car. *Please don't let me get carsick.*

"I hope you like lobster," he said, breaking the

silence.

Oooh. That was a conversation starter. Me, who lived on ramen noodles and an occasional macrobiotic dinner out, courtesy of BFF Lauren, who was forever going through a raw diet phase, didn't know the first thing about eating lobster. All I knew was that it was a big red shellfish with big, scary claws that I could never afford.

"Yes," I lied.

"Good. We're going to The Palm, my favorite restaurant."

"Cool."

This was not going well. Despite my intimate encounter with this gorgeous man only hours ago, I now felt at a loss for words. Remembering one of my favorite sayings, "Speak only when spoken to," I peered out the tinted window, gazing at the spectacle of cars, cabs, and pedestrians that made New York the city that never sleeps. A thought crossed my mind. I could see them, but they could not see me. Somehow, I thought Trainman's piercing blue eyes could see right through me yet mine could not penetrate him. He made me feel naked.

Trainman's voice diverted my attention. "Would you like a drink?"

"Um, a coke would be nice."

Trainman smirked. He reached for a bottle of wine, already corked, and poured some into two crystal goblets. He handed me a glass and then clinked his against mine.

"Cheers. To you and a fine meal." His eyes stayed fixed on my face.

I put the goblet to my lips and took a sip of the wine. It was chilled and delicious. It didn't taste like the acidic or oversweet "house wine" I occasionally ordered when I was out with Lauren. No, it tasted perfectly balanced and velvety. I glanced at the label on the bottle; it was in French. So, Trainman liked fine cars, fine wines, fine food...and fine women?

The limo was heading east across 42nd street, the driver expertly weaving in and out of the insane Friday night midtown traffic. I imbibed more of my wine.

"So, Saarah..."

There he was saying my name with that slow sexy lilt. My breath caught in my throat.

Holding the glass of wine in one hand, he slowly ran the manicured fingertips of the other down my right leg, all the way down to my ankle. His caress gave me goose bumps.

"...You didn't wear any pantyhose," he purred, his hand rubbing up and down my ankle.

I swallowed hard. I was too nervous to say anything.

"I hope you're as hungry as I am."

"I'm famished," I squeaked. Suddenly, I was craving a heaping portion of his cock. My stomach emitted an embarrassing growl.

He responded with that bemused smile.

His hand glided back up my leg and made its

way under the silky satin of my little black dress. His middle finger toyed with my button. I was getting hot. Very hot. And very wet.

"You're salivating. You *must* be starving."

I bit down on my berry-stained lips to suppress a moan.

"Open your mouth," he growled.

Hesitantly, I parted my lips. Removing his hand from between thighs, he slid his middle finger, wet with my sex, across my tongue. "Just a small taste of what's to come."

I steadied my wine in my hand. I feared one way or another I was going to end up with a large wet stain on my new black dress if we didn't get to the restaurant soon.

The limo turned north on Third Avenue and, after a couple of turns, pulled up behind a cab in front of The Palm. The driver got out and the door opened. Trainman slid out and I followed, aided by his hand. I really was hungry.

Inside, The Palm was a noisy, bustling restaurant with white-table cloth tables and a colorful array of caricatures of well-known celebrities lining the walls. At the reception area, a jovial heavyset man, with half-moon glasses, who looked to be in late 60's, greeted Trainman with a warm handshake.

"Good to see you, Mr. Golden. Your regular table is waiting for you."

So now, I knew Trainman's full name. Ari Golden. Fitting for the golden-haired warrior. Later tonight, I would google him and find out everything there was to know.

Holding my hand, Ari followed an attractive, mini-skirted receptionist who kept looking back at him, past the jammed bar and table after table of chicly dressed couples and businessmen devouring lobsters. I managed to keep up on my heels and again prayed I wouldn't do something embarrassing like breaking my ankle in front of all these diners.

Several stunning, well-dressed women stopped Ari along the way, eyeing me curiously. Ari politely acknowledged each of them with a quick smile and a nod. *Former passengers on a train?*

The booth to which we were led was in the far corner of the restaurant. It could easily accommodate four more people, but we had it all to ourselves. I sat on one side, Ari on the other.

A waiter came by shortly, and Ari ordered for the two of us. Two Manhattans, Caesar salad, and a four-pound lobster to share.

I was happy when the Manhattans arrived at our table. I still felt super-nervous in front of this man. I didn't know what to talk about. I took several consecutive gulps. The velvety cold liquid, another first, went down smoothly and loosened me up. A little.

Twirling his Manhattan cherry by the stem, Ari eased into conversation. "Sarah is a beautiful name. It means 'princess' in Hebrew."

My mother had told me that once, but I was the last thing from being a princess. Tomboy, geek, plain Jane, yes. But not princess. "Thanks," I said in a tone that was more dubious than flattered.

He removed the cherry from his drink and flicked it with his tongue. "I've seen you a few times before at the 30th Street Station."

I gulped. He had been spying on me? He really was a stalker.

"Were you visiting someone there?" He popped the cherry into his mouth and swallowed.

I nervously nodded.

"Oh, a boyfriend?"

"No, my mom," I replied, taken aback by his question. "She's being treated for cancer at the Hospital of the University of Pennsylvania."

All the emotions I had bottled up broke loose. I don't know what caused it. The wine. The Manhattan. The cherry. Or a combination of all three. Tears that had been welling up in my eyes on and off all day streamed down my cheeks.

Before I could apologize for my emotional outbreak, Ari leaned into me and brushed them away with his thumbs. With a tenderness that surprised me.

"I'm sorry," I sniffed.

"Don't be." His voice embodied genuine compassion. "I lost my father to cancer several years ago."

So we had something in common. Or close enough. Fingers crossed, my mother would go into remission.

"What kind?" I asked hesitantly.

"Lung." Sadness filled his voice. "He was a smoker."

"My mother has lung cancer too, but she never smoked a day in her life." Anger from this unfair fate rose fast and furious inside me. Just in time, the Caesar salads arrived. I picked at mine, my appetite suddenly gone. Trainman dug into his, sheepishly gazing up at me with each forkful.

"Sarah, cheer up!" It was almost a command. "Here comes the lobster."

My eyes grew wide at the sight of the monstrous red-shelled creature that our waiter set down in the center of our table. On either side of the platter, he placed a couple of nutcrackers and pickers. Tying ample plastic bibs around our necks, he bid us, *"Bon appétit."*

My anxious eyes darted back and forth between the lobster and Ari's face. I had never eaten a lobster before and had no clue where to begin.

He was a god. And a mind reader. "Watch. Use the nutcracker and start with the tail. The most succulent part." Squeezing the utensil, he skillfully cracked the creature's tail and then plunged one of the slim two-pronged forks into the meat. "Taste," he ordered after dipping the snowy meat into a side of melted butter.

I opened my mouth and let him feed me the buttery piece of lobster meat. Oh, God, it was good. Rich, melt-in-your-mouth good. I instantly wanted more.

"Your turn." A wry smile curled on his face.

"But, I want you to crack a claw. The next best piece of meat."

Taking the nutcracker, I wrapped it around one of the lobster's large claws. I pressed hard, but the shell would not crack.

Suddenly, under the table, I felt Ari grab at a naked calf. He pulled off my Jimmy Choo and moved my foot to the crotch of his expensive jeans. The soul of my foot sat directly on the warm bulge between his muscular thighs. Gripping my ankle, he rubbed my foot up and down. Slowly. Then faster. The mound hardened and expanded while my foot caught fire.

I fumbled with the nutcracker. I still couldn't crack open the damn claw. I was totally distracted.

"I'm hungry," growled Ari. He rubbed my bare foot faster and harder against his member. The rigid rod beneath his jeans tensed further, then finally gave way to a series of short spasms. Absent-mindedly still working on the claw, I gazed at the man sitting across from me; his eyes were closed, his lush lips parted and his back slightly arched. His member thrust deep into the arch of my foot...

And at that very moment, the claw cracked opened, the tender white meat inside exploding through the shell. I plunked the two-pronged fork into a chunk and slid it into Ari's parted lips. His eyes remained shut as he moaned, "Mmmm."

I delighted in the pleasure I could give this gorgeous man.

He savored the meat in his mouth and then opened his eyes. I watched him swallow.

"My princess, that was delicious."

I flushed at his compliment. And he called me his princess!

"And now for dessert." With a hungry smile, he picked up a spoon and let it fall under the table. "Whoops. Excuse me."

Puzzled by his behavior, I watched as he gracefully slid his sculpted body under the table to retrieve it.

Remembering my bare foot, I quickly wiggled my toes back into my shoe. A hand gripped my ankle and yanked my foot out before I could set my heel down. A moist, warm mouth descended on my big toe and sucked it up and down feverishly. Tingles shot up my leg, all the way up to my crotch. Oh my God! Dessert had arrived.

Having enough of my big toe, he nibbled and sucked the rest of them. Delicious pain followed by delicious pleasure. He bent my foot backward, and moved his mouth to my heel. His tongue glided, like a slow rollercoaster across my high arch, making its way back to my toes. The sensation sent a shiver up my spine. Who knew that the souls of my feet were so sensitive?

Holding my foot gently in his palms, his tongue continued its journey up my long, naked leg. The sensation was ticklish, yet strangely erotic. I did my back arching of my own. When it reached my thigh, his hands firmly pulled my legs apart. Oh,

God. Here came the icing on the cake.

Instead of the warm tongue I was expecting, the back of the spoon pressed against the folds of my pantyless crotch. The unexpected chill of the metal jolted me. He circled the spoon around my genitals, arousing me further. I clenched my fists and moaned inwardly. Oh, God. What this man could do me!

Pulling up my dress as high as it would go, he let his tongue take over. It figure skated across the surface of my folds, performing all kinds of tricks, from spins to figure eights. My patch of ice was melting, turning into one steaming hot wet river. His ever-so fit tongue stroked furiously. The pressure between my legs mounted—I wanted to scream! —and finally an explosion gave me the relief I'd been craving.

He re-emerged from under the table, with the spoon tipped in his luscious mouth, as if he were savoring the last bit of sweet creamy frosting. Removing it, he languidly rolled his tongue over his upper lip and murmured, "Saarah, I hope you enjoyed dessert as much as I did."

"It was amazing," I gasped, still vibrating below.

His lips curled into a dimpled, satisfied smile.

I stared at his beautiful face, realizing that I still knew so little about this man who had robbed me of my virginity and made me explode with ecstasy, already several times.

"What do you do?" I asked, finding the courage

to interrogate him.

"I'm a businessman."

"So, you were on a business trip to Philadelphia today?"

"No, my company is based there. I commute back and forth everyday."

That was a big distance to travel twice a day, but obviously his employer made the trip worthwhile.

"And what do you do?" he asked, his voice flirtatious.

"I work for—"

Before I could finish my sentence, Trainman leaped up from his seat.

My eyes followed him as his long legs strode to the front of the restaurant. And then my heart leapt into my throat.

The gorgeous redhead! And she was in Trainman's arms.

My emotions skipped over jealousy and sprinted straight to rage. How could he do this to me? And so shamelessly right in front of me?

Without putting on my other Jimmy, I jumped up from the table and hobbled over to them. If people were staring at me, I was oblivious. The redhead regarded me suspiciously. As if I were in a league below her and didn't belong here.

His face, however, brightened. "Saarah."

"Don't 'Saarah' me." In a single smooth move, I yanked off my other Jimmy and flung it at him. "You can keep your damn shoes," I shouted. As I stormed out the front door, I was pretty sure I would not be returning to The Palm any time soon. Make that ever.

With tears pouring down my face, I headed west on 45th Street. I had not brought my messenger bag with my wallet, so I was going to have to walk home barefoot. Fortunately, the night was still warm.

Tears kept coming. Past Third. Past Lexington. Past Park. Happy, laughing young couples, taking advantage of the fine weather, passed me by, but they were just a blur.

I wanted to get him out of my mind. Erase him forever. But I couldn't. The inner throbbing just would not go away. I hated him. I hated her. But hated myself most of all. How could I be so stupid to fall for this callous man? To give him my body, pure and unadulterated? To trust him? My mother had always told me to wait for someone who really loved you. She made the mistake of not—and had to raise me as a single parent. I should have listened to her words of wisdom. And right now, there was nothing more that I wanted than to talk to my mother. To tell her everything. To hear her consoling words. And feel her loving embrace.

When I got home, I was going to take a scissors to his little black dress and tear it to shreds. I was going to go back to who I really was. Sarah plain and tall.

27759060R00183

Printed in Great Britain
by Amazon